"We like to have this first advising session because a lot of people find the atmosphere at Babylona challenging," Ben said gently.

She made herself meet his eye. "Oh, but that's what I signed up for. I mean, it is an institute for sex professions." She was trying to sound cool, but saying "sex professions" while looking into the deep green eyes of a gorgeous man was very different from seeing it printed on a prospectus. She tried to get back on the right track. "Anyway, I think I'll get used to it soon. It's not that different from my life back home. I mean, it is! But I'll catch up in no time. I mean, it'll be fine, because—"

To her consternation, a broad grin was spreading across Ben's face. Suddenly, he burst out laughing. She couldn't help it—she started laughing too.

"Okay, I *am* a little frightened. Is that okay?"

He laughed again. "It makes me feel better. I was terrified when I first got here."

Then suddenly she felt a light touch on her bare thigh. It was Ben's hand, that same large, masculine hand that had gripped hers with such strength and certainty. Now it was brushing against her tender skin, sending electricity up her thighs and straight to that patch of wetness in her silk panties.

"So do you think you . . . ?" he said, his voice hoarse.

She heard a voice saying, "Yes," in a husky whisper, only it was her voice. And that was her heavy breathing as his hand traced shivers up the inside of her thigh. . . .

Pleasure U

Carole Hart

HEAT

Heat

Published by New American Library, a division of
Penguin Group (USA) Inc., 375 Hudson Street,
New York, New York 10014, USA
Penguin Group (Canada), 90 Eglinton Avenue East, Suite 700, Toronto,
Ontario M4P 2Y3, Canada (a division of Pearson Penguin Canada Inc.)
Penguin Books Ltd., 80 Strand, London WC2R 0RL, England
Penguin Ireland, 25 St. Stephen's Green, Dublin 2,
Ireland (a division of Penguin Books Ltd.)
Penguin Group (Australia), 250 Camberwell Road, Camberwell, Victoria 3124,
Australia (a division of Pearson Australia Group Pty. Ltd.)
Penguin Books India Pvt. Ltd., 11 Community Centre, Panchsheel Park,
New Delhi - 110 017, India
Penguin Group (NZ), 67 Apollo Drive, Rosedale, North Shore 0632,
New Zealand (a division of Pearson New Zealand Ltd.)
Penguin Books (South Africa) (Pty.) Ltd., 24 Sturdee Avenue,
Rosebank, Johannesburg 2196, South Africa

Penguin Books Ltd., Registered Offices:
80 Strand, London WC2R 0RL, England

First published by Heat, an imprint of New American Library,
a division of Penguin Group (USA) Inc.

First Printing, August 2008
1 3 5 7 9 10 8 6 4 2

Copyright © Carole Hart, 2008

Heat is a trademark of Penguin Group (USA) Inc.

LIBRARY OF CONGRESS CATALOUGING-IN-PUBLICATION DATA
Hart, Carole, 1965–
Pleasure U / Carole Hart.
p. cm.
ISBN: 978-0-451-22413-2
I. Title.
PS3614.E66P57 2008
813'.6—dc22   2008001011

Set in Centaur
Designed by Ginger Legato

Printed in the United States of America

Without limiting the rights under copyright reserved above, no part of this publication may be reproduced, stored in or introduced into a retrieval system, or transmitted, in any form, or by any means (electronic, mechanical, photocopying, recording, or otherwise), without the prior written permission of both the copyright owner and the above publisher of this book.

PUBLISHER'S NOTE
This is a work of fiction. Names, characters, places, and incidents either are the product of the author's imagination or are used fictitiously, and any resemblance to actual persons, living or dead, business establishments, events, or locales is entirely coincidental.
The publisher does not have any control over and does not assume any responsibility for author or third-party Web sites or their content.

The scanning, uploading, and distribution of this book via the Internet or via any other means without the permission of the publisher is illegal and punishable by law. Please purchase only authorized electronic editions, and do not participate in or encourage electronic piracy of copyrighted materials. Your support of the author's rights is appreciated.

To Millie Simpson

Pleasure U

Chapter One

From the outside, the wall surrounding the Babylona Institute was elegant and anonymous, a genteel facade of slate-gray brick. On the inside, however—and it almost made Lila lose control of her car when she first saw it in the rearview mirror—the wall was covered in a shockingly realist mural depicting a daisy chain of oral sex. Lila slowed the car and finally pulled up onto the side of the drive to look back at the mural. Each figure was stretched out with its hands clasping the thighs of the next figure, its mouth sunk into the genitalia of the next person, the tongue curled suggestively out. It was like an illustration in a book she'd had as a child of elephants parading in single file, each with its trunk clasping the tail of the elephant ahead. The sucking circle went boy-girl, boy-boy, girl-girl, boy-girl, all along the wall and out of sight. The nudes were all shapes, colors, and sizes, but all shared a dreamy, blissful expression, and identically pink curling tongues that peeped out of their mouths to deliver what the artist somehow managed to suggest were masterful, intricate strokes of pleasure to the cocks and pussies involved. The background was green grass—so like the grass of the expansive campus lawns that it must have been intentional.

The mural wasn't even erotic—not exactly. There was something about a mural that was basically not erotic, the idea of it. But it was pretty and sensuous, a little bit comical in its extravagance. Most of all, it was a happy scene. It was sex without the shame, the anxiety, the morning-after regrets. And the fact that such a thing could exist, so publicly, on such a scale, gave Lila a giddy, don't-look-down feeling. It was like one of those old comedy movies where the characters crash-land on Venus and find it populated by sex-starved bikini-clad girls. This was it, for real: Planet Sex.

From the moment she had enrolled at the Babylona Institute of the Sexual Professions, she'd been fighting a mounting sense of panic. When she'd lied to her parents, saying she was going to work at a friend's ski resort in Colorado, she'd felt that panic. She had never lied to her parents about anything, but she wasn't sure how they'd react to this—she was only sure she wasn't going to change her mind. So why upset them for nothing? Then, when she'd entrusted her sister with the secret, and seen the half-admiring, half-alarmed look in Bethany's eyes, she'd felt the panic more powerfully. Bethany had said, "Are you sure you're ready for . . . you know?" She'd wanted to shout "No!" but she'd bit her tongue and equivocated, saying, "I've made up my mind." And she'd felt the panic most of all in the nights she spent studying the college catalogue, which was illustrated with full-color photographs of students, naked and in the midst of the sex acts that formed the bulk of Babylona's curriculum.

It wasn't as if Lila had always dreamed of studying sex. In fact, coming to Babylona was a last-minute decision. It was a break with her whole life up to that point; a break with the timid, quiet girl she'd always been. A girl who'd met the man she knew she wanted to marry when she was only fifteen. Up until six months ago, she'd had her whole life mapped out. She was going to take a year off after high school to marry Tad, her high school sweetheart. Then they would go to school together and get jobs and somewhere along the way they would have two children and—what else? Oh yes, live happily ever after.

She'd built her life around Tad. It had seemed like the natural thing to do. He was so faithful, so kind to her, so good about things like buying birthday presents and noticing when she'd bought a new dress. She'd lost her virginity with Tad, and the idea that he was going to be the only man she would ever share her body with had never bothered her. In fact, it seemed sexy, in an all-absorbing way that made her sorry for other girls. It made sex into a secret world that only the two of them would share. And if she had sometimes thought about sex with other men . . . if in fact, she had often thought about sex with other men . . . if she had several times every day thought about sex with various other men, in exhaustive detail . . . well, that was just thinking. And the beautiful thing was, she knew Tad wasn't thinking about other girls that way. He'd told her so. And she'd never known Tad to lie to her.

Maybe she'd been naive. But she'd always been the sort of person bad things just didn't happen to. Her mom and dad were still in love. They lived in a quaint two-story colonial house in Maine, in a sleepy seaside town where everyone's mom and dad were still in love. Her big sister, Bethany, was her best friend. Like her, Bethany got straight A's and spent her summers working as a lifeguard at the public beach.

But even Bethany once burst out in irritation: "Well, guys just fall all over you; you don't know what it's like!" In the tearful heart-to-heart that followed, Bethany confessed that she'd always been especially jealous of Lila's looks—her thick silky dark hair, her generous breasts that formed exactly the right hourglass outline with her nipped-in waist . . . For years Bethany had been bringing home dates who became tongue-tied when they met her voluptuous green-eyed sister. Then Lila entered high school and immediately bagged Tad, the town's official hottest guy—official because the girls of Parville High had a tradition of running Hot Charts on their blogs; every Valentine's Day someone took on the task of collating all the charts and producing an official top ten. Tad's broad-shouldered frame and perfect chiseled features had won him the number one spot when he was still a sophomore.

Lila had said, "But Tad and I are just like each other. It's not like that at all. It's not because I'm—whatever you think I am." She could feel herself blushing furiously.

"Oh, Lila," Bethany sighed with an irritating older-and-wiser smile. "What's crazy is, you really believe that."

That exchange was the first major shift in Lila's outlook. Because she had always been scared of meeting people, she never realized that anyone could see her as popular. She didn't think of herself as especially good-looking. When she was younger, guys tended to overlook her because she didn't talk. And since she turned fifteen, there had been Tad. If guys paid attention to her, she cut it short nervously. She liked it a little *too much*, and it made her feel so guilty and confused that she just wanted to escape.

In fact, she thought of herself as the girl who didn't like to go to parties because the loud music made her nervous, and the drunken flirting made her uncomfortable. Some of the girls at Parville seemed to think they were auditioning for *Girls Gone Wild* whenever they had a drink. There were the hookups in bedrooms, bathrooms, and closets; there was the public groping. The skimpy clothes made Lila uncomfortably horny. She didn't like being horny in the middle of a gang of people; it made her feel like she might at any moment forget everything and have sex with one of those people. She felt like if she just had one too many beers, she could find herself in one of those hookups, her legs spread for some drunken football player in the middle of the dance floor.

At one party Lila had gone to, the class slut, Becky Falkner, had spent the latter half of the evening topless, walking around completely casually as if she didn't notice every guy in the room leering. For weeks afterward, the vision of Becky's chubby breasts with their delicate apricot nipples haunted Lila. Somehow the fact that Becky was standing among so many fully clothed people made her breasts seem especially, deliciously naked. Every time the scene went through Lila's head she felt a tingle in her own nipples, as if—because this was what she'd kept expecting to happen to Becky all that night, until Lila's panties were utterly, embarrassingly soaked from the anticipation—a boy had just dragged one finger through the chilly condensation on a beer and then stroked the wetness across Lila's nipple . . . no, Becky's nipple . . . and at that point, whether because she felt guilty toward Tad, or because she was genuinely dis-approving of Becky's behavior, Lila had vowed that she wasn't going to parties anymore. Of course, it didn't help that she always went to parties with Tad, and that Tad was also mesmerized by Becky's per-formance, and all the similar flashing, flirting, groping performances that went on there.

Anyway (she would always break off the train of thought here), of course she much preferred to spend the night alone with him. Tad would have been enough for anyone. Parties were just a lot of drunken, raucous, playacting around the idea of sex—even the tor-rid, spur-of-the-moment fucks that occurred at those parties were, from what her friends told her, barely worth the embarrassment the morning after. And even though theoretically Lila had no basis for comparison, she was instinctively certain her sex with Tad was as good as it got. From the very first time, they'd had a natural chem-istry that made it easy for Lila to accept things that she thought would be uncomfortable—like him going down on her. When she'd thought about it before it ever happened, it seemed like she would be embarrassed, that she would feel too exposed. It was the sex act that seemed the most obscene to her. But with Tad, everything felt so natural that she'd given herself over to his searching lips and tongue without even thinking about it. She was just dizzy with pleasure, whimpering without knowing what she was doing, coming so hard she writhed and felt like she was fainting. And she accepted her loss of control as part of her love for Tad. He could make her lose her mind, and it was still all right.

The night they broke up had been no different—at first.

Since it was August, they'd decided to go down to Rockwell Beach to swim that night. The only way to get to that beach was to cut through the woods behind Lila's house. It was a quarter mile's walk, and for that reason, the beach was empty all year round. There was no need to wear a bathing suit; they would strip to the skin as soon as they got to the water, and often have sex on a blanket before they even got their feet wet.

It had rained the night before, and it was cool for that time of year. Lila went ahead, barely aware of her surroundings; she was lost in a dream of their wedding that was planned for November, for the day of her nineteenth birthday. She had picked out her wedding dress that afternoon, a classic white silk dress with a fitted bodice covered in eyelet lace that pushed her breasts up in a way that made their creamy lushness seem romantic instead of—as Tad liked to say of her figure—"porn star stuff." Going down the dirt path with this in her mind, Lila began to pull off her T-shirt slowly, idly, thinking of Tad watching from behind, gradually realizing what she was doing.

She pulled the T-shirt off over her head as she walked and let it hang over one arm as she unhooked her bra. Becky Falkner flashed through her mind as she felt her breasts spill free and begin to bounce gently as she walked on through the dark woods. The chill made her nipples immediately pinch into erectness, and she felt a thrill run right down her belly and into her pussy. It stabbed deep inside, and she almost made a sound.

Tad said behind her, "Baby, what are you doing? You trying to drive me nuts?"

Lila kept walking for a while without saying anything, imagining herself at that party, walking naked with dozens of men's eyes feasting on her exposed flesh. Her breasts tingled as if not only were those guys staring at them, all of them (this was what Becky must have been thinking!) getting stiff in their jeans, but as if one of them—someone she had never seen before but who somehow had the nerve to do this—was letting his fingers run over her breasts, tickling the skin into maximum arousal before letting himself take a good, lustful handful and squeeze it, savoring the firmness and shape. He would be staring at her breasts shamelessly, not caring what anyone thought . . .

"Come on. Don't stop," Tad said behind her, his voice husky.

She had already begun to unzip her skirt when she saw the movement in front of her. She came to a stop, and simultaneously let her skirt drop to the ground. Then she saw a man's face flare into focus as he sucked on a cigarette. Beside him, she could make out the shadowy figure of a second man. Both of them were older—in their thirties, probably—and wearing swim trunks, obviously on their way back from the beach.

She recognized them from town; they were tourists who had rented a holiday cabin out by Bartlett's Grocery. They were always coming into town in swim shorts and T-shirts, driving a custom-built convertible that was half fascinating, half offensive. Like, it was bad enough that some people had enough money to buy sports cars. But to have enough money to have a sports car especially built for you, like not just a vanity license plate but a whole personalized automobile? It made them seem like some kind of exotic and morally dissipated foreigners. It was the kind of thing that made serious Bethany fume. But she, like Lila, always stared at the men in the car. They were lean, deeply tanned, and muscular. They always had a day's stubble on their faces. They were both blond in different ways: the one a perfect blue-eyed pretty boy with a snub nose and a permanent smile; the other had a gaunt, slightly arrogant face that looked subtly British, or even British military—if you were casting a film, for instance. Bethany used to sum them up by saying, in a pert, phony way: "Oooh! It's the playboys!" But when she and Lila giggled about it, they laughed way too much, and there was more excitement in it than real mirth.

Now Lila stepped out of her skirt and something inside her shifted gently. For that moment it still seemed as if the two surfers wouldn't really look up and see her. That was still impossible. It was a thing that couldn't happen to her, a thing she wouldn't let happen. No strangers would ever see her naked breasts. Her naked body was only for her husband, forever and ever, a secret world just for the two of them. That was what Lila's heart had been set on for the past three years. But Lila—the Lila she had always been—would already have been hiding behind Tad, scrambling to put her blouse back on.

Now she moved quickly, as if to get it done before she could fully realize what was happening. She slipped her cotton underpants down her thighs and bent quickly to grab them and her skirt. Then she walked forward with her clothes bundled in the crook of her elbow, with her breasts, her ass, and her pussy fully exposed. She felt Tad's fingers lightly graze her left buttock, sending tight waves of sensation through her ass and into her bared cunt. The cool night air made the wetness between her legs prickle with cold, feeling all the more exposed. It sent sparkles of pleasure into her, as if it were a stranger's hand touching her, just barely, teasingly, tickling her clitoris and labia with a finger that was chilled . . . from being deliberately drawn through the cold condensation on a beer can. And on she went, into the semiclearing where the men were now hidden, with the faint, guilty thought: *Tad won't know I saw them. I could have missed them completely in the dark.*

The first thing that happened was that the harsh-looking man, the one who made her think of a British army officer, stepped out into the path directly in front of her. For a second he looked almost panicked as he caught sight of her. Then he was staring at her body, his face rigid with desire. His baby-faced friend was saying, "What? Mike—" until he stepped out beside him and saw Lila, too.

Before she could stop herself, she had let her eyes lazily droop half shut and licked her lips, slowly, luxuriously. And she was staring at the swim trunks of the British army man—Mike—thinking of how his dick would be growing harder, longer, in his wet swim trunks, how it would feel to mold it in her hand inside the wet fabric. Then she could just slip her hand up into the leg of the trunks and . . .

"Jesus!" It was Tad, behind her. In a second, he had pulled her back against him and was covering her breasts, grabbing at them clumsily in his haste. Lila felt the hand crushing her breast, making her feel the delicious crinkling in her hard nipple, red-hot with sensitivity, and her pussy spasmed, halfway to coming. She gasped and pressed back against Tad, feeling his hard-on in his jeans. Then his other hand came down and pressed against her cunt, trying to cover her, but incidentally sweetly crushing her clit. That was all it took—she came, and for a moment she was thinking only of the surfer guys' eyes on her *as* she came, their hands reaching forward to her; the excitement of a stranger losing control and just grabbing what he wanted—spasm after spasm went through her pussy, while her knees went weak, and she let Tad hold her up; it was like she was crushing her orgasm into his strong hand, tricking him into squeezing more and more pleasure out of her cunt.

"Lila," Tad was hissing into her ear, "get behind me, for Christ's sake." He was pulling her around, getting in between her and the other men, who were now looking away, muttering to each other.

"Of course, yeah," she said, beginning to wake. He let go of her and she immediately crouched down to put on her panties—and to hide her confusion. Her pussy was still ringing with a sweet soreness as she moved. She began to put her clothes back on clumsily, like a sleepwalker. They suddenly seemed strange to her. The whole idea of wearing clothes seemed strange. The skirt was a weird tube that you put around yourself—why exactly? Struggling to get the bra on properly, Lila longed to just throw it all away and go on naked to the men. Then Tad would watch as they took turns with her; in the fantasy Tad was approving of what she was doing, getting off on the idea of other men enjoying his fiancée's tight pussy.

But at the same time another part of her was insisting sensibly that all this was crazy, and those men would be talking about her tomorrow. People would find out; she was going to be a laughingstock. She was going to be like Becky Falkner, the kind of girl who had strange guys pulling up in front of her house at night, honking their car horns for her to come out. And then she was going to go out

to the cars in nothing but her underwear; she was going to mount
guys in the front seats of their cars and fuck them then and there,
without even knowing their names—no! God, no! This was all just
prewedding jitters.

At last her clothes were on again, and she felt the everyday Lila
returning, with a mingled sense of relief and disappointment. The
strangers were smoking again and they'd withdrawn a little into
the woods, backing away from the path, leaving Tad and Lila room
to pass without too much embarrassment. Lila began to feel the
beginnings of the deep shame that was in store for her. *Even these
men*—the "playboys" Bethany used to make fun of for their cheesy
penis-mobile sports car—were embarrassed. They were hiding, they
were so embarrassed. She made herself look at Tad, who seemed
stiff, either with anger or nerves. She said quietly, "It's okay, Taddie.
Let's just get to the beach." Her voice sounded strangely calm. She
reminded herself to make a point to him later of how shocked she'd
really been. She could say she was too shocked to move. Too shocked
to even realize.

Tad started walking forward, and she followed him, wretchedly
ashamed. It seemed to take forever to enter the semiclearing and
walk through it. The moon shone down clearly on her as she went
through, and her mind reran the scene of her nudity. The men must
be staring, remembering her naked body. Or would they be looking away in disgust, thinking of her as a crazy woman who exposes
herself to strangers?

Tad went forward rapidly, ducking his head, so she had to hurry
to catch up. She didn't dare look to the left, where the men were
standing. She could smell the sleepy smell of their cigarettes. The
moonlight came down clearly, the sleepy silver color that went with
that languid smell. And at last she was ducking again into the darkness of the woods, out of the stares she imagined coming from
the men, when one of them called out almost reverently: "You're
beautiful!"

Although she didn't know, of course, which one had called out, the voice was, in fact, British. And in the dark, Lila smiled, unreasonably relieved and grateful. Tad in front of her hurried forward still more, muttering under his breath. A pang inside her warned her that Tad was going to make her sorry for that. But it wasn't her fault—it wasn't *that much* her fault, anyway. And she found herself lagging a little behind, longing to look back and smile at the man who had called to her. But she made herself go on, and soon the men were too far behind, and even the smell of their cigarettes had faded.

Then they came out onto the beach, and the calming, familiar rush of the waves greeted her. She was half relieved to feel that it was actually too cold out here by the ocean to swim. She could leave her clothes on now. And what had happened back there had just been a matter of circumstances. It wasn't that she was really interested in other men. Maybe she had an exhibitionist streak—that was all it could be. And that was fine; that was something she could share with her husband. She could even go to those classes where you learned how to strip for your boyfriend. It was absolutely normal; it was even a good thing that would add excitement to their marriage.

But would Tad see it that way? She stole a glance at him as he spread the blanket out on the sand. The wind kept whipping it back the wrong way, frustrating his attempts to get it flat on the beach, and he was beginning to lose his temper. A gust of wind suddenly flung the blanket up and over his head. It briefly wrapped itself around his head, and he had to struggle to get free. She couldn't help grinning, and when he saw her, for a second, he grinned back. But then some thought seemed to pass over his features, and he turned back grimly to his war with the blanket.

Lila went to help him, and between them they got it down on the sand flat; Lila sat down before it could fly away. Then she looked up at Tad, who was frowning at the moonlit sea and the streaks of pale cloud in the black sky. She said softly, "Hey. I guess it's too cold to . . . make love out here. Right?"

Tad shuddered and looked down at her as if he were trying to figure out who she was. At last he shook his head and said, "I wouldn't
say that. It's not too cold for us, is it?"

That was his usual tone, and Lila relaxed. She said, "No, never
too cold for us. I just thought you . . . you seemed like you were in a
bad mood, after that mishap."

Tad sighed and looked back at the surf tumbling in, the whitecaps
flickering in the faint moonlight. He said, "Well, it was weird. You
seemed like . . . you were obviously turned on by that. That's all."

Lila thought about it. Of course she should say what she'd
planned, that it was just shock. But this was the man she was going
to marry. He was going to be her best friend, a friend even closer
than Bethany. He would be the one who would share all the problems and talk her through all the confusions of her life. Well, maybe
it should start now.

She said, "I was. I don't know what happened to me. I was really
turned on. I hope that doesn't upset you. It's not that I wanted to
sleep with them or anything like that." But her voice rang false at the
end, and she giggled nervously.

He turned to her with a scowl. The wind from the sea kept sweep-
ing his dark hair back, so his features stood out more clearly than
ever. He had the most beautiful brown eyes, sweet and long lashed;
they would have seemed feminine if it weren't for the rough mascu-
linity of the rest of his face. Then there was his thick, muscular neck,
which she sometimes thought was her favorite part of his body, if
only because it was what she was kissing, licking, biting, as he made
love to her. She sighed with the rekindled idea that this was the man
she would spend the rest of her life with. But he was still glowering, and when she reached forward, wanting to touch his cheek, he
grabbed her hand roughly and pressed it to his bulging crotch.

She caught her breath. He was hard—really hard. She could feel
the entire shape of his cock through his pants fabric, its elegantly
shaped head and the slightly bowed length of it, the strong vein that

widened as it led down to his balls. He held her hand there firmly and moved his hips forward to grind his cock into her palm a few times. Then he pulled her hand aside and unzipped his fly, saying, "Go on. Suck me, Lila."

She couldn't help taking his dick in her hand; she had to feel the fine hot skin on it, she had to feel for herself that he was rock hard for her. But then the tone of his voice got through to her. He was talking angrily, as if he was disgusted with her. It was what she had expected from the strangers, but it was coming from him. Before she could say anything, though, he had grabbed a handful of her hair and was guiding her head down to his prick.

She let herself fall into the spell of his cock then; the sweet taste of his precome welcomed her as she took the glans between her lips and applied the tip of her tongue to his penis opening. The smoothness of the skin there, and the salt/sweet taste, always made her feel faint with desire. She flicked her tongue over the head of his cock greedily, her body responding as she felt in imagination the pleasure she was giving him. He turned slightly and began to thrust into her mouth, still holding her head steady by her hair, fucking her mouth with a feverish need. He was muttering, "Yes, suck it hard. Suck it hard, baby." She let herself close her lips tight around his shaft, feeling the satisfying rock hardness of his dick, the slick shape of it making her tighten her mouth over him as if her mouth were a sensitive, responsive, second pussy. Without even thinking, she was imagining the same feeling in her vagina, how he would fuck her this hungrily, but harder, swiping her clitoris with each thrust, building and building . . . He was shoving his dick deep into the back of her throat now, and she struggled not to choke. She bent her head back, and his dick began to slide halfway into her throat, deeper and deeper. She let her tongue play up and down the shaft, flicking up to taste the glans with each outward thrust. He was moaning, and his thrusts had become convulsive, out of control. "Yes . . ." he moaned. "Yes, that's my good little cocksucker. Good girl."

Lila froze; he had never talked to her like that before. But before she could do anything, he had thrust one more time deep, deep into her throat, and as she somehow managed to swallow it, swept up in his desire, he came with deep jerks of his whole cock, sending the delicious sperm into her throat; some spilled down her chin and she couldn't help shutting her eyes with pleasure. It was as if she could feel what he felt. Whatever he said, out of anger or just crude lust, they were still on the same wavelength; that was proved by the flood of gratification she felt when he came.

At last he let go of her hair and she sat up, smiling at him as she wiped her chin. "I love you, darling," she said.

But he was still looking at her darkly. There was even a hint of disgust in his eyes, and she felt more ashamed than at any time this night. It was as if sucking his cock had made him look at her as a whore; as if what she had done made her dirty in his eyes. But that was crazy; they did it all the time. It wasn't like it would suddenly shock him that she was willing to give him head!

For a moment, though, she was sure he was going to say something like *I guess that's what you wanted to do to those guys back there.* And then she would be stuck back in the same dilemma; should she tell him the truth or lie? Which would do more damage to their marriage in the long run?

But what he said finally was, "I guess that shocked you, right?"

At first she was caught off guard. Then she realized what he was talking about; it was the way he had talked to her, called her *cocksucker.* She smiled, relieved. That was something she could tell the truth about without worrying. "Oh, a little bit," she said. "But no big deal."

"Yeah, but you didn't like it, did you?" he insisted, almost pouting.

"Come on, Tad. What if I didn't like it?" Then she thought better of it, and hastened to add, "It's more that it took me by surprise. If you want to talk dirty to me, I mean . . ."

"Yeah, I guess no one ever talked to you that way before," he said triumphantly, as if she'd proved his point.

She laughed. "Well, I think Bethany maybe called me a cock-sucker once. But I think she was too young to know what it meant."

"Cute," he said heavily. "Cute. But you're missing my point."

"What point?" she said, forcing her voice to remain cheerful. He was staring away at the surf gloomily, and she began to realize that this wasn't the first time he'd been like this recently. It had bothered her before, but it was more that he wasn't having fun, and she kept trying to get him to have fun. Now it appeared to her in a different light. What if it wasn't just that he wasn't having fun, but that he was having second thoughts about her? She swallowed and said, "Hey, what's this all about?"

He sighed and crossed his arms. Then he turned to her with a stagy seriousness, like an actor steeling himself to deliver dreadful news. He said, "I have to tell you, it's been getting pretty boring."

"Boring?" Her mind went in all directions, trying to find what could be boring. Maybe it was because they stayed home more now. She would understand if he wanted to go to more parties without her. They could go on vacation; maybe that was the kind of thing he was missing.

But all the time the only answer, the impossible answer, stared her in the face. He meant that sex with her was boring. But how could he think that? Especially after what she'd just done? She almost retorted that his problem was that she wasn't boring *enough.* Instead she began to babble. "Well, we can definitely—role-play, and whatever you like. If you wanted to tie me up again. I mean, I'm open; you really just have to ask for . . . Anything that makes you happy makes me happy. Because, I mean, I love you," she finished up lamely, and put her hand out to rest on his thigh.

He flinched, but let the hand stay. Sighing again, he said, "You just don't understand. It's not that. It's nothing as crude as that. It's your whole . . . sexuality. It's just so small town, so high school. It's . . ."

Suddenly her face felt hot. "Compared to what? Tad? Are you . . . You're not comparing me to someone, are you?"

Then his jaw set. He said with a tragic air, "I really didn't want it to be like this."

"Oh my God," said Lila. "It's true? Who was it?" She'd already begun to cry. The whole beach felt like it was spinning. The relentless crashing of the breakers, tumbling up the beach, made her feel giddy.

Slowly he began to explain, his voice patient and condescending in a way that sounded pointed. It was as if he were deliberately conveying his complete contempt to her. But what was worst of all was the story itself.

He said that when he'd gone to New York with Jim and Ray last month, they'd all gone out to a strip club. (That all by itself shocked her: Even if he'd wanted to do that, she could have sworn he would tell her about it.) He'd had a little too much to drink, and at the end of the night, the hottest stripper in the place "actually kind of threw herself at me; she was following me out to my car." Well, of course he didn't intend for it to go anywhere. He didn't even *mean* to screw her in the grass behind the club. It had just kind of happened. But the stripper couldn't get enough of him; she'd wanted to come home with him, and she'd kept on calling him day after day until he caved in and slept with her again. And again. And when it had happened enough times, he began to realize that the stripper, with her experience of acting in porn films, with her hundreds of previous lovers, was—"sorry you have to hear this, but she was ten times more exciting to fuck than you." It was a matter of technique, yes, but that wasn't all. She was so free with her body, she made him feel—

Here he broke off and looked at Lila as if she were something very, very small, for which he only had pity. She had been crying for a long time now and here she sobbed out, "So—the wedding is off? It's over?"

He said with the same condescending care, "Lila. After what I just told you, don't you have too much pride to stay with me? Really? Show some self-respect."

At this she scrambled to her feet and ran past the clearing where, she was half disappointed to see, those men were gone—no opportunity to run off with them for a night of revenge sex, of being *free with her body*—and on home, where she'd taken a two-hour bath, continually letting out the water as it got cold and refilling it until her sister banged on the door to ask if she was all right. She'd lied that she was fine and crept off to bed before anyone could ask her any questions.

It was the very next morning that she saw the TV spot about Babylona. It was really about local protests against the school, and how they'd been overcome by even greater local support. A girl student was interviewed, a skinny black girl in a filmy halter top who kept flinging her exquisite slender arm around the reporter's shoulders and squeezing him against her, flirting relentlessly. She ended by suddenly saying, "Free sample, free sample!" and going down on her knees, out of shot of the camera. The reporter grinned uncertainly and said, "This really isn't what it looks like." But then he froze, went a little cross-eyed, and the shot abruptly ended.

The story picked up from a completely different place. The reporter's hair was wet, and he was wearing a different shirt. "It seems that here, in rural New Hampshire, the sexual revolution is still going strong," he said, grinning over his microphone as he stood in front of a patch of that mural, his head neatly X-ing out the crucial section of painted crotch.

Lila, who had never felt more battered in her life, sat forward with a burning conviction. She pulled her favorite old terry-cloth robe (the one with the ducks embroidered inexpertly on the lapels by her twelve-year-old self) tight around her. She hadn't even told Bethany what had happened yet. She hadn't told her mother or father. And she'd never felt less like being free with her body—she felt like she didn't really have a body, but just a dirty, old, crumpled rag that belonged in the garbage. But something about the green, lush campus, the girl who seemed to have never heard of fear or shame—something made her absolutely certain that Babylona and only Babylona could save her.

Now she was here. She took a deep breath and carried on down the main drive. Now she was driving through a little patch of forest. Lila half wanted to stop the car and go lie down under the trees and shut her eyes. She could have let herself drift off, inhaling the clean scent of pine, just letting the tension of the past few weeks float away. Without intending to, she'd let the car slow down again, and then she saw something that made her coast to a stop.

Some of the lower branches of the trees were festooned with slinky scraps of lingerie. Underneath the trees, she could see various socks, jeans, shirts—it was as if someone's laundry had been spilled in the middle of the woods. But the owners of the clothes were in plain sight, just a little farther off the road—a complicated tangle of naked limbs. It was a little too far off to make out details, but even from here, Lila could see one pair of buttocks thrusting purposefully, again and again. And then a head popped up, looking directly at her—a hand beckoned. She hurriedly took her foot off the brake and drove away with her face bright red.

Lila suddenly realized why they might need a wall around this place. For one thing, the locals might be creeping around, trying to get a glimpse, or even an invitation. For another thing, the students might easily wander out of bounds, happily nude and open for business—and occasion another protest like the one she'd seen on television.

Again, she had that giddy feeling. When she'd seen the black girl laughingly say "Free sample!" and fall to her knees, she'd felt a wonderful sweet liberation. That girl wasn't just sexy; she was adorable, she was charming, she was elegant. She was everything that porn, in Lila's experience, wasn't. She had no qualms about studying the art of being that playful and graceful about sex. It would have been impossible, Lila thought, to think that girl was cheap, or obscene, or anything bad.

But was she anything like Lila? And could Lila be anything like her?

At last she saw the sign for Advising, and pulled into the little parking lot with a sense of help being near. She looked down at the clothes she had chosen to wear—a thin blue sweater and a midthigh-length skirt. She'd thought that it would be cheesy to show up at the sex school dressed—well, for a sex school. Now she wondered. Was she going to look like a terrified virgin, a spinster who was going to crack up at the first improper nudge?

But then she saw her face in the rearview mirror, the black-fringed green eyes and the full lips that added a touch of filthy to her sweet heart-shaped face. Well, she told herself, that girl looks like a sex champion. I've just got to be that girl a little more, and the terrified almost-virgin a little less. With that resolve, she opened the car door and headed up the path to the Student Services building.

From the outside, it was a stately neo-Classical mansion with a rosy tone to the stone of the facade and the broad pillars evenly spaced along the front. The statue of Venus that reclined by the door was carved from a pure white stone, and the contrast with the pink lime-stone of the floor she was placed on made the whiteness seem more like real pale skin. Lying with one hand pressed to her left breast, Venus had her mouth half open in invitation and her legs spread to show a faithfully rendered vulva. Lila remembered that the many statues of Venus scattered around the campus were based on the same model: the Babylona who had started the school and given it its name, a call girl who had become a millionairess and sex toy mogul. For a moment she paused, studying the body of the woman who was about to become her benefactress. The rounded, obviously muscular buttocks and heavy, pointed breasts seemed somehow wrong both for a mogul and for a Venus. What came through overwhelmingly was the call girl; there was no difficulty imagining the original of this statue charging and getting thousands of dollars for sex. Finally Lila shook herself out of her reverie and carried on into the building.

Her appointment was with Ben Hartford, student adviser. As she walked along the rose-colored limestone floors of the arched corridor, she tried to imagine what the student adviser would look like in an institute that trained people for sex professions. Although so far everything about Babylona had been rather elegant and tasteful—in fact, it conveyed an almost intimidating sense of wealth—Lila couldn't help imagining a sleazy swinger type from an old movie: a middle-aged man with dyed hair and gold chains, wearing a satin shirt open to his waist. But no, in reality, it would have to be the opposite, someone in keeping with the distinguished building. An image of a bearded psychoanalyst flashed through Lila's mind. He would refer to the sexual aspects of the curriculum with words like "conjugation" or "frottage." No, it would be a woman, a kindly Ruth Westheimer type with . . . a name other than Ben. Her mind reverted to the bearded authority figure. Maybe he wouldn't mention sex at all, she decided; that would be easiest.

When she found the office, the man sitting at the desk was nothing like what she'd expected. He was only a few years older than she. And at a glance, the first, startling impression she had was that here was the brother of the green-eyed, black-haired temptress she'd seen in her rearview mirror. He had the same olive skin that made his green eyes blaze out startlingly and set off his sleek black hair. But when he stood up, the resemblance faded away; he was easily a foot taller than she, with the muscular, lithe form of a Hollywood action hero. His sleeves were rolled up, and she couldn't help noticing his thick, powerful forearms, the light coating of hair on them making the smoothness of the tanned skin seem even more striking.

She took a deep breath and made herself smile as naturally as she could. "Hi. I'm Lila Anderson. You're Mr. Hartford?"

"Lila, hi," he said. "Please, call me Ben." He came around the desk with his hand extended. She shook his hand and at the moment his skin touched hers she remembered walking into that clearing in the woods. She looked away a little guiltily, aware of the size of his hand as it gently pressed hers. For that second, the entire painful memory of Tad's infidelity and the collapse of her marriage was gone. Instead, she had the distinct impression that she'd decided to come to Babylona at that moment in the woods as she walked toward the strange men naked—or at least to do something that would mean the same thing, that would mean that she could hold a man's hand like this and be ready to sleep with him that instant. And instead of regretting her breakup, she was regretting not going back to those men in time, not acting out the fantasies that had made her lose control that night.

Then she caught herself. She wasn't here for that. Or . . . she was here at Babylona for that, but not *here* at Advising . . . Then the thrilling idea flashed through her mind that here, for the first time, she would never have to be worried about wanting to sleep with a stranger. No one would ever make her feel embarrassed about being interested in someone. It wasn't cheating—she had no one to cheat on. It didn't make her a slut, or desperate, and it wouldn't even matter if the guy didn't want her. It would probably only mean that he'd already had sex three times that morning. And the next guy definitely *would* want her, and have her, and like her for it.

She couldn't quite figure out what it all meant in the long run, but at that moment, it made all the tension in her seep away into the strong, reassuring grip of Ben's hand.

As he let go of her hand, he smiled at her as if he knew everything she'd been thinking and—yes!—liked her for it. He gestured at a leather armchair that was pulled up in front of his desk and she sat down, feeling an intensification of the elation that had been growing in her. To top it off, everything in the room was gorgeous and expensive; she was beginning to realize that the college catalogue had been understating the truth when it referred to "elegant surroundings."

The chair she was sitting in had the soothing, exaggerated comfort that came with an outrageous price tag. It was broad and had stylish, simple lines, and the leather it was covered in was softer than she'd realized leather could be. Ben's desk was likewise beautiful: huge and made of reddish polished wood, with little mother-of-pearl inlays for detailing. Behind him, a big arched window showed a courtyard with a garden full of lavender and Japanese maples, with paths made of shiny white quartz pebbles and elegant wooden benches. Lila had never thought of herself as caring about expensive things, but the sheer beauty of everything here was making her relax deeply. Her body and mind felt a general, happy gratitude.

"So how do you like Babylona so far?" Ben said. A slight anxiety entered his voice, as if he were braced for a negative answer. He added, "You can be completely honest; I've heard it all before, so don't worry about hurting my feelings."

"Oh, I just got here," Lila said. "I mean, literally. I just got off the road. But it's so beautiful. I didn't realize it would be so beautiful." Then she suddenly remembered the orgy—that's what it must have been—in the bushes, and looked down at her lap, flustered. It didn't help that as she looked down at her lap, she was naggingly aware of the red silk panties she'd put on that morning, in honor of her new life. As she recrossed her legs, she couldn't help noticing that those panties were now noticeably wet at the crotch.

Recognizing her discomfort, Ben said gently, "We like to have this first advising session because a lot of people—not just girls, either—find the atmosphere at Babylona challenging. At first."

She made herself meet his eye. "Oh, but that's what I signed up for. I mean, what we all signed up for. I mean, it is an institute for sex professions." She was trying to sound cool, but saying "sex professions" while looking into the deep green eyes of a handsome man was very different from seeing it printed on a prospectus. She added, trying to get back on the right track, "Anyway, I think I'll get used to it soon. It's not that different from my life back home. I mean, it is, but I've had sex, so, I'll catch up in no time. Or, I mean, in time. And if I don't, it'll be fine, because—"

Then she broke off completely. To her consternation, a broad grin was spreading across Ben's face. Suddenly, he burst out laughing. She couldn't help it—she started laughing too.

When their laughter died, she said, "I'm not being very convincing, am I?"

"Not really."

"Okay, I *am* a little frightened. But—is that okay?"

He laughed again. "It's more than okay. It's great. At least, it makes me feel better. I was terrified when I first got here."

"Oh, so you're a—former student?" Her image of both him and Babylona shifted subtly. If Ben was typical of the students here, everything would be all right. The very idea that she was following in his footsteps made her feel better about her decision. He was so obviously smart and together and nice.

And on the other hand, she was facing a gorgeous, charming, gorgeous, gorgeous man who had effectively just told her that he was in the habit of having sex all the time, with everybody he met. Her panties suffered accordingly, and Lila stopped herself just in time from squirming on her increasingly sensitive pussy.

"Graduated two years ago," Ben was saying. "But I'm still not ready for the outside world yet. It's not the sex," he said. "It's just that it can seem cold out there after Babylona."

"Is it partly because . . ." Lila paused, thinking of how to put it. The thing that had almost stopped her coming to Babylona was her worry about what she could do with her degree afterward. Alumni, the brochure boasted, got lucrative and respected posts as sexual surrogates, porn professionals, sexperts, sex researchers, and "hyperescorts" in Amsterdam and Tokyo, often set up for them before graduation through the Babylona Abroad program. But Lila wasn't sure she wanted to spend the rest of her life in the sex industry. So she said at last, "Was it because you weren't into working in the sex industry?"

"Not exactly," said Ben. "I think I wasn't into working in any industry. After a few years here, you get spoiled. It's not just the luxury—though one thing I always want to point out to incoming freshmen is that we are probably the only school in the nation that has a hot tub that's filled with champagne . . ."

"Oh, wow."

"So that's hard to beat. But the other thing is that this place is very . . . innocent."

"Innocent?" Lila laughed, although she already had an inkling of what he might mean.

Ben smiled at her, and for a second they locked eyes and Lila felt a strange warmth spreading through her body. It wasn't a sexual feeling, either. It was more like the feeling of meeting someone who's going to become your new best friend. At that moment, Lila would have stayed at Babylona just to be near Ben.

"You'll see," he said. "Or I hope you'll see. If you stay."

"Oh, I'll stay," she blurted.

He blinked and for the first time seemed a little shy. "A lot of people don't stay. Every year we lose between ten and twenty percent of our freshmen."

"Even though it's innocent?" she said, teasing.

He shook his head and looked at her very seriously. "I think our brand of innocence isn't for everyone. You have to be able to accept people as they are, somehow. You can't hold yourself back from people the way you do in the outside world. What I learned in the end is that when you make sex your life's work, it doesn't stop being intimate. You just learn to be intimate with people as a default, instead of—" He caught himself. "I'm sorry. I'm getting carried away. I guess I maybe believe in my sales pitch a little too much."

"No," Lila said without thinking. "That was wonderful. I think you're being really wonderful."

Then they were both embarrassed. Ben began neatening the papers on his already painfully neat desk. At last, still busying himself aligning a stapler precisely with the edge of his desk, he said, "Anyway, you can take that as a demonstration of what can happen when you get used to being intimate with *everyone.*"

"And I think it's wonderful. So you can take that as a demonstration that I'm going to stay here."

Ben smiled at her, relieved. "I hope so."

She sat back in the armchair, letting her bare arms slip luxuriously over the creamy leather. She was feeling more in control now, and she remembered now what she had promised herself to ask when she got here. "Actually, one thing that I think would make me more comfortable is if I knew exactly what would be expected of me. I mean, the catalogue kind of tells you, but . . . it's not really focused on the things you're going to be scared of."

Ben was nodding. "No, I know exactly what you mean. I felt exactly the same. Let me just find something on my computer . . ." He began to work at his keyboard, squinting into the computer screen.

"So lots of people are frightened?" Lila asked. "You were frightened, too?"

"People who *aren't* frightened when they get here—actually, I think they're a little weird. And a lot of them leave; they realize this isn't what they wanted. And then there are the people who were already sex workers."

"Is that bad?"

"Not bad." Ben looked up from what he was doing. "It's not that it's bad, and maybe those people actually help, because they're already comfortable with basic things like nudity. But I think for a lot of them, that's because nudity doesn't make them feel anything anymore. And that's not the same as feeling what nudity makes you feel and being comfortable with it."

Lila tried to imagine it. Her body began to fill again with that all-over tingling she'd had in the woods. She said softly, "I think I see what you mean."

Once again he blinked shyly. Then he said, also softly, "I guess

I'd better find this stuff for you. Just give me a second." He bent over the computer screen once more. It gave her an opportunity to study his face, the fine olive skin in which his parted lips showed a row of glistening white teeth. If this conversation were happening under any other circumstances, Lila might have been plotting to date him. But here at Babylona— First, she didn't even know if people *did* date. It seemed like that whole world of dating would be irrelevant here. And on the other hand, he was still a student adviser, an employee of the school. So at a normal school, he wouldn't be *allowed* to date her. She had no idea if rules like that meant anything here, and of course there was no way she could ask.

But all the while she couldn't help thinking of putting her hands on his face, of kissing him. She could easily imagine how soft his lips would feel—softer than the leather on her palms. How she would shut her eyes and her head would tilt back as he took her in his arms. It was silly because it was such a sentimental fantasy she was having; it was like the fantasy a thirteen-year-old girl might have about a teacher. She wanted to kiss him on the lips and feel his strong arms around her—it was completely corny. But all the while her panties were getting wetter and wetter at the thought of it.

"Okay," Ben said. "These are some pictures of projects from the last group of first-year students. If you come around here, I can talk you through them."

He gestured for her to come to his side of the desk, and she got up, suddenly feeling vulnerable, sure she wouldn't know what to say. She stood beside him, painfully aware of the closeness of his shoulder in its clean white shirt.

On the screen, she was relieved to see a simple picture of a naked man. His penis wasn't even erect.

"This is kind of a silly one. This is Jake giving himself a hard-on with the force of his mind. He's got it down to fifty seconds."

"You're kidding."

"No, I'll run the film." He clicked the PLAY button at the bottom of the frame, and the man in the picture raised his arms straight out from his sides as if to say: look, no hands! At the bottom of the frame, the time began to run down from one minute and two seconds . . . fifty-eight seconds . . . forty-five seconds . . . and the man's penis began to stiffen and twitch. Gradually it filled out, getting chubbier and chubbier until it stood, seemingly magically, in the air—with twelve seconds to go! At that point, applause and cheers came from what Lila assumed was a student audience. She was laughing now, and Ben started laughing, too. He said, "It's a contest we have every year. But usually the first years don't compete. Jake is kind of a phenomenon." He closed the picture and clicked on another one.

Lila gasped as she saw that this film began with a close-up of a vagina with two fingers in it.

"This is similar," Ben said, his voice quieter as if he'd caught her anxiety. "This is Annie having an orgasm in a minute and ten seconds."

He clicked the PLAY button and the fingers began to move, playing around the glistening clitoris and shoving in and out greedily. There was the sound of a girl's light, frenzied breathing. Lila was all too aware of her own clitoris stiffening and throbbing. And when she saw the hand convulse and press hard into the pussy on the screen as the pink vulva began to spasm, her cunt cried out for a similar release.

Ben's voice was husky as he said, "Okay, I'm just going to show you one of the exhibitionism projects . . . It's just sex, but *because* they're exhibitionism projects, we film them."

This film began in a classroom that was much like the classes at Lila's high school except that the desks and chairs were much nicer—like a designer's idea of the school desk rather than real school desks. For a flash, she saw the faces of the students, all smiling as they leaned forward, concentrating on something at the front of the class. Then the camera pivoted to show what they were seeing.

A slim blond girl stood there, slowly unbuttoning a long white man's shirt, which was apparently all she was wearing. From time to time she paused to mold the shirt's thin fabric against her small round breasts. When it was completely unbuttoned, she let it fall open to show her blond pubis, the hair trimmed to a thin stripe. Then a man stepped into the frame, a Latino guy who was already bare to the waist. He took one side of her shirt and pulled it open to reveal the girl's breast. Then he bent his head and began to lick the bared nipple.

Lila was staring at the screen, frozen, full of the idea of doing that in just—how long would it be? Did they start with actual sex the first week? Then suddenly she felt a light touch on the back of her bare thigh. It was Ben's hand, that same large, masculine hand that had gripped hers with such strength and certainty. Now it was brushing against her tender skin, sending electricity up her thighs and straight to that patch of wetness in her silk panties. Even the tips of her nipples prickled as his hand stroked inward, cupping the inside of her thigh and beginning to creep up between her legs.

"So do you think you could . . ." he said, his voice hoarse. He continued to look only at the computer screen as the blond girl let the shirt fall off her shoulders to the floor.

She heard a voice saying "Yes," in a husky whisper, only it was her voice. And that was her heavy breathing as his hand traced shivers up the inside of her thigh and one finger arrived at the damp crotch of her panties. He caught his breath when he felt the wetness there. Then the finger began to stroke against her pussy, teasingly tagging her clit again and again as it felt the richness of the wet silk.

She said, "Yes," again, though he hadn't asked anything. Then his finger had hooked around and pulled the silk away, nosing up into her dripping-wet pussy. She gasped as it slipped into her cunt. It turned inside her, feeling all the folds of her as she involuntarily pressed her hips down, plunging it deeper.

She kept her eyes trained on the couple on the screen; the blond girl was perched on the edge of one of those fancy school desks, her legs spread to let the Latino guy shove into her. His dark cock could be seen clearly working in and out of her cunt. The girl's face had an almost fierce expression; she leaned back on the desk, arching her back to let the man run his hands over her breasts. And Ben got up from his chair. His finger slipped out of Lila, and she cried out, one slight, sweet note of disappointment. Then he had pulled her skirt up and he was gently tugging her panties down over her ass.

Both of his strong hands were stroking her ass then, appreciating its firm full cheeks. When she heard his zipper, she almost cried out; the sound alone sent pleasure coursing from her belly down her legs like adrenaline. There was an awful pause while she waited and almost came to her senses—she couldn't be doing this! This was absolutely wrong! Then she felt the head of his penis pressing against her wet cunt lips. And a second later, he had thrust deep inside her, and she bit her tongue, trying to contain the cry of pleasure that almost tore its way out of her. He pressed into her as deeply as he could go. Then he was actually fucking her, his cock going deeply into her; she had to grip the edge of the desk to keep her balance. With every thrust, her whole body rang with the pleasure in her cunt. He had reached around her and slipped a hand under her sweater, and soon he was pulling her bra down to free a nipple, which he took between his fingers and gently twisted, while his other hand pulled her hips back toward him. Tears were coming to her eyes with the pleasure; she had never felt anything like it. It was blow after blow of joy that resonated through her whole body until even her fingertips were buzzing with it. The couple on the screen were fucking with the same rhythm, the blond girl wrapping her legs around the man's back now to let him go even deeper into her. And Ben was going deeper and deeper into Lila, his long cock finding stores of pleasure she didn't know she had.

At last she felt him stiffen and drive into her even harder, his hand tightening on her breast. She came, her vision going dark and fuzzy with the intensity of it, as she felt his cock jerk, spurting his come hotly into her. Her cunt went on orgasming, squeezing his cock dry as she moaned, no longer aware of what she was doing. "Oh, Ben . . . oh my God . . . thank you."

His cock slipped out of her, and before she had time to think or feel ashamed, he had turned her around and was kissing her. His fingers sank into her hair and she was kissing him back passionately, feeling the deep dark warmth of perfect physical release flooding her body, relaxing her to her toes. Her hands found the strong broad muscles in his chest and slid down to his hard belly.

He kissed her ear and murmured, "Lila, sweet Lila . . ."

And then something in her woke up. Maybe it was that she'd only ever heard Tad's voice in those circumstances. But the first thing she thought about was the phrase "intimate with *everyone*" and some part of her announced clearly and nervously that she didn't know how to do that! The fact that she'd just done it didn't prove anything except that she was out of her depth. She pulled back against his arms, already smiling anxiously.

He was looking at her with a drowsy delight; one of his hands was still under her sweater, fondling her breast. She almost impatiently pushed his hand down, and as he let her go, backing away with a hurt expression, she tugged her bra back into place. Then she was pulling up her panties. In a moment everything had changed; she was smack back in her old reality, realizing that this was the *second man* she had ever had sex with, the second one she'd given herself to. A man she'd met only half an hour ago! A man who had shown her dirty pictures (never mind that he was only doing his job; or maybe that made it worse) and then made the crudest possible pass at her. A pass that she had accepted unthinkingly . . . Was this what she was really like? Was this what she would have to be like?

"I'm sorry," she mumbled. "I don't know why I . . ."

"No, I'm sorry," said Ben. The look on his face was still baffled, but becoming quickly cooler. He narrowed his eyes and said, "I know that was . . . unprofessional of me, but I felt . . ."

"No, I understand." Lila forced a laugh. "It's what we're here for, right?"

"No, not really. Not with me. That's not what this was . . . That's not my job. Don't think that."

Lila wouldn't meet his eyes. She wanted to put her arms back around him; she wanted to believe what he was saying. But she couldn't. Not now; it was too much, and she still didn't understand what she'd just done. So she said, "I think I'd better just go find my dorm room. It's all a little sudden for me."

For a flash, she looked him in the face, and his green eyes, now pained and concerned, almost made her succumb. But then she just took a deep breath and said, "Thank you for your help, Mr. Hartford. You've been great." And then, before she could fully appreciate the ridiculousness of what she'd just said, she turned and walked back out of his office, rushing as fast as she could down the corridor and out to her car.

Chapter Two

Lila slept fitfully that night. It was the first night she'd spent away from home, or at least the first night she'd been away *alone*. Many times she'd spent the night at Tad's, especially in the six months after they'd announced their engagement. And then there were the camping weekends, the trip to New York City—so many memories that were lying in ambush for Lila the second she was alone.

She'd half hoped, half feared that her new roommate would already be there, but when she arrived in the room, it was empty. Though empty was really the wrong word, because it was more lavishly furnished than any room Lila had been in before.

There were two brass beds, with fluffy white comforters and pristine white silk sheets. Each had four down pillows on it, and on the top pillow was a little welcome kit, with travel-size toothpaste, shampoo, and shower gel, a note wishing students a *delight-filled stay!* and three chocolate truffles, all in a little satin drawstring purse. There were matching lamps on the floor and desks, with matching rose-fringed lamp shades, and the curtains on the windows were of the same rose taffeta, with the same darker fringes. There was an intricately patterned Persian rug on the dark hardwood floor, which had woven into it a picture of odalisques and peacocks in a lush garden. There were two desks, both of them either antiques or extraordinarily good replicas. One was a cherrywood rolltop desk, which Lila mentally reserved for herself. (She'd *always* wanted a rolltop desk; surely she couldn't have the bad luck to be rooming with another girl who'd *always* wanted a rolltop desk.) There was even a little family of orchids in dainty lacquered pots clustered in the corner of the room.

The room had a private bathroom as well, which featured an enormous sunken bathtub and a little mosaic of mermaids worked into the floor tiles. One wall of the bathroom was taken up with a mirror, and there was an incredible number of incredibly plump towels neatly hung over a brass rail. All the enamel was a faint rose pink that reminded Lila a little uncomfortably of the Student Services building and the abandoned scene she had just played there with the uncomfortably enchanting student adviser.

And on two opposite walls of the bedroom hung oil paintings: one a landscape of a French village, and the other a portrait of Babylona herself, the patron saint of the institution. In this portrait she was uncharacteristically fully dressed, wearing a white summer dress and sitting on a rolltop desk that was the twin of the one in the room, and pursing her lips as if to blow a kiss at the viewer. Again, Lila got a sense of the woman, a carefree, scapegrace lover of men. What came across was not just her sexiness—though that was plain—but a sense of well-being and grace that seemed like a natural continuation of the beautiful grounds of her institute.

The lavish atmosphere at Babylona was all the work of that lady, perhaps the most successful prostitute of the twentieth century. She had begun life in a family of carnival owners, traveling from state to state in near poverty. At fifteen, she had run away with a man who would remain her good friend for the rest of her life, James Parris. He had been her lover but had also given her her first job in the sex industry, working (on fake ID) in the topless-bottomless place he owned in San Francisco. In her autobiography *A Life on All Fours*, Babylona, who was then called Nancy, described how she realized that, despite her love for James, she had a vocation for sex work:

> *I'd been serving a table of Marines who were getting rowdier and rowdier. One of them kept squeezing my butt whenever my back was turned.*

Another one made a grab for my tit when I was putting down his drink. I jumped away, giggling, but he still copped himself a good feel.

And the manager, Mandy, took me to one side and said, "If those boys are bothering you, I can chuck them out. Don't worry about it. It happens all the time. I don't want you putting up with any crap. It's not worth it." Well, I just stared at her. It had never occurred to me that someone grabbing your breast could be a bad thing. I'd been dying to stand there and let him grope to his heart's content. But I was worried that I'd get behind on my drink orders—I was at work, after all!

That was when I realized I just wasn't like other girls. And it didn't take long before I figured out that that difference could be the foundation stone of my fortune.

At first James was distressed as he saw our wedding plans evaporate in the heat of my newfound craze. But soon he came to love me even more . . .

Lila fell asleep reading that autobiography, since every new student got a copy of it tucked under the fat down pillows of his or her bed. And when she woke up, the first thing that greeted her eyes was a page describing Babylona's trapeze act: *Then I swung in on my trapeze and Fabulo caught me by my feet and impaled me on his . . .*

She sat up in bed, startled. For a second she thought she was in Ben's room, though in her muddled state she wasn't quite clear about who Ben was. Then it all came flooding back. She had a flash of chagrin, a flash of excitement, a flash of pure fear . . . then so many flashes of so many different feelings she didn't know whether they were good or bad. Finally she looked at the clock and realized that she'd slept through her alarm; she had only fifteen minutes left before her first class, Satisfaction 101. All her feelings resolved into the familiar panic of being incredibly, hopelessly late.

Ten minutes later, she was rushing up the stairs of the main building, Parris, clutching a notebook. Her hair was shoved into a sloppy ponytail and she was wearing jeans that were clean but had clear fold marks from being packed and a wrinkled T-shirt showing her high school mascot—a turkey—brandishing a hockey stick, over the slogan PARVILLE GOBBLERS—not exactly the first impression she would have most liked to make.

And as she took her seat, she couldn't help noticing that everyone else was dressed very differently. Where she had assumed that dressing sexy at a sex school was—well, so *obvious*—everyone else seemed to think that obvious was just the beginning. They'd gone past obvious to blatant, and on to eye-poppingly filthy.

Hers was clearly the only bra in the room. There was a girl who was wearing a net shirt with daisies embroidered like polka dots over it that, either strategically or by pure chance, barely covered her nipples. But the remainder of her breasts were not only exposed but kept quivering as she giggled at whispered remarks from the crew-cut blond man behind her, who obviously spent most of his waking hours in a gym. And the rest of them perhaps in a tanning booth. He was actually wearing gym shorts. Only. Lila took a deep breath and realized that one of the more trivial things she would have to get used to was being at a school where it was completely normal to go barefoot. And shirtless, as half of the men in the room were. A corollary of this realization was the realization that the school authorities, obviously anticipating this state of affairs, had heated the building to such a toasty warmth that Lila was feeling hot in jeans and T-shirt.

The classic store sign, NO SHIRT, NO SHOES, NO SERVICE, flashed through her mind. Here it would be NO SHIRT, NO SHOES—FULL SERVICE. Where Full Service meant the high jinks described so lovingly in *A Life on All Fours.*

Lila looked around surreptitiously, a little overawed by the incredible array of low-cut blouses, the pierced navels and short shorts cut high enough to reveal a pale curve of buttock when the owner stood up . . . and Lila, in her T-shirt.

A girl suddenly plumped down in the seat next to her, with a loud "Oof!" Her hair was platinum blond and she wore plush gym shorts with a bikini top that seemed more like a garnish than a garment on her enormous breasts. She grinned widely at Lila and said, "I'm the walking wounded. I think I had one too many Long Island Liquors last night."

"Long Island Liquors?"

"Yeah, it's what you call a Long Island Iced Tea when the only ingredient you got is vodka. That's my kind of ladylike way of saying I drank straight vodka all night and woke up in the grass at ten a.m.—with a man asleep on top of me. Ouch." She put out her hand. "My name's Brandi."

Lila shook her hand, saying, "Lila."

"Well," said Brandi, sighing. "I guess you win best dressed. Look at us!"

"Oh, I thought . . . I feel like a slob."

Brandi shook her head. "No, honey. You win hands down. The problem is, you're the prettiest. I hope you don't mind me saying it. Keep in mind I have a big mouth, so what I say doesn't mean the same as a normal person. Anyhow, so you're prettiest, and now you show up dressed like an everyday person. Well, it makes the rest of us all look tacky. If you were plain, just a little bit plain, even anything close to ordinary-looking—but no such luck." She grinned. "No hard feelings from me, though. I realized a long time ago my problem is, I just try too hard. But I can't stop trying too hard. I got cheesy in my blood." She looked around the room. "Well, at least I'm among my own kind here."

Lila was straining to think of some rejoinder, but she was saved by the arrival of the teacher. The woman, a startlingly beautiful thirtyish woman with dramatic cheekbones and slanting brown eyes, shut the door behind her and turned to face the class with one hand on her slender hip. She was wearing a black slip dress that hugged her lithe body tightly. Her honey-blond hair was cut short, but that only accentuated the perfection of her features. She smiled and cocked her head as if she were pausing before delivering a deadly piece of flirting to a lover whom she was facing over a martini. At last she said, in a husky, sultry drawl, "Hello, I'm Miss Foré. Welcome to Satisfaction."

The class laughed, a little uncertainly. Lila thought to herself with a certain relief that at least now she wasn't the prettiest. The teacher smiled, licking her crimson lips, and walked to the blackboard, her gait in sky-high heels a luxurious feline stalk. She picked up a piece of chalk and began to write on the board.

"In Satisfaction, we study the *feelings* that are associated with sexuality. The emphasis is not on the *acts themselves* but on what the body and the mind experience during them." She paused in the middle of writing the word "arousal" and looked back over her shoulder at the class with an air of complicity. She said, "Of course, as Babylona will tell you herself when she visits later in the year, the key to sexiness is in what you feel, not what you do."

Brandi stuck her hand in the air boldly. Miss Foré seemed to hesitate, but at last she said, "Yes, do you have a question?"

Brandi folded her arms under the great prow of her breasts and said, "Well, but wouldn't Babylona be talking different if she was some big fat ugly thing? I mean, what you do and what you feel is all very well, but what you look like . . ."

The class tittered a bit, but they all shifted uncomfortably, obviously expecting some swift retribution.

Miss Foré squinted and said, "Why don't we talk about this after class?"

Brandi's jaw dropped open. "I'm just saying, because I think it's important to get these things up-front. And sometimes, when I was working in movies, you know, I'd just be feeling sore. I wouldn't be hot at all. But the shots came out okay. But when I was *looking* like hell, like this morning for instance—'cause I didn't get a whole lot of sleep, you know—well, we were just throwing film away on that. It wasn't sexy at all, unless you were a necrophiliac. I can look pretty bad in bright lights, take my word. So—"

"After class," said Miss Foré calmly. She turned back to the board and went on writing.

Brandi looked around her in consternation. Most of the other kids avoided her eye, but Lila gave her a grimace of commiseration. Brandi leaned toward her and whispered, "Never mind. I'm going to give her an earful after class. She's probably right, as far as it goes. But not in a movie. In a movie, it's all about what shows on film. She'll see my point; I bet you anything."

Miss Foré had written "Arousal," "Peak," "Climax," "Relaxation" on the board. She now turned to the class and said, "For our purposes today, these are the basic phases of *satisfaction.*" Then she looked up into the air dreamily and said, "I think everyone is familiar with arousal and climax. And probably you can guess what we mean by relaxation. But what is peak?" She cast her eye around the class languidly, as if she were about to saunter down the aisle running her fingers through the students' hair.

A boy in front raised his hand shyly. Miss Foré nodded at him, saying, "Yes, and would you tell me your name?"

"Hi, I'm Judd, ma'am. And I was thinking that peak is probably just before you come, and . . . you can't stop anymore. Is that it?"

"Marvelous," said Miss Foré, actually seeming to wriggle slightly with the pleasure of getting the right answer. Then she said, "Judd, would you give us an example of the first two stages from your own experience?"

"Ma'am?" said Judd, in a terrified voice a full octave above the voice he'd used before.

"Just a story," Miss Foré purred. "A story about a time that you were aroused until you reached a *point of no return.*"

Judd, a slender boy with the frame of a swimmer, looked around the room as if he were asking the other students to interfere on his behalf. Everyone just looked back at him blankly, and finally his face altered, looking intent as he seemed to snatch a memory from thin air. He cleared his throat and began: "Well, I think this is what you want, ma'am. So, when I was fifteen was when I had my first experience with a blow job. I was staying with my girlfriend's parents for the summer. They had a place on the beach in North Carolina and we'd spend the whole day on the beach. I was, well, I was fifteen, ma'am, and I used to have a lot of trouble with all the nubile bikini-clads around—that's what my girlfriend's father used to call them, the nubile bikini-clads, 'cause he was an English professor, ma'am."

"And . . . ?"

"Oh, yes, ma'am. I'll get to the point. So I spent half the day on my stomach trying to hide my hard-on, is what I was saying. And my girlfriend, Dana, wouldn't let me get past second base. So one afternoon Dana was gone to the doctor with her dad and me and her mom were having brunch together . . . and I have to say Dana's mom was kind of a knockout, really. She was, well, she had an amazing body, just the most incredible . . . ass, if you'll excuse my French—"

"We're partial to French here," said Miss Foré.

"Thank you for saying so, ma'am. So Dana's mom, I guess, was partial to French, too, cause we'd had two mimosas each on the porch of their beach house, and, well, I was helping her clear the table, and I'd just put down the dishes I had and turned around and walked right into her. And I guess she felt my hard-on, 'cause she'd been sitting there in her bikini and I was, um . . ."

"Hard," Miss Foré purred, letting her hand drift into her cleavage.

"Yes, ma'am. Hard as stone. My dick was hurting in my jeans, and I guess she felt it, because she kind of says, 'Oh, do you need some help?' and then she touched my zipper. Just lightly, she was letting her hand run up and down my bulge there. I was dying. And I say, though I didn't mean it, 'You shouldn't do that. Dana could come home. You shouldn't do that. You shouldn't do that.' But I was staring at her boobs and just repeating myself and before I know it I'm touching her breasts through her bikini top, and she's moaning and then . . . well, she gets down on her knees. And when the zipper unzipped, well. I was at peak."

There was a moment of silence while everyone waited for the rest. Then the class groaned. Brandi muttered, "Kiss-and-tell-us interruptus."

Miss Foré said, "I think you might have left us hanging here, Judd. Would you like to say what happened next?"

"Oh." Judd shrugged his shoulders. "Just, Dana walked in, but it was too late and I came all over her mom's face. Boom!" He made a gesture, shooting his hand up from his crotch and then wriggling the fingers in the air. Then he shook his head and said, "Busted!"

"How difficult for you," said Miss Foré.

"Oh, not actually, ma'am," said Judd. "The fact is, though I never got to go back to that summer house, Dana solved the problem, once and for all, by having sex with me herself from then on. So we all patched it up okay."

"Oh, I'd like to hear Dana's side," Brandi said. "Patched it up okay, hell!"

Judd turned around and addressed her seriously: "No, you don't understand, 'cause Dana turned out to be a chip off the old block. Dana was sleeping with every Tom, Dick, and Harry in town by Christmas. I got to say that Dana *and* her mom were an inspiration to me. They're the reason I'm here with you today."

"Amen," said Brandi.

"Amen is right," said Judd, nodding thoughtfully. His sky-blue eyes misted over with emotion.

Here Miss Foré broke in and said, "I think that's enough for our first day, class. I'd like you to do a little bit of homework for me, though." She shut her eyes and seemed to drift off in erotic imaginings for a moment. When she opened them again, there was a languorous smile teasing the corners of her lips. She said, "Would you please go out"—she gestured vaguely at the window—"in the real world and *experience* the stages of arousal and peak for me. Which, naturally, means experiencing the other two stages as well." She winked. "But this is about *feeling*. So *ignore* your climax and everything after, please. I'm sure that will be straightforward. And be prepared to discuss arousal and peak based on your experience. But no need to mention any names, of course." She winked again.

Then she pointed at Judd. "Would *you* please stay behind for just a minute?" Then at Brandi. "And of course I want to see *you* as well. For the rest of you—till next Monday."

Lila gathered her books and noticed several students looking at the clock, a ludicrously ornate thing of filigree gold with rhinestone numbers spreading from it, and rhinestone-encrusted arms. Only ten minutes of class time had passed. She didn't know whether to feel cheated or relieved. At least she hadn't had to recount any experiences of "peak" in front of her new schoolmates. But there was part of her that was actually left with the craving to do just that. She had prepared a story about Tad finger-fucking her under a coat he'd spread over their laps in the movies. When he'd started, it was a night scene in the film, and no one could see anything. Then it changed to a scene in a bright white office, and the woman sitting next to Lila had stared rather oddly at the rhythmic movement under the coat. Lila had pushed his hand away but . . . well, she was at peak, and after a long painful minute of suffering, she had to finish the job herself. And walking out of class, she felt that telling that story in front of everyone might have put her into the same condition. Which made her wonder what exactly Miss Foré had kept Judd behind for, and whether he, at least (and Brandi?), would get to complete the last two stages of *Satisfaction*.

Kiss-and-tell-us interruptus, indeed. Lila walked out into the balmy autumn day on the crest of a wave of erotic longing—and fresh self-confidence.

Chapter Three

Brandi sat back in her chair and watched the other students file out to freedom. That cute Dominican guy, Miguel, smiled at her commiseratingly as he went, and she had a miniflashback of his tensed gleaming butt, with the rounded balls peeping lusciously from between his thick muscular thighs and pulsing as he drove it home into Nina, the Russian girl. Well, last night she'd got along with everybody just *fine*, she thought, sighing. She'd promised herself she would keep her big, fat, stupid mouth shut at least for the first month. Give people a chance to get to know her before she started arguing and causing trouble. And yes, "get to know her" might mean get to know how good her pussy tasted ("like whipped cream . . ." her first boyfriend had said, starry-eyed ". . . or lobster"), or how good it felt spasming around their cocks. Okay, that was her usual method of winning friends and influencing people, and maybe it was a little cheap. Maybe some people would look down on her, in fact. But if it ain't broke, why fix it?

But here she'd gone and opened her trap already. And she was sure if she hadn't had *quite* so much vodka last night, or let five guys take the Brandi taste test (*lobster* won), she would have been able to keep her promise to herself. She was pretty sure anyway. Though after all—she watched Miguel's broad bare back pass by, admiring the deep ridge between his crests of back muscle—what did she come here for? If she was honest with herself, she didn't think she had that much to *learn* about making love, exactly. She'd come here less for study than for a kind of an internship.

That poor kid Judd turned around almost superstitiously and

met her eye. She flashed him a reassuring grin. She mouthed, "It's okay!" but he snapped his head back to the front of the class, as if scared to be seen associating with her. Oh well.

He hadn't been there last night. And that precious little green-eyed kid, Lila—she hadn't either. Probably they would be the hottest ones in a month, though. Despite her own outgoing nature, Brandi tended to think that still waters ran hot. Anyhow, she couldn't help thinking about walking home with Judd. His pale skin, the kind of milky white skin that promised a delicate, baby-pink nipple, and a cock that would blush in subtle gradations of color as she gently, slowly, teased it into hardness . . . yum.

Now all the other students had disappeared, and even the sounds of their chatter had gone from the hall. Miss Foré shut the door again and turned to Judd and Brandi, smiling. "Why don't you come up here so I don't have to shout?" she said, with her hand tracing delicate circles on her flat belly.

Judd got up awkwardly and Brandi followed, beginning to wonder if this wasn't quite the kind of dressing-down she'd expected. Miss Foré perched on the edge of the teacher's desk, her tongue drawing a slow, deliberate line across her upper lip. One dress strap fell lightly off her shoulder. She cocked her head and said, "I guess you're wondering why I asked you to stay . . ."

Judd said, "Ma'am?"

He and Brandi were standing side by side in front of Miss Foré. Brandi could tell Judd was struggling not to stare at the fallen dress strap . . . and the breast under the thin fabric that was beginning to peep up from the slowly dropping neckline of the black dress.

Brandi cleared her throat and said, though she was aware of a slight double entendre creeping into her tone, "Are we going to be punished, Miss Foré?"

Miss Foré shrugged, letting the dress fall so that it was barely hooked above her visibly erect nipple. She said, "I think *you* should be punished, young lady. But I don't see why Judd should be punished, do you? Perhaps Judd should do the punishing. So I don't have to get my hands dirty, if you see what I mean."

Brandi said, "Oh, I see." She smiled broadly. Everything was working out more or less exactly as she had hoped. Her bottom was already tingling with suspense.

Judd said, "Ma'am, are you . . . I mean . . ."

Miss Foré coughed politely into her hand, and her dress neckline made the final tiny leap, letting her entire left breast appear nude. It was large and teardrop shaped, with a silky mauve areola surrounded by a speckling of light freckles. The nipple was just barely erect, and as Miss Foré took her hand down from her mouth, she let it gently tweak the erect nipple, and her whole body stiffened and then released in sympathy. Then, as if tiring of the pretense, she shrugged the other strap of her dress off and the whole dress fell to the floor, revealing her complete, pale, gorgeous nudity. A patch of honey-colored pubic hair was shaved into a perfect Valentine shape over her slightly protruding cunt lips.

Judd gasped. Brandi wanted to cheer. This was exactly what she had come for. Her internship was about to begin in earnest. She said, "What kind of punishment did you have in mind?"

Miss Foré said, "Well, first I'd like you to do a little chore for me. And maybe while you're at it, I can think of something for Judd to do for me, too. Just a little something like . . . clapping erasers." She let her hand snake up and down her body and perched once more on the edge of the desk, letting her thighs fall open to expose the wet pale pink folds of her cunt.

Brandi immediately fell to her knees without thinking and began to nuzzle Miss Foré's tender inner thighs. The skin was smooth and hot against her burning lips. She could already smell the musky scent of the teacher's pussy waiting, and her breath began to come fast and hard. She was so ready for this.

She let her tongue play up inside the sensitive join between the thigh and the pubic bone, suppressing a smile of gratification as she heard Miss Foré gasp with need. Then she nosed gently against the clitoris and let her tongue dip in between the soaking hot lips. First she thrust as deep as she could and held her tongue still, letting Miss Foré wait for it. Then she made the tongue squirm lightning-fast and pulled it up over Miss Foré's clit. And again. She built up a rhythm, working it softly, softly, then harder and faster . . . Then she would hold her tongue still again until Miss Foré squirmed in need. Brandi would begin to play the teasing game again, tongue-fucking slowly, then faster and faster, letting the slender older woman come to the brink of orgasm again and again. She was giving her "peak" in spades.

Then Miss Foré's hand suddenly grasped Brandi's hair and pressed her mouth hard into her pubis. And the sultry voice was saying, "Judd, I think this girl needs to be taught a lesson. Would you . . ."

From the shadow that played over her expectant head, Brandi knew that a gesture was explaining to Judd what he should do. And of course she wasn't surprised when she felt her skirt being lifted up to expose her ass, and then the always exhilarating slip of her thong down, down, to let the cold shock of air meet her bare-shaved pussy. She moaned helplessly, and her tongue struggled against the delicious cunt of her teacher, fighting as if making Miss Foré come would free her.

Brandi pressed her eyes shut and felt the faint breeze before Judd's hand came down to spank her bare bottom. She almost laughed at the pleasure she felt at the light smack; it made her vulva sting with the anticipation of his cock. And again. She was writhing, and her tongue was writhing against Miss Foré's clitoris, making her writhe too . . . all caught at that tormenting moment just before orgasm. And then, at long last, Brandi heard the sweet sound of a zipper being pulled down. The image she had created before of the girlfriend's mother ravenously unzipping the fifteen-year-old-boy's zipper went through her mind. And then she couldn't think at all as the cock plunged deep inside her, and Judd began to fuck her with a rapid-fire frenzy, almost machine-gun fast. His dick was so long that it was giving her deep G-spot a beating, hitting it so hard it couldn't quite come to its senses enough to come, and she was trapped at that moment of perfect sensuous insanity. Miss Foré pulled her hair gently, lifting her head an inch away from the teacher's dripping, luscious crotch, and Brandi's tongue began to flick frantically over Miss Foré's clitoris, as she worked the teacher into a sudden, bursting orgasm. Miss Foré groaned as her cunt began to fire spasm after spasm, and her body began to release, her thighs falling even farther open, letting Brandi play her tongue all over her wide-open cunt.

At the same moment, Brandi felt Judd's thrusting begin to slow and he began to moan helplessly, bending forward to grasp her breasts. He was squeezing them, at first hard, then with more attentive appreciation, and a fresh current of bliss opened between her tits and her pussy, sending her over the edge into her own shuddering, wild orgasm. A moment later, Judd gasped deeply and his hands clawed deeply, deliciously, into her breasts as he pressed almost painfully deeply into her, overwhelmed by his own spurting orgasm.

Brandi gradually let her head relax, resting against the teacher's soft thigh. She felt Judd's hands also relax, stroking her breasts affectionately as he pulled out of her with a sigh of farewell. Miss Foré's hand eased out of her hair.

In a moment, they were all standing again, and Brandi pulled her thong up within reach with a practiced hook of her lifted foot. Judd zipped up with a dreamy expression. But Miss Foré walked away to the blackboard, wearing only her black high-heeled sandals, with as much composure as if she were wearing a floor-length gown. She lifted an eraser and tossed it to Brandi, who caught it reflexively.

"Clean the board for me, darling," said Miss Foré. "Oh, and both of you"—she looked them up and down with a lingering appreciation before winking once more—"this *doesn't* count as the homework."

Chapter Four

By the time she got back to her dorm room, Lila's elation had given way to worry. It had sunk in that she had actual homework—homework that gave her a stark choice. Either she had to have sex with another stranger within a week, or she had to be willing to masturbate and describe the results to her new peers. Not that she was ashamed of masturbating. But she wasn't sure she wanted to discuss it in public—not just yet. Plus, wouldn't that be a little like shirking? Just a little bit like stealing your essay off of Wikipedia?

She opened the door with every fiber of her being ready to throw herself down on the fluffy bed and give way to dreams of home . . . or at best, to another couple of hours whiled away with *A Life on All Fours*. But she froze in the doorway. The room had been transformed.

Her first impression was that an underwear bomb had gone off; every surface seemed to be covered with some kind of lace, satin, or . . . yes, that was a red leather bra on the floor. In the midst of all this, a suitcase that was almost as big as the double bed lay agape, with a tangle of high-heeled sandals on top of a heap of clothes.

For a second she thought she'd actually got the wrong room. Perhaps there was some mistake, and the locks were the same on two of the doors? Perhaps all the locks were the same, the better to facilitate impromptu midnight visits.

But then she heard a light voice humming in the bathroom and realized it was her roommate. She came in a little tentatively, calling, "Hello?"

There was a little yelp and the sound of glass breaking from the bathroom. Then there was the sound of a cool alto voice saying, "Fuck."

Lila stepped gingerly into the room. A slim girl with short black hair, in shorts and a white tank top, was standing in the bathroom, a perfume bottle shattered at her feet. "I'm sorry," Lila said. "I didn't mean to startle you."

"Oh . . . no, it wasn't your fault at all. I was just trying to unpack too many things at once and . . . ran out of fingers." The girl shook her head ruefully. "I should be apologizing. I'm afraid we're going to be suffocated by Diorella for the next week." She smiled, and Lila noticed that her mouth was unusually full and red; with her slanted dark eyes and turned-up nose, she looked a little elfin.

"That's okay," said Lila. "It kind of goes with the decor."

The girl laughed. "That it does. I'm Anna. And I guess you must be my new roommate."

"Oh, yes. I'm Lila." Lila put her hand out and Anna took it. The grip was warm and firm, and Lila felt a thrill almost like recognition. Strange though it seemed after only ten seconds, she felt certain Anna was going to be a real friend. When Anna released Lila's hand, the palm glowed with something like a sweet aftertaste.

"Well, have you tried the champagne hot tub yet?" Anna said.

"No."

"You know about it, though?"

"Oh, yeah . . . Ben . . . the student adviser told me."

"Ben!" Anna wolf whistled gently.

"Yes," Lila said. "He's kind of . . ."

"He's not *kind of* anything. He's *absolutely* beautiful. Honestly. But wait a second, I brought something just for my new roomie," Anna said, stepping carefully over the broken glass and walking over to a gaping suitcase. She sat on the bed beside it and began rooting among various frilly and strappy garments, pausing to hold up a pair of pink handcuffs for Lila's inspection, then tossing them to one side and pulling out a bottle of champagne. "There you go," she said. "Even if you're not ready for the champagne hot tub, I hope you drink it?"

"Of course," said Lila, secretly grateful that it wasn't the hand-cuffs she was meant to try.

"Well, if you look in that silly cabinet behind you . . ." Anna pointed to a dainty gilt cabinet embellished with a painting of a turquoise and pink peacock that echoed the peacocks in the Persian rug. Lila opened it and found an array of wineglasses. She took two out and turned, smiling, to Anna, who was busily tugging at the champagne's cork. "Now, stand back," Anna said. "I've broken enough glass for one day."

Then the cork popped and Lila dashed forward to catch the spurting liquid. Some of the champagne spilled, cold and fizzy, over her fingers before she got the first glass into position. When the glasses were filled, Anna said, "Hey, let me lick your fingers. I love that."

Lila balked, but obediently put the glasses down on a desk and held out her hand. Anna took her wrist lightly and lapped the wine off Lila's fingers, shutting her eyes with pleasure. Lila was surprised to find how pleasant the sensation was. When Anna was done, she sat back licking her lips for good measure. "I hope that's not gross," she said. "I just really like the champagne and the skin salt. I'm like a dog, I think."

"No, it was kind of nice. But . . . maybe a little forward," Lila said. She put her hand back in her jeans pocket again.

"Oh. I freaked you out." Anna squinted. "I'm truly sorry. I'm always doing the wrong thing."

"No, never mind. You brought the champagne. That was absolutely the right thing. And I guess . . . well, it's very Babylona, anyway."

"That's true. I can blame this place. It does change you after a while."

"After a while?"

"Oh, yes. I'm an old-timer. A sophomore." Anna reached forward and snagged her champagne. "You know most people keep living on campus all four years."

"No, I didn't know." Lila got her champagne and sipped it. The bubbles coursing down her throat soothed her, and she felt an afterglow on the hand that had been licked.

"Yeah. I think it just seems too weird to go back into civilization at the end of a day of Babylona." Anna tossed down her champagne in one gulp and set the glass back down on the desk. Then she threw herself back on the bed and hugged herself, shutting her eyes. "Mmm. I'm *so* glad to be back, actually. I might just end up living here the rest of my life. I'll turn into a staffer. Like beautiful Ben." She opened her eyes again, blinking happily at Lila. "Though the tragedy of that is, if you're a staffer, you can't sleep with students anymore."

Lila was in the middle of taking another sip of champagne, and she almost coughed it up in her surprise. She said, "You—you can't?"

"Yeah. It's what they call the Parris Rule. After Miss Babylona's lifelong, long-suffering boyfriend. He used to be the dean here, in the old days. And while Our Lady of Babylon slept with literally thousands of men and women, she was jealous as hell. So James was supposed to keep his paws off. And he did, mostly. The reason was, Babylona may have slept with other men; she may have even had favorites who lasted for months and years. But she was *never* jealous of anyone but Parris. So it was a kind of trophy for him, I guess. Then he finally got fed up with it and left her, though. Just a couple of years ago. And he wrote a nasty tell-all memoir about her."

"Really?"

"You got it. *A Love on All Fours.* It's his answer to her *A Life on All Fours,* you know. Anyway, there's a legacy now. But hey, I think the no-sex-with-staff rule probably helps, after all. I mean, it stops people like me from trying to stay here forever, having ten lovers a day. And it's one of the few rules that stands between us and round-the-clock free-for-all orgies . . ." Anna stopped herself. "I honestly am not trying to freak you out."

"Oh, do I look nervous?" Lila laughed in what she was irritated to notice was a nervous tone.

"Um. Not nervous, but maybe alarmed. Or petrified. Or ready to wet your pants."

Lila sat down on her bed and finished her glass of champagne. "Well. That's probably because I'm terrified."

"Give me your glass." Anna sat up and began to pour a second round of champagne. Handing Lila back her refilled stem, she said, "Here's to losing *all* our fears in the course of a single day."

Lila laughed uncertainly but touched her glass to Anna's. After she'd taken a sip, she asked, "A single day?"

"Well, that was exaggerating. But it's worth a try. What if some-how, just by saying that, I hypnotized you and you lost your fears?" Anna tilted her head, and her full lips curved into a foxy smile.

Lila laughed. "It's worth a try."

"Exactly!" Anna nodded approvingly. "Anyway, the first step is telling me all the things you're scared of—I mean, about Babylona. I don't care if you're scared of spiders." Anna kicked off her thong sandals and shifted to sit cross-legged on her bed.

"Well . . ." Lila immediately thought, *I'm scared of myself. I'm scared of losing control.* But she decided she couldn't say that, so she avoided the question. She said, "You know, the thing is, before I came here, I'd only ever slept with my boyfriend."

Anna's eyes opened wide. "Never!" She drank off her second glass of champagne and put the glass down on the floor. "You're lying."

"No, honest." Lila made a face. "It wasn't . . . It just kind of hap-pened that way, because we were going to get married."

"You were going to marry the only man you ever had sex with?" Anna said in almost fearful astonishment—as if Lila had told her that she was born of the unholy union between a woman and a jackal.

Lila was a little annoyed. "Well, once you decide to marry, you can't very well then go, 'Oh, but I want to sleep with a dozen other guys.'"

"Yes, you can!" said Anna.

"You . . . you can?" Lila blinked. "But people get jealous. I mean, I would get jealous." She thought of the stripper who had been *ten times more interesting*, and gulped.

"Oh, I'm sorry. Listen, I'm only saying that because that's what *I'm* doing. I mean, I have a boyfriend at home, and yet . . ."

"Oh. I see. So you have an open relationship." Lila relaxed. Somehow putting a name to it made it seem less threatening. And she couldn't exactly say what made the idea of she and Tad in an open relationship seem so wrong. Perhaps it was just because it touched the same nerves that were so raw from his having cheated on her. Perhaps she now couldn't imagine a man sleeping with another woman and then still wanting Lila. *Boring*, she remembered. Her blow jobs, of all things, were *boring*.

She looked at Anna, her eyes a little misty, and decided that she wasn't quite ready to share that with a stranger, even as likable a stranger as Anna. So she just said, truthfully, "Hey, I'm glad I'm sharing with you. Maybe you can help me adjust."

"You got it." Anna stretched forward and grabbed the champagne bottle again. "Any adjusting you want done, I'm your girl."

"Well, there's one thing." Lila thought of the *Satisfaction* homework and sighed. "I just had class today. With Miss Foré."

Anna hooted with laughter. "Uh-huh. And she sent everyone home early. Except for the two she wanted to screw."

"Oh. She did? Yes, I guess . . . that is what she did." Lila thought about Brandi, Judd, and Miss Foré in a tangle together. Immediately she wondered why she hadn't been chosen, and had to remind herself to be grateful she hadn't been chosen. Because, at this very moment . . .

"Classic," Anna said. "Sorry, she's renowned for that. And

before you ask—she's faculty, not 'staff.' Faculty can sleep with students. A, they kind of have to sleep with students to do their job. And B, Parris never taught here." Anna drank off her third glass of champagne, squinted at the glass again, then put it back on the desk empty and took a swig straight from the bottle. "Sorry. Carry on."

"Oh, so we got our first homework, and it's . . . well, in a nutshell, we're supposed to have sex with someone."

"Mm, I remember. Stage of arousal, stage of peak. Gotcha. What's the—" Then Anna's eyes flew open again. "No! You never slept with anyone but your boyfriend before? Still?"

Lila debated with herself and settled for a meek, "More or less."

"Well." Anna looked oddly satisfied. "We won't unpack *that* statement too much. Okay. And now you're freaking out because you have to jump into the water before you feel ready."

Lila swallowed. "That's about it."

Anna shook her head. "Listen, I'll make you a deal. When's your next class?"

"A week from now."

"A whole week? Well! If you haven't had sex with anyone by the night before class . . ." Anna put her finger to her lips, thinking. Her eyes rested on Lila's with what appeared to be a filthy surmise.

Lila said hopefully, "You'll do my homework for me?"

Anna burst out laughing. "No dice. I'm not going to be responsible for slowing down your development. But there won't be any need for that. I was going to say, if you haven't had sex with anyone by next week, I'll give you a thousand dollars. Then you can tell Miss Foré the dog ate your homework, with a smile."

"You mean you're that sure that I'll—"

"I'm good for the money," Anna said. "But I'm not going to need it."

"What if I decide I'd rather have the thousand dollars?" Lila smiled, already feeling better.

"Yeah. Not going to happen." Anna stood up and put out her hand to Lila. "Deal?"

"Deal," said Lila, and shook her hand.

"I have homework, too, and unfortunately, you're not it tonight. I have five minutes to get to Megan's room, where I have a date with a banana. Lame." She pulled her tank top down and shook her head. "You're really hot, you know that? Take it from your elders: You're a natural for this place. After a year here, you get a sense for these things."

"Really?" said Lila. There was something about Anna's certainty that was contagious. She thought about the scenes Ben had showed her on his computer. Could she really be one of those people? Then her mind slipped to a flashback of his hands on her thighs, him lifting her skirt, his dick sliding into her. She shuddered with the memory and realized there was no way she was leaving here. She wasn't going anywhere as long as there was a chance that Ben would sleep with her again.

Chapter Five

A s Lila walked into the first session of Groups and Growth, she immediately noticed Brandi sitting in between two men—on the lap of a third. Brandi spotted her, too, and put on a face of mock astonishment and disapproval as she registered what Lila was wearing. She shook her head, pouting, and then let her face lapse into its typical toothy grin.

Lila couldn't help laughing. She'd borrowed an outfit from Anna this morning. According to Anna, there was no point wearing anything at Babylona but underwear—except in winter, when you put a thick overcoat on over your underwear, until you got to class. "You probably noticed they keep the classes heated to, like, ninety degrees. They have to, or half of the students would be turning blue. Around Christmas all the freshmen get the bright idea of going naked. But don't you do that, kid. Leave something to the imagination for the first five minutes, right?"

So Lila was wearing a green satin baby doll over matching lace panties. She'd brushed her hair out loose so it cascaded over her slender arms in glossy black waves. She felt a little self-conscious, because she'd always felt like her thighs were a little too plump; but Anna assured her that that was sexy, and perfectly balanced out her ample breasts. "Like an Indian goddess," Anna said approvingly. "Your body is nothing short of filthy. Go get 'em."

Walking across the grass barefoot in sexy underwear, in plain sight of a hundred other students rushing to classes, was one of the most unsettlingly wonderful experiences of her life so far. In some ways it was like the time she'd gone to a nude beach with Tad. But being naked out-of-doors soon came to seem natural, nonsexual, like being a furry animal gamboling in the sand. Whereas the silky underwear that left her breasts free to bounce and shiver disturbingly as she walked did, as Anna had suggested, leave something to the imagination. Only in this case it was Lila's imagination, which felt every breeze that stroked the crotch of her panties, and even the sun on her half-exposed buttocks, as if they were the touch of lustful fingers. The shy skin around her panty lines was especially sensitized, and the touch of the air alone made her persistently imagine a man trailing a finger along the line of the fabric there, then tugging . . . inserting . . . By the time she joined the flow of similarly outrageously dressed students heading down the hall to class, she realized to her embarrassment that not only was she breathing heavily, she was more or less panting through her mouth. She shut her mouth hastily and tried to smile at the other kids, some of whom looked equally disoriented and, well, needy.

She wondered if most of these kids were spending all their free time hooking up with one another. Maybe smiling at someone here was the first step to . . . tugging . . . inserting. She swallowed, thinking automatically that she could never be like that; she was way too timid. Then the memory of how she'd been exactly like that with Anna only yesterday made her smile. And the next thing she saw was Brandi in a knot of laughing men, and the next thing she knew after *that*, she was sitting on the lap of the man to Brandi's left in her underwear, as if this was how she'd been behaving since she was old enough to wear a bra. And it was becoming increasingly obvious that the man who was giving her the hospitality of his lap, Andy, was enjoying the experience. She could feel the distinct swell of his growing hard-on.

Groups and Growth was held in the Attahoosa Lounge, so named after the Indian tribe that had adopted Babylona as an honorary member after her slightly unconventional initiation into their sweat lodge practices. One end of the room was taken up by a water bed the size of a small stage; several students were lying there, flat on their backs, trying to create waves by coordinating their movements. Brandi and company were taking up one of the several velvet couches heaped with velvet cushions and pillows in an array of colors that might have been intended to be Native American themed: russet, pink, sea green. The couches were distributed around the room in a semicircle around an absolutely ordinary teacher's desk, a cold-looking metal affair that was the first charmless thing Lila could remember having seen here. It gave the impression of a student body completely run to decadence, while the teacher alone remained a strict disciplinarian.

Brandi had already renamed it the Acapulco Lounge for its reddish mood lighting, and was happily recounting, frame for frame, the film <i>Spring Break: Cancun</i>, which she claimed had changed her life. "Honey, it wasn't great art, exactly. Okay, it wasn't great art one bit. It was more like the right drug for my condition." The guy whose lap she was sitting on, Miguel, had given up resisting temptation almost immediately and now sat with one hand on each of Brandi's breasts and a sleepy smile on his face. From time to time she arched her back to remind him, and then he began to stroke her tits again, muttering, "It isn't fair." One of her breasts had nosed out of her halter top, which had almost reversed itself from all the pushing and shoving that had gone on under it. Its nipple poked out of the arm hole and rested in between Miguel's fingers, its smooth tender skin faintly lavender in the ruddy light. Even Lila had to restrain herself from testing its texture with a fingertip. Her own breasts began to ache, and she longed for the nerve to ask Andy to touch her in the same way.

She began to think about a time she had been sitting on Tad's lap at a party. It was when they'd first begun to have sex, and every time she touched him, that stunning fact electrified her, making it almost impossible for her to think of anything sensible. In fact, it was impossible to do anything but wait with bated breath for the next time

Tad would take his clothes off. Her hands smelled like sex all the time, and she used to zone out sometimes with her face in her hands, inhaling the memory of his cock in her.

It was summertime, and he had come to that party in a pair of baggy cutoff shorts that used to drive her crazy because she knew that, the minute they were alone, she would be able to let her hand glide up into the leg of those shorts and cup his cock and testicles, feeling them instantly jerk and respond to her caress. She could even work the shorts up far enough to get the very tip of his dick out and lick the taut hypersensitive glans, sometimes coaxing out a pearly drop of come before he lost patience and shoved her away so he could get undressed.

That party hadn't been the abandoned kind that had made her uncomfortable in the old days. It had been just a dozen people getting together to listen to emo records and unwind in the basement of Tad's friend Eric's house. She was trying to follow a conversation between Tad, Eric, and Eric's girlfriend, Heidi, about which Matt Damon movie Matt Damon had been best in, but all the while, she was overwhelmingly aware that Tad had a painfully beautiful, perfectly rigid hard-on, and that it was fitting beautifully, perfectly, painfully deliciously upright in the groove of her pussy and butt. It was all she could do not to shove back on it, riding it, trying to ease the longing she felt.

Tad was growing increasingly silent, too, and at last Eric got bored with their silent company and he and Heidi went to see if there was any tequila left. Then Tad leaned forward and whispered in her ear—and she could still remember the exact damp heat of his voice that turned into chills as she heard it: "Will you come to the bathroom with me?"

She got up without a word and went to the bathroom. She felt Tad's presence behind her, and the separate, enticing presence of his cock; she could still feel its outline as a line of pleasure drawn up the base of her spine. When they got to the bathroom, it was mercifully empty. Tad pushed her inside and had the door shut and locked in a second.

She was saying, "We'll have to hurry—" and he already had his shorts down around his ankles and was shoving her against the sink. He pulled her skirt up and was grinding his rock-hard cock against the wet crotch of her panties. He was biting his lip to keep silent, and his face expressed a painful intensity of need. At last he pulled away and snagged her panties desperately, pulling them down until she could kick them off one ankle and let him in.

Then he paused again, and she let out a slight, suppressed yelp of disappointment. He was staring at her exposed cunt, his mouth open in near awe. She felt like that second lasted forever; it was a moment when she was pure cunt, and the only question that existed in the world was whether he was going to get down on his knees and press his mouth against her, or just fall on her and shove his big cock home.

And then he reached his hand out, still with that look of utter devotion on his face. She was watching his strong tanned hand with the delicate ridges of veins that ran along the back, and there was a feeling about that moment as if what was happening would change her forever. He reached forward and just touched her clitoris with the tip of his index finger.

Lila came instantly, in jolts that made her skin go hot and cold. And in that instant, Tad moved toward and over her, and she felt the tip of his cock pressing against her slit, sending another course of blissful shocks through her clitoris from below. He froze for a moment with the head of his cock teasing her opening with its hard width, and then he was shoving into her all the way. That set her off on a new, deeper and darker, plummeting course of pleasure, and she was biting her lip fiercely with the effort of not making a sound. There were actual tears of pleasure in her eyes. Then he was fucking her, strong and sure, his fingers digging into her hips as he drove into her.

Lila blinked and she was back in the Acapulco—Attahoosa—Lounge again, noticing the pink and maroon cut glass in the chandeliers that was reflecting that reddish, soothing light. She leaned back against Andy's muscular chest and his arm came around her, pressing into her stomach companionably as he went on talking, apparently unaware that she'd been off in such a powerful daydream that she wasn't sure how much time had passed.

Andy was a sophomore, and he was playing the old hand, telling the others about the professor of Groups and Growth, Mr. Banks. "Legendary. The guy was a soldier in the first Iraq war who had just come back and started college, okay. Babylona met him in a bar when she was passing through Texas on a speaking tour and took him to bed. And on the spot she offered him a six-figure salary to work for her. Apparently he was the *most* incredible lay she'd ever had. And he was only twenty-one. That's fifteen years ago now." He raised his eyebrows significantly.

"Oh, I get your point," Brandi said mock innocently. "So now he can't stand the sight of one more butt."

Andy kicked her in the shin, and she squealed and kicked him back several times, her breasts escaping from Miguel's care and boinging frantically around, in and out of her halter top.

"Yo! No fighting," Miguel said.

"Oh, yes fighting." Brandi laughed. "But I'll take this one outside, after this."

"No more outside," Andy groaned. "I think I've got permanent grass stains on my knees."

Then all of a sudden the class fell silent. The students who'd been lounging on the water bed began to scramble, floundering awkwardly over the sloppy surface, to the edge. One by one they slipped out and slunk almost shamefaced into the more proper couches. Mr. Banks had arrived.

He was a dark, gaunt man with pale blue eyes and a look of ingrained silence about him. Although he was not especially big, he moved with a certain tensile grace that gave the impression of unusual physical strength. Without thinking about it, Lila slid off Andy's lap and went to find a seat on a nearby couch, and what was more amazing, Brandi did, too. Furthermore, Brandi adjusted her clothes so that she looked almost respectable.

For the next forty-five minutes, everyone sat spellbound while Mr. Banks explained the course, outlined a simple history of group sex from ancient Greece to the present day, and discussed the psychology of exhibitionism and orgies. Throughout, he said nothing that was in the least explicit or even (Lila was shocked to realize afterward) all that unusual; it was about as dry and factual as a sex class could get. And although he was a good-looking man, many of the guys in the room were much more handsome. Still, the whole class hung on every word. And when he finished, and glanced at the clock, there was a tangible sense of disappointment and even sadness. Everyone in the room had been experiencing the same sudden crush, for the past three-quarters of an hour.

Mr. Banks summed up by saying, "Tonight I'd like you all to meet back here for the most elementary, primary form of group sex. What is that?"

And, to Lila's horror, he had addressed this first, last, and only question to her. His calm, assessing blue eyes were boring in to her, and a slight, dry smile was playing on his mouth.

"Me, sir?"

Everyone in the class was breathless with envy or sympathy; Lila couldn't be sure. She was cruelly aware of them all staring at her, though, and of her mind being an utter blank. "Yes, Lila. The most elementary form," Mr. Banks said.

Then there was a further stage of breathlessness as everyone wondered how he knew her name. Did he know everyone's name? Had she been singled out?

Lila was thinking desperately. Mr. Banks prompted her. "Something that most of us have done when we were very young."

"Spin the bottle?" she blurted.

He looked around the room again without further comment. He said, "Eight o'clock, spin the bottle, here. This room will be left unlocked. See where it takes you."

The class had all relaxed, as if every one of them had been put on the spot and passed the test. And in that moment Lila wondered whether this was all calculated—there was such a strong synchronicity in the group now, that they might have been people who had been through a personal tragedy together, or just grown up in the same neighborhood.

And in the meantime, Mr. Banks had left without anyone noticing. It was as if along with the power to command attention at will, he had the power to become invisible. He had masterfully deflected them onto thinking about themselves as a group, and they were all looking at one another, thinking about where spin the bottle could take them, when they looked up and realized he was gone.

Chapter Six

Brandi had been a passionate fan of Babylona's work from the time she was a teenager, starting her own career in stripping. Of course the sex industry she knew was a far cry from the exalted spheres in which Babylona moved. Brandi had danced in a couple of clubs around her hometown of Gallup, New Mexico, and then made a couple of no-budget porn movies with her gang of drop-out friends. In those years, she even had a sugar daddy of sorts, who'd not only bought her a car and taken her out nights but been a real lover, someone who made her feel funny and shy and beautiful all at once. Only then he messed it up by wanting to marry her.

That was the thing that had finally given her the impetus to come to Babylona. She'd loved Phil more than she could imagine loving anyone again. But the thought of spending her whole life with one man . . . well, maybe she would feel differently when she was older. But at twenty-two it made her take her work seriously for the first time. Sex wasn't just about the money for her, she realized, it was something that made her look forward to each day. It was something that she wanted to be the best at in the world—like Babylona was.

Now she walked away from the class in deep thought, holding hands with Andy on one side and Miguel on the other. She felt inspired all over again, and the warm pressure of her new friends' hands reminded her of the new sense of connection she'd just experienced. She was imagining that not only could sex bring people closer together, but it could transform them into more powerful, self-confident, loving people. Like Mr. Banks. Or Babylona—Brandi could learn that refreshing openheartedness that shone out not only in every page of Babylona's book, but in the way every detail on the campus had been lovingly arranged to please.

Miguel said, "Wow. This school is so much better than I expected."

"Yeah, I thought it would be sleazy before I got here," Andy said. "I almost chickened out and didn't come. The only reason I didn't was because my brother applied, too, and didn't get in."

"What?" said Brandi, laughing. "How does that make sense?"

Andy shrugged. "Well, we were kind of competitive . . ."

"So you did it just to piss off your brother?" said Miguel. "That is *cold.*"

"Oh really, smarty-pants?" said Brandi. "Why did you come here?"

Miguel shrugged. "It was this or premed."

"No way," said Andy. "You chose this over being a doctor?"

"I can always be a doctor later on, right?" Miguel shrugged. "Somehow, getting laid for four years seemed more urgent."

They had come to Miguel and Andy's dorm building, the all-male dormitory that had formerly been Babylona's year-round home. Her lavish apartment on the top floor was kept exactly as she'd left it, for her occasional visits, which were never announced beforehand. When Babylona wasn't visiting the college, Perkins House (named after her friend and gynecologist, Lisa "Perky" Perkins) was strictly hetero male only, a tradition that the brochure claimed was responsible for a "special atmosphere that residents come to treasure." Andy, speaking as the know-it-all sophomore, had told them on the first night that the special atmosphere referred to the smell of unwashed socks.

"But seriously," he'd added, putting on an air of profound experience that they, as callow freshmen, wouldn't be able to fathom. "It makes it a different experience, to have a zone where friendships are just friendships."

Now they had come to the front door, where a staff member or

Perkins Brother usually sat, typically reading a textbook like *Promiscuous: Past and Present* or *Hygiene—Is It for Me?* and signing people in. But today the post was unmanned.

Brandi instantly said, "Well, look at that. I'm coming in."

Both men instantly let go of her hands. She looked from one to the other and said, "What?"

"Brandi, come on," said Andy.

Miguel smirked and said, "The special atmosphere is at stake."

"It's just that rules are rules for a reason."

That made Brandi and Miguel crack up. "Andy, for real," said Brandi. "The reason rules are rules is so you can *break* them."

"Yeah," Miguel added, "that's probably the whole secret reason. That's what we're going to treasure, man, is sneaking Brandi in."

"Look," said Brandi. "What other kind of sex would actually be taboo?"

"And taboo," Miguel said, "is the spice—"

"Okay, okay. Fuck off. You're not going to make me be the uncool guy," Andy said. "If you want to sneak in . . ."

Brandi said, "Hey, I wasn't asking your permission."

"Ooh," Andy mimicked her. *"I wasn't asking your permission."*

But Brandi had already passed into the building, with (though she would never admit this) a certain fear and chagrin—what if Babylona somehow *knew?*—and was walking down the hall with a firm *clack! clack!* of her platform shoes, leaving Andy and Miguel scurrying to catch up to her. She actually felt a little light-headed at the thought that her idol might disapprove, but she reassured herself: *Hell with that. Even if it is her rule, she would break it if she were in my place.* And with her five years' constant reading of *A Life on All Fours* to fortify her belief that breaking rules was always the Babylona way, Brandi managed to keep going without faltering.

"Hey!" Andy hissed at her. "You already passed our room!"

"Oh!" Brandi stopped dead. From the open door of a dorm room, a couple of guys gawked at her from their beds, gradually beginning to grin as they registered her cartoonishly lush figure. They were both dark-haired and brown-skinned, and looked almost frighteningly similar, as if they were brothers. Brandi couldn't help grinning back at them. She said (a joke she never got tired of), "No, they're not real. You're dreaming."

"Hey," one of them said, "you've got to get out of here, if any part of that body's real."

Brandi took a deep breath and made a decision. She went straight into the look-alike guys' room as if she'd been invited. She let Andy and Miguel follow her, noticing in passing that both of them were at least as terrified as she secretly felt herself. (She hoped she wasn't actually trembling, like Andy.) Then she turned as boldly as she could, and shut the door behind the three of them, as if this was exactly what she'd planned to do all along.

"Hello, boys," she said, trying to copy Miss Foré's purr. "What are you called?"

Andy said flatly, "This is Drew and Barrymore. But Barrymore isn't Barrymore's real name. It's a joke."

"People call me Barry," said the man who'd originally spoken to her.

"Drew Barrymore," Brandi said. "Right."

Drew was standing by the door, looking anxious. "Anyway, you'd better get out of here. Before anyone finds out."

Brandi thought about it. She'd already broken the rule. But somehow it didn't feel like she had. It felt more like a little casual bending. She still felt only half satisfied. What would Babylona do? she asked herself.

She stretched back and lay down on the bed, letting her knees fall gently open. "Oh, well. And if someone finds out, what'll happen?"

There was a pause. She was waiting for someone to say that she would get expelled from school. She honestly didn't know what could happen, and she also didn't know if getting expelled would be threat enough to make her lose her nerve.

But no one said that. She heard Andy saying, in his faint (Florida, she remembered) Southern accent: "Oh, you get a fine, I believe."

"Oh, dear," she said.

"Okay, I don't know," Andy said. "It could be worse than that."

She took a deep breath and said, "Well, we were in the middle of a conversation."

Miguel laughed and sat down next to her on the bed. "What were we talking about, again?"

"What brought us here," said Brandi.

Barry said, "Okay, if you want to stay. I mean, I'm okay with that. Okay?"

There was a pause. She looked up at Drew, trying to stare him down, but her eyes somehow ended up straying down his body, thinking about what he was going to look like naked. That turned out to be the best way to stare a man down though. Drew almost immediately said, "Oh, fuck. Okay."

Then Andy sat down, too, and Brandi turned slightly onto her side to look at them all. "So what brought me here."

"That's no big mystery," Andy said.

Everyone, including Brandi, laughed. "Come on. I have a story just like everyone."

"So tell us your story," Barry said, sitting down next to her and letting a hand fall on her knee.

Brandi thought about all the things that had brought her here, and made a split-second decision. She would tell them a story, but it wouldn't have the purpose of confiding her deepest darkest secrets. It would be intended purely to light a flame. She would tell the story of her first porn film.

"Well," she said, "how I very first got the idea. I was just eighteen, and I had a couple friends, let's call them . . ." She blinked drowsily around the room. "Well, say, Drew and Barrymore."

" 'Cause you couldn't use their real names," said Andy sarcastically

"That wouldn't be confidential," said Brandi. "So Drew and Barrymore were old friends of mine from high school. In fact, I lost my cherry with Drew," she said, shooting the Drew who was present a sultry look. "Which is a *whole* other story." Her hand felt its way over her thigh, not quite at the level of her crotch, but close enough to be handy.

"So, after you lost your virginity?" Miguel said, with laughter in his voice.

"Well, Drew and Barrymore had a sort of business idea," said Brandi, closing her eyes as if to remember better. "Drew had a video camera, and Barrymore . . . well, he had the biggest cock in New Mexico."

"This you established scientifically how?" Miguel kicked her foot.

"Hm, I think it mighta been an Internet thing. I don't exactly remember," Brandi said, and stuck her tongue out at him. "Anyway, so we got together, and we made up a little story about a girl who's living with a creepy roommate who keeps on looking at her funny, until one day, she comes home and he's lying in wait for her."

"And steals her wallet," said Andy.

"Don't interrupt. You know very well what he does. And he does it a bunch of times, and then he lets a friend do it. Only one friend because we didn't want to tell anyone else, not yet." Brandi let her hand steal a little closer to her pussy, which she could feel beginning to respond predictably. She tugged her miniskirt out of the way and let one finger poke just the other edge of her labia experimentally. Her panties were already awash with juice. She couldn't help it; she brought her hand to her nose and pretended to scratch her lip, inhaling the ambrosial fragrance of . . . well, the four-way fuck she was promising herself.

She let her hand fall back down to her thigh. "So Barrymore with the enormous dick . . . It was really incredible. Not only was it nine-ten inches long, it was thick as a cucumber, and the shape of it, honest to God, I personally could have an orgasm looking at that bad boy. It was a good deed, getting that Wonder of the World on video, really.

"And so Drew gets the camera rolling, and I'm dressed just about like this—little miniskirt, halter top with no bra, you know. And I walk in all unawares. There's Barry—boom! He's being the horny roommate, and he grabs me by the wrists and says, 'Hey, where do you think you're going?' And I go, in this little scaredy-cat voice, 'I don't know. To my room. Is that okay?' And he laughs and takes a big handful of tit and says, 'Not until you pay the toll.'"

The whole room erupted in laughter. Brandi opened her eyes and peered around. She said, "Goddamn, somebody come here and lie with me."

Barry lay down on his side next to Brandi on her back, stretched out as if she were alone in her own room. She immediately appropriated his hand and brought it back with hers to her inner thigh. He began to lightly stroke the velvety skin there with his thumb. Brandi sighed and opened her eyes slightly to look at him. Her eyes lingered on the swelling pectoral muscle under his white undershirt, graced with a nipple that made a tiny bump, just the faintest shadow. With her free hand she reached over and ran her fingers over that bump, then on down over his belly. His chest was absolutely smooth and hard, while his belly had a delicious shallow layer of fat over toned muscle. She went on: "So, then quick as anything, he ties my wrists together with a necktie. And I'm pretending to struggle and saying, 'Ooh, I can't believe you're doing this. You don't dare. You're a terrible man!' And Barrymore is laughing and stroking himself in his boxer shorts, which is all he's wearing. He was a skinny guy, actually. Not like you," Brandi said to Barry, and without thinking, she let her hand sweep down all the way to the tent that was beginning to form in his sweatpants. But she stopped herself just as her hand encountered the bulge, pulled it back primly to her own chest and said, "But you know. That just made his dick more stunning. And, keep in mind, this was my first time on camera. So I'm obsessed about what I look like while Barrymore is tying me to his bedpost, okay. But then—this wasn't in the program—he pulled out a big pair of scissors and just starts cutting my clothes away. And then I started to actually fight—that was twenty dollars worth of Kmart designer wear he was destroying, you know. But he just took a scrap he'd just cut off my own top and shoved it into my mouth as a makeshift gag and that was that.

"And then I forgot about everything because I was naked on that film. My . . . oh, hell." Brandi pulled her halter top up a little bit, baring the round lower swell of her pale, full breasts. Then she looked around the room, registering the intent expression of each man in turn, before pulling her shirt up over her nipples and letting it rest there, slightly pressing down on her tits so that the breasts swelled up below the constraining fabric, making the nipples point their stiffening peaks up as if straining out toward the men's eyes. Then Brandi took Barry's hand and used it to brush against her purplish fine-skinned nipples, bringing them to full erectness. And at that moment, it crossed her mind that she still had to do her homework for Satisfaction 101. She'd promised herself that if she had to tell her classmates about one—and only one—sex act, she was going to make it an affair to remember. Well, here was her chance. She would just leave out the part where it happened in the forbidden zone of Perkins House.

She pulled Barry's hand back down to her thigh, then took it the extra two inches to the thin crotch of her panties. With just the slightest movement of her wrist, the skirt was pulled out of the way, revealing the openwork lace and the pink moist folds behind. She heard a sharp inhale from a couple of the men. Everything was going to plan.

Then Barry took the initiative. His hand squirmed free from hers and began to explore under the stretch lace, invading the delicate slippery folds of her creamy pussy. As his finger slid down, exciting the hypersensitive flesh, Brandi made herself focus and return to her story.

"Mm . . . so, well, Barrymore had me tied up and he cut off my top first. So then he was sucking on my tits." She paused to moan as Barry began to act out what she was saying, pressing his hot mouth to first one nipple, then the other, suckling gently as if he wanted to suck all the pleasure right out of her. She caught her breath and said, "And all the time Drew was watching and getting this on film. And I was dying. I was biting down hard on that cloth in my mouth and trying to beg Barrymore to fuck me. I didn't care anymore if he cut up all my clothes."

Now Drew sat down on her other side and his hand joined Barry's in her cunt. She heard him groan as he felt the wetness, and paused to savor the feeling of two different hands, two sets of fingers playing inside her, fingers slipping in and out and past each other, too fast to keep track. One of them had his thumb up over her clitoris, gently slipping back and forth and worrying it. She made herself go on talking, her voice now soft and weak.

"And so then Barrymore pulls out his huge dick, right out of the gap in his boxers, and he gets up and he presses it against my mouth. And of course I can't get it in, cause of the gag, but I try, and I manage to get the very tip into my lips when I see that Drew has abandoned his post.

"So Barry's pressing the bottom of his big cock against my cheek when I see Drew appear down below, with his jeans halfway down, and his cock rising out, all beautiful and hard and flushed . . ."

Here Miguel cracked and got down on his knees in front of Brandi, between her thighs, which were now wide open as if to invite all four men inside. He opened the fly of his jeans and had his cock in his hand, darkly swollen. Gently he stroked it and Drew and Barry pulled their hands aside. Miguel just pressed the rock-hard tip of his dick against the fabric of Brandi's panties, though; he pressed the tip in hard, as if he were going to force his way on through the panties, then pulled away and pulled the crotch of the panties to one side, pressing his mouth there instead. He was just beginning to lap away expertly, making Brandi moan in high-pitched ecstasy, when an angry pounding came at the door.

"Oh, shit!" said Andy, who had also succumbed to the spell, and was in the midst of stroking the bulge in his pants into full erection. "Goddammit, Brandi!"

Brandi half sat up, not ready to give up so easily. She whispered, "Just act like no one's here!"

Then a cold voice came through the door, "Is there a girl in there with you? Hello? Drew? Dolphin?"

Barry made a face and suddenly his hands were primly folded in his detumescing lap. "Asshole. He always calls me by my real name."

"It's Ben," Drew said in a lowered voice that rang with fatalism. "We're doomed."

All the men were suddenly standing up—abandoning her. Brandi said, "Hey, where's everyone going? Chicken . . ."

"Okay, I can hear her in there," Ben said outside.

"She's just leaving!" Andy blurted.

Miguel began to laugh helplessly.

"It's not funny!" Andy hissed at him.

"Damn right it's not funny," Brandi said. "Who's going to stay here with me? I'm dying."

"Cut it out, Brandi," said Miguel in an indulgent tone. "You've got to give up now. We all respect your dedication . . ."

"Yeah," whispered Drew, with his hand on the doorknob. "Best thing you can do, when I open the door, just cover your face and run. We won't tell on you."

"Yeah, I never caught your name," said Miguel.

"All I saw of you was, um . . ." Barry cleared his throat, staring sadly at Brandi's still-exposed boobs.

"Oh, hell," Brandi sat up and pulled her shirt down. She was beginning to feel ridiculous. But privately she had no intention of going anywhere. Once this Ben, whoever he was, came in, she was sure she would be able to convince him to make a fifth in her favorite game. It wouldn't be the first time she'd had to convince a man against his better judgment. There was the junior minister, and the policeman, and then there was the gay guy—the gay guy had actually resisted, granted, but that didn't bother her. It was pretty hard to make Brandi feel self-conscious. The fact was, she thought it was funny about that gay guy (who she was *sure* had just a little bit of straight in him—he wasn't even all that good-looking!) turning her down and snapping at her, "Just keep your hands to yourself. Can't you get it through your head, already? You do not turn me on—not one iota!" Plus, that gay guy was the only one she'd ever failed with. It was like the exception that proved the rule.

Well, maybe Ben was gay, though then *he* wasn't supposed to be here either. (She could use that argument.) And otherwise, the smart money was on Brandi. So she decided, and gestured at Drew to go ahead and open the door.

He mouthed, one—two—three—at her, and then threw the door open. Brandi, who had been poised as if about to take to her heels, sat stolidly, smiling at him. Then she turned to smile at Ben, who was glowering in the doorway.

"Hi, Ben," she said. "Would you care to join us?"

Ben crossed his arms and said, "Okay, guys. I'd like to talk to Miss . . ."

Brandi sighed. "I don't have a Miss. I'm Brandi. My family was too poor for last names."

"You want to talk to her alone?" said Drew, obviously relieved. "Does that mean we're . . ."

"Are you in trouble? That depends," said Ben. "Let me just talk to Brandi alone for a minute."

The boys all began to file out, shamefaced. As he slipped out last, Miguel gave her a complicated hand signal. Brandi didn't know what it meant, but she guessed it was some version of "We're with you in spirit!" and smiled at him gratefully. She would have winked, but Ben was staring her down.

And it was just beginning to sink in to her exactly how good-looking this man was. In a place where most of the men were gym addicts, and many of them were strikingly handsome, nonetheless this man stood out, and made everyone else look ordinary. Just standing there with his white office shirt a little rumpled and a glare darkening his fine features, he radiated the charisma of incredible good looks. His hair was black, and his skin was a natural deep olive color; the light stubble on his cheeks cried out to be stroked. His green eyes were the most stunning of all. Brandi wasn't sure if she wanted to fuck him or just stare at him hour after hour.

No, that wasn't quite true. She wanted to fuck him.

He shut the door behind the retreating guys and stood leaning back against it. "So, Brandi. I haven't met you, have I?"

"Hell," she said, laughing. "You saying if you'd met me, you wouldn't have remembered me?"

Ben said dryly, "I'm trying to say you were supposed to come for an orientation talk with me."

Brandi's jaw fell open. She suddenly realized that this was the Ben Hartford she'd blown off to go drinking with Miguel the first afternoon she'd arrived. It was only some official thing, after all. And Brandi, of all people, didn't need any orienting at Babylona, any more than a fish did when you threw it into the water.

She shrugged. "Well, you got me there. I should have canceled, anyway."

"You should have come to see me," Ben said coldly.

She smiled. "Well, now that I do see you, I realize that. But I didn't know you were going to look like that. You should've ought've put that in the letter."

Ben stared at her, unmoved. And said nothing.

Brandi narrowed her eyes. She felt like she had met a worthy adversary—who she was going to damn well beat. So she began, ever so gently, ever so phonily, to let her lip tremble. "I'm sorry," she said in a plaintive voice. "I didn't mean to do anything wrong. I guess I'm just stupid."

"I'm not calling you stupid," said Ben, a little softened.

"Oh, I know you're not," Brandi said, letting her voice crack with what she hoped was a convincing sob. "But I just do everything *wrong!*"

Then she buried her face in her hands, sobbing heavily—and surreptitiously pulling out a couple of her own nostril hairs, which she'd learned in her brief, glorious, homemade porn career was the quickest way of bringing on tears. Sure enough, her nostril stung unbearably, and her eyes started to tear. She looked up miserably (she hoped) at Ben and whimpered, "Are you going to—throw me out?" Then she sneezed—but only a little. And she was able to compose her face back into a mask of sorrow lickety-split.

His face went soft, and he shook his head. "No, I'm not going to throw you out," he said.

"You—you promise?"

"Oh, Brandi." He came over and put his hand on her shoulder. "I promise. Don't cry. It's all right. You just have to learn to follow the rules."

"Oh, thank you!" she cried and leaped to her feet, pressing him gratefully to her very generous and very aroused breasts. Then she was a little taken aback at how good he felt in her arms. His hair had a warm, fresh smell, and his skin had a slightly sweeter scent that made her want to turn it into a taste. She let her cheek press into his neck, and felt the delicious connection of flesh with flesh there. His body felt wonderfully masculine in her arms; she was aware of the strong muscle of his shoulder tucked under her chin. Without thinking, she brought her groin forward to press lightly against his. And moved her hips from side to side, teasing him, feeling for the luscious swell of his cock.

He let go suddenly and took a step back. Caught unawares, she pouted and said, "Oh, no fair!"

Ben sighed with the unruffled air of a man who had played this scene many times before. He said, "Listen, Brandi, sit down and let's talk."

"No," she said. "I can't just sit down. I'm going to level with you: I was in the middle of . . ."

"I guessed as much."

"Getting off," she said evenly, huskily, suggestively, and looked pleadingly at his crotch. She couldn't be sure, but perhaps there was a slight bulge there. She licked her lips, willing the bulge to grow.

He crossed his arms again, looking distinctly uncomfortable. "I can't help you with that," he said.

Her eyes flew open wide. "Are you kidding? Who, in your opinion, would be *better* equipped to help me with that? You could have been *born* to help me with that! I could have ordered you to specification to help me with exactly that!" Her mind immediately supplied an image of his cock—with a somewhat darker olive skin, velvety, swollen, and nodding slightly as she caught its taut end between her lips—and sucked hard, tasting it, before slipping its whole hard, sweet length down into her throat and letting her tongue steal out to tease his balls . . . mmm.

She met his eye, trying to telepathically show him what she was thinking. Maybe he saw it—he gulped and hugged himself still more tightly, looking so beautifully stern and resistant that she shifted from foot to foot, longing for him. She breathed, "Please? We could . . . make it my meeting with you, just a little delayed?" And she lifted her skirt up, showing the darkened patch of lace where her white panties had long since been soaked through with her juices.

"If you'd come to your meeting, you'd know why . . . Don't do that."

His voice was getting hoarse, she noticed with delight. "What?" she said, using her other hand to lightly lift the lace away from her cunt, showing him the waiting opening. She opened her thighs a little and dipped one finger into her pussy, biting her lip with the desire she was feeling.

"Brandi. Stop showing me your cunt," he said. "Staff aren't allowed to sleep with students."

"Mm, that's sick," she said happily. "Don't obey any such sick rules. Babylona wouldn't." She began to shimmy her panties down; the constriction of the fabric was beginning to feel claustrophobic. She didn't want anything between her pussy and his eyes. His dick.

"Sit down, Brandi, please."

She met his eye, which was cooling again. She let her skirt drop, but kicked the panties away in annoyance. They fetched up on his shoe, and he cracked a smile, obviously despite himself. Then he straightened his face and said, "Thank you."

"You're welcome," she said, with a tragic air. "You can keep the panties. They've failed me, and I never want to lay eyes on them again." And she sat on the edge of the bed, absolutely crawling with the idea of his hands on her ass, her breasts . . . ouch.

He said, "Listen, Brandi, this is a special kind of school, and we have rules here to make sure that people feel safe. You may not have the same needs as other students . . ."

" 'Cause I'm a big dumb slut," she said petulantly. Then she caught his look of concern and said, "Oh, don't worry. I'm just rattling your cage. I know what you mean. Some people have sensitivities. *I* don't understand it, but I know it happens . . . It's like being allergic to chocolate. Or having asthma," she finished up brightly, and smiled.

"Right. So just as you don't smoke in an enclosed space, because some people have asthma and they might have a negative reaction—"

"Do *you* have asthma?" she asked solicitously.

There was a long pause. At last he said, "I have a job."

"And you never, ever, ever, broke that rule even a little bit? Like, maybe you just nibbled the corner off of it?"

He reddened, and Brandi felt triumph. Why, the little devil! He was holding out on her! She said, "Okay, maybe you're perfect and you never broke any rule, even a tiny little bit, even when it seemed irresistible, but I'm not so perfect. And *if* you don't mind, I'm going to finish what I started. I'd *love* your help, but I don't want to give you an asthma attack, so I won't insist."

And with that, very delicately, she slipped one hand underneath her skirt and let it meet her now-desperately panging cunt. She moaned with the release of finally touching her clitoris, and began to flick it with her index fingertip, digging her other three fingers deep into herself. Before she knew it, she was out of control, chasing her orgasm. *Peak*, she thought feverishly, *peak*. But how was she going to explain this to Miss Foré? Well, cross that bridge when she came . . . yes, came . . . yes . . .

Ben said, "Brandi, come on."

"I'm just . . . minding my own . . . business," she gasped. Her skirt had ridden up, and she felt his eyes locked on the work her hand was doing. Then hers strayed to his sweet unavailable crotch, and she gulped—he had the biggest bulge in his pants she ever saw. She stared longingly, and her mind sketched his cock again, giving it all her favorite properties. A gentle upward bowing that would tag her G-spot with every stroke and saw away sweetly at her clit all the while. Sweet cushiony balls that she would feel against her ass as he fucked her deep, deep, deep—and her climax hit her, rocking her with an amazing flood of sensation. Ben was staring at her silently, obviously in an agony of lust. His frustrated desire seemed to seep into her pleasure, prolonging it and adding spice to the delicious anguish of it.

As the bliss was ebbing, leaving her cunt slightly sore and delightfully sloppy, Ben sat down on the opposite bed and groaned slightly. Brandi caught her breath and said in a weak voice, "Hey . . . never too late."

"No!" he said sharply, and then gritted his teeth.

"Aww," she said, and let her skirt fall back into place. "I'm sorry, I probably come on a little strong." She sniffled, feeling the pain where her nostril hairs had been ripped out.

"A little," he said wearily.

"Well, but listen, if you're really really determined not to fuck me . . . ?" She gave him one last mournful look, but he just gave her a stony look and nodded. "Okay," she said, sighing. "But then you've got to tell me who beat me out."

"Excuse me?" He raised his eyebrows. "Listen, we have to talk about you breaking the rules, about you missing your meeting, about you being in this room at all . . ."

"Oh, forget all that. I'll come to your office to talk about all that stuff. Hell." Brandi gave him a disappointed look. "Look, you cheated me out of *five* screws today. Don't leave my curiosity with all blue balls, too."

"Five?" He frowned, then realized. Suddenly he seemed to give up entirely. He started to laugh.

"That's it," Brandi said. "And you know, now I come to think of it, why am I guessing everybody was only going to do me once? Dammit, you cheated me out of *ten* screws!"

"At least," said Ben.

"There you go. So you owe me something awful. You ought to be my *slave* for a month. That's what we would do where I come from."

"Slow down."

"Okay, just tell me your secret then." Brandi folded her hands in her lap. She felt like a million bucks, like she always did after an orgasm. Everything was rosy with physical well-being, and Ben was her favorite person. She smiled at him sunnily. "I won't tell anyone. You ought to know after fifteen minutes in my company—I have a mother of a strong will. If I decide to keep a secret, it gets kept."

"Yes," said Ben, seeming to ponder something troubled within himself. "That's probably true."

"So spill. Who'd you break the rule with?"

"What makes you think—"

"What makes me know for a fact. Don't try lying to me."

He looked at her with friendly consternation.

She said, "And you lost your beautiful hard-on. Look at that. This afternoon began so great, and now you cheated me out of fifteen fucks, and you even lost your hard-on . . . I don't know what I'll do if you don't make good on your promise to tell me."

"I didn't—"

"Yes, you didn't promise, but I feel just like you did. Which is basically the same thing."

"Listen. First things first. Do you know what the penalty is for a girl coming into Perkins?"

"Spanking?"

"Chastity."

Brandi just stared at him imperviously.

At last he said, "Did you understand what I said?"

"I understand the *word*," she said. "But I don't understand how you're going to enforce any such thing. My daddy never could."

"Well, you aren't allowed off the premises. And no one's allowed to sleep with *you*. So I'm not going to enforce it. Everyone here will."

Brandi balked. She remembered how quickly the boys had deserted her in her moment of need. Was it possible—could it be that in a whole institute full of sex-loving kids, she was the only one who understood the importance of breaking all the rules? What if no one would sleep with her for real? She said, "Well, break my heart, why don't you. So how long is that supposed to carry on?"

"A week in the first instance. But if it ever happens again . . ."

"Oh, you're just being mean. And anyway, I've got to get going so I can get laid before you have time to tell anybody. Damn." She stood up, giving Ben a haughty, disapproving look. "And—just in case you think you got away without telling me—that girl you broke the rules with, you're in love with her, right?"

"I just met her!" Ben blurted out.

"Ha!" Brandy said triumphantly. "A freshman, huh? I knew I'd get *something* out of you. Now, Mr. Ben, good afternoon. And you may have won this round . . . but I'll have you yet—in the biblical sense. Punishment or no punishment." She winked and flounced off out of the room, already plotting ways around the impossible seven days of abstinence.

Chapter Seven

The Attahoosa Lounge was empty when Lila arrived, apart from Andy, who was sitting on a couch in front of an array of wine bottles. The teacher's desk was gone, leaving a carpeted space in the middle of the floor where she immediately imagined a circle of kids watching a couple awkwardly French kiss. As she walked in, Andy was cursing and tugging a corkscrew from a bottle of red wine. He looked up and said, "Hey, Lila. Do you know how to work one of these things?"

She said, "Oh, about as well as you, I guess. Are we the first ones here?" She sat down next to him.

He handed her the bottle with a grimace. "Yeah. And Brandi's not coming."

Lila froze in the middle of picking a bit of broken cork out of the bottleneck. "She's not?" She'd somehow counted on Brandi to get her through this. Just being around Brandi made her feel more fearless. Now the lounge seemed to grow around her, into a formidable and enormous hall. She felt like turning tail and running back to her dorm room.

For some reason, this evening's assignment had tapped into all her fears. Maybe it was too close to the parties that used to intimidate her in high school. She'd ended up changing her outrageous costume of the morning for a cotton dress whose belted outline showed her lush figure without hugging the exact contours. She would have been in a sweatshirt and jeans if she hadn't thought that would be like announcing to everyone that she was terrified.

Andy made a face. "Brandi's grounded. Or spayed. Or something. She got caught in Perkins, and so she's off-limits for a week."

He briefly sketched the events, and Brandi's untouchable status. He was obviously feeling guilty about his part in the affair, and he summed up, "I don't know why we didn't get in trouble. I think Ben had it in for Brandi for some reason."

Hearing about Ben made Lila feel even more flustered. Every time she thought about him, she remembered him with her whole body. His hands on her ass, on her nipples—every part of her body chipped in with a sense memory, leaving her confused and tingling. She didn't know what it would be like when she saw him again. Now she applied herself fiercely to the corkscrew, and managed to draw most of the cork out of the bottle on the second try. The remainder had broken up into crumbs that floated in the wine. She said, "Glasses?"

"No, no glasses," said Andy.

"Oh. Is that . . . some policy?"

"Babylona moves in mysterious ways." He smiled at her. "How are you doing here, by the way?"

"Oh. Great. Terrible. Mostly okay. Freaking out half of the time."

"And the rest of the time—"

They said in unison: "Happier than ever."

Lila laughed. "You know the feeling?"

"Hey. I almost left the first week I was here. Last year." His blue eyes smiled at her.

"Oh." She smiled back at him. In the semidark of the lounge, she felt close to him suddenly. Maybe she could make it through this, after all. She said, "Were you daunted? I mean, 'cause I'm daunted."

"I guess I'd bitten off a little more than I could chew. I came here thinking I was some kind of stud, and when I got here I realized I was a little afraid of talking to strangers."

Lila laughed. "I'm not afraid of talking to strangers. But I'm still not sure about fucking strangers."

Andy put his arm around her and squeezed her. "Oh, don't worry about it. Everybody feels like that around here at some point. Except Brandi."

Maybe because they'd just been talking about having sex with strangers, Lila immediately felt a sensual warmth from his arm around her. She snuggled in, noticing that Andy was considerably bigger than Tad; he was built like a football player. Everything about him was big. Even his fingers were twice the size of hers. She put her hand in his and felt the strong muscles in his palm. "Well, I don't think I'm going to leave."

"I hope not," he said, with a tender awkwardness in his voice. Then he turned and kissed her on the cheek. She flushed hot all down her face, her neck . . . and the heat even reached her thighs.

"Thanks," she said. Then she turned to him to find his face still hovering there, his expression soft and amorous. She put her hand to his cheek, which had that smooth, clean-shaven feel that went with the familiar scent of aftershave. And his big quarterback arms pulled her in for another kiss, on the lips. She felt tiny and fragile in his embrace. Her mouth seemed to melt into his, and when his tongue invaded her mouth, the whole world disappeared for a long, long minute.

Then she heard laughter behind her. "Hey, kids, spin the bottle isn't a game for two players, you know."

She and Andy detached from each other, smiling guiltily. Miguel and a couple of girls were standing there. Everyone said hello, and Miguel came and sat on the other side of Lila. He shoved Andy's arm off of her. "You have to wait and spin the bottle like everyone else."

Andy rolled his eyes. "You know, I'm going out on a limb, but I feel like this is a little elementary for us."

"Ouch," said Miguel. "That's harsh."

Lila said, "It's not elementary for me. It's exactly my speed."

A chubby redheaded girl said, "Amen. I'm ready to go hide under the bed."

"Oh, you guys are such lightweights," said a slim blond girl Lila remembered from Miss Foré's class. She was wearing a silk robe, doubtless with nothing under it, and she flashed a pretty, careless smile at them all. "I was just saying to Missy"—she nodded at the redhead—"that we should turn this into a spin the bottle for something worthwhile. Like, at *least* fucking."

Lila groaned before she could stop herself. Everyone but the blond girl laughed.

"And I think we should do what we were told to do," Missy said.

"See where it takes you." Miguel winked.

"So, Ginny, you've been at a lot of orgies, is that what you're saying?" Andy said.

There was a short silence, during which Ginny just glared at him. At last Missy said, "I sure haven't."

Miguel said, "That's what our tuition's paying for. Bring on my first orgy."

Other students were beginning to arrive, and they fell silent, watching the new arrivals, some of them nervously, some of them lustfully. Andy had moved his hand onto Lila's knee, and there was a current of warmth running from it up her thigh again. She sat back in the soft couch, trying to relax, trying to tell herself that everything so far had been easy, even the things she would have thought would be impossible for her to do. Miguel began to tell the story of what had happened to Brandi, and the students who were arriving gathered around, laughing at the high points. Lila tried not to listen—she already knew all this!—but every time Ben's name was mentioned her attention was yanked back, and soon she was doing nothing but picturing him: the straight dark brows that made his green eyes look so startling, the lips that would press onto her bare back gently, and then kiss their way down her back, her hip, until . . .

no, she couldn't think that way. She still didn't have any idea what had really happened between them. If it was against the rules, did that mean that he'd gone out on a limb with her? Or did it mean that he was breaking the rules all the time . . . in the same way . . . with all the freshmen? She studied the faces of the other girls, trying to spot a reaction in their eyes that was anything like hers. But she couldn't tell at all, and all the while, she was confused by the increasing attraction she felt to Andy . . . which made her feel guilty, as if she were going out with Ben, who doubtless had never given her another thought.

Now everyone was there; Andy stood up and did a quick head count, while a few people hurriedly uncorked bottles. The bottle Lila had opened was already empty, and Andy grabbed it from the floor at her feet, smiling at her reassuringly. "Ginny," he said to the blond girl in the robe, "do you want to take charge?"

"Me?" she said, apparently taken aback. "But I'm a freshman." For a moment she looked like a tightrope walker who'd been told at the last moment that tonight, for the first time, there would be no net.

"Yeah, but this is too easy for you."

She made a face at him. "Okay, fine." She took the bottle from him and clanged it against a bottle she was drinking from, until she had everyone's attention. The room fell silent, everyone looking up at her with an odd excitement.

Lila, looking around at all the faces, felt that excitement too. It was a strange out-of-bounds feeling, a sense of staying up past your bedtime, of being out late at night, with no adults present. Anything could happen.

Ginny's voice shook a little with nervousness. "Well, we're all here, and . . . I guess we all know what we're supposed to do." She paused, and looked at Andy for help. He looked back at her innocently. At last she said, "Well, what is there to say?"

Everyone laughed. They all began to applaud her, and she shook her head and walked off to the place where the schoolteacher's desk usually stood, and bent to place the bottle squarely on the floor. She called back to them, "Come on!"

It began like any game of spin the bottle anywhere. There were the same awkward jokes, the same clumsy clinches. But when Andy and Missy were kissing, and someone shouted out, "Go all the way!" mimicking a drunken teenager, Lila found herself holding her breath, waiting to see if they would. And when they separated, she felt a soft, sinking disappointment. She was waiting for someone to do it, to go all the way, in the center of a circle of voyeurs, well-wishers, people who might just join them, too. She was waiting, if she was honest, to be the one in the center of the circle, and to let the longings of the circle of people be embodied in her. To be the focus of everyone's desire.

Finally, the spinning bottle pointed to her, and she found herself crawling on all fours to meet a slim Latino guy with a black ponytail who kissed her furiously, and whispered into her ear before she could escape, "I've been wanting you all week . . ." Then she was safe back in place in the circle. She'd been sitting there for a minute when she met his eye and got a delayed response, a thrill that went from her lips down and made her smile right at him. He smiled back, delighted, and it occurred to Lila that she would probably sleep with him someday. Someday very soon. And then she realized that the same was true for all the men there.

It had crossed her mind before, but this was the first time it was really real to her. And it was perfectly okay. It was more than okay. It was like someone telling her, "You know that guy you have a crush on? He likes you, too!" She felt the wine running through her blood now, making her dizzy and boozy, and felt like she truly belonged here. She felt as if she were already experiencing the hands of everyone in the room roaming over her naked body, over her stiff nipples, into her cunt and out again to feel the plump firmness of her ass. It was about how you felt, like Miss Foré had said. Something opened in you, and it was like suddenly being able to speak a language.

Then, before she could think about it any longer, someone handed the bottle to her. She leaned forward and put it down deliberately on its side. She realized she must look very serious, maybe even soulful, but she didn't mind. Then she got the bottle spinning, and couldn't help noticing a certain intensity on the faces of some of the men as they watched it spin. They wanted her . . . "I've been wanting you all week." Her lips formed the words "You too."

The bottle glittered and spun, shifting slightly to one side as it twirled. At last it began to slow, and everyone leaned forward. It made a few last lazy circles and fell still, pointing at Andy.

Lila looked at him and knew immediately what she was going to do.

He came crawling forward, smiling at her in a friendly way; maybe he still remembered how she'd talked about her anxiety. He was probably trying to reassure her. But she was feeling smoky and strange with lust. Crawling to meet him, she was aware of the seductive motion of her hips. And when he was close enough that she felt the warmth coming off his skin, she heard herself whimper with desire, so softly only he heard.

But he had heard. His eyes went darker with passion. They kneeled in front of each other and began to kiss. Then his big arms went around her and their bodies pressed snug against each other from the knees up. She felt the musculature of his chest and his stomach, his big thighs . . . and then thrust her hips in, meeting his, to feel the growing pressure of his dick.

They fell on their sides and Lila was pulling his shirt up, feeling his bare chest. He was still kissing her, with that same fierce power that had made her feel like she was tiny and helpless before. And she let her lips trail up his cheek to whisper into his ear, "I want to fuck you. Now."

He pulled back slightly and looked at her; then his face filled with a feverish desire. One of his hands left her and he was unbuckling his belt. Just watching him do it made darts of heat shoot through Lila's cunt.

She wanted him. Part of her was aware of the faces all around, intent, urging them on. She squirmed down and pulled up his T-shirt to kiss his belly, willing him to hurry as he unzipped his jeans and pulled them down. Then his cock was free, and she let her lips touch it, kissing the tip, the sides, the fat vein running down to his balls. Her tongue played lightly around his testicles, winning a rough moan from him . . .

And then she heard an answering moan from the watching circle of students. It sent a crazy arrow of heat through her. Electrified, she took the head of his dick in her mouth and put one hand on his hip, pulling him in to thrust into her mouth. She gobbled hungrily, her tongue playing over the velvety surface as he pressed it all the way in, filling her throat. Then it was coming out again, and she had a chance to fully appreciate the straight, hard thickness of it. It was like the rest of him; it had a bulk and power to it that made her feel weak and pleasurably frightened.

He was fucking her mouth slowly, deliberately, pressing his dick into her sucking mouth with an emphasis that made her feel his pleasure even more than the soft sounds he had begun to make. His hand stole down to shape itself around the back of her head, and she again felt the strength, the size, of that hand. Someone in the audience said, "God, that's . . . that's so hot."

Then Andy had closed his fingers on a handful of her hair and was pulling her up. She felt his cock slip out of her mouth with a keen shock of loss. But she knew that the best was about to come. And she was already pulling down her panties, a black scrap that seemed to melt away into the darkness as he turned her onto her back and moved his powerful hips between her thighs. His cock found her pussy opening. For the first time she fully appreciated its width; it stretched her open almost to the point of discomfort. Then he had pressed his cock in with the same slow deliberate appreciation with which he had fucked her mouth.

Lila gasped with the overwhelming feeling of being filled. His body pressed down on her with a weight that made her feel that she was pinned, gratefully paralyzed as he continued to fuck her, gaining speed, with that dick, which he drove in with such certain aim and power. And she opened her eyes, and looked from underneath him at the eyes that surrounded her. As her gaze met that of the Latino man who had kissed her before, she felt the pleasure in her cunt spread suddenly in a bomb flash to fill her to the skin. Every inch of her was alive. It was as if the eyes on her were all conveying a charge of pleasure that flowed from Andy's cock, which was pummeling her, through her cunt, and then somehow between her nerve endings and their intense, passionate attention. They all leaned forward, experiencing it with her, longing for her, for him, all part of the experience.

His thrusting began to call out layers of pleasure from her, as if her cunt were being strummed, and each string gave out its note of ecstasy. And before she knew it, she was coming. But he was still fucking her, as the waves of her orgasm clutched his prick, making him thrust faster and faster, losing control and pounding her so hard now she felt that fear again, a wild thrilling fear that turned her orgasm into a near faint of delirious physical joy.

Finally he was freezing above her, his back arched as his cock strained all the way into her cunt, and she felt the kicking of his cock as he spurted the warm come into her. She moaned, another wave of orgasm hitting her. Her half-lidded eyes saw the open mouths of the watchers, and she felt as if their panting, their desire, was following her into the dark of her new orgasm.

She shut her eyes, and when she opened them again, it was over. Andy pulled out of her, kissing her once more on the cheek, and began to fumble with his zipper. She pulled her skirt down almost by reflex, and then she looked around her again.

Suddenly she felt where she was. In a strange room, surrounded by strangers, filled with a stranger's semen. The faces around her looked different now, coldly calculating, as if they were figuring out exactly how well she had performed. She imagined them holding up numbers, like Olympic judges. And she remembered Tad's judgment of her: *Boring. Your blow jobs are boring. Sex with you* . . . These kids, all future sex professionals, would surely judge her even more harshly. *So boring,* she imagined the blond girl, Ginny, saying. *Elementary stuff, and even that* . . .

She crept back to her place in the circle. Only then did she realize that Andy had switched seats with someone, and he was waiting for her there, with a warm, sloppy smile on his face. She sat next to him and couldn't bring herself to meet his eye. But his big arm caught her again and crushed her to his side. He whispered into her ear, "Thank you, Lila . . . That was great. You were amazing."

She caught her breath, and burrowed her head into his neck suddenly, clutching him to her hard. At last she whispered, "I wasn't— boring? You know what I mean?"

He flinched and then he was scowling at her in amazement. He whispered, "Boring? Are you crazy? If dying of pleasure is boring, Lila, you got it. You're unbelievable. And unbelievably sweet and . . . don't get me started."

She sat back, trying to smile at him in a way that conveyed that he was unbelievable, too. (But hopefully sophomores didn't need reassurance. God, how she wanted to be a sophomore, and not need any reassurance!) Then she was watching the next couple kissing, their hands snaking over each other. She realized that she had put the bar higher for everyone. From now on it was going to be round after round of public sex.

And then some part of her gave way. Whispering, "Thanks . . . you were great . . . thanks for everything," to Andy, she scooted back out of the circle. Then, only at that last moment remembering that her panties were still lying discarded somewhere on the floor of the lounge, she fled, slipping as soundlessly as she could out of the door, down the hall, and into the night.

Chapter Eight

Lila stumbled across the grass, her head tipped back so that she could see the stars above. Since Babylona Institute was a dozen miles from the nearest town, the stars and even the Milky Way were plainly visible, and they gave Lila a soothing feeling of calm and beauty. Somehow the peace of the night made what she had just done seem all right again. The tight warm wetness between her legs, where she was still feeling subtle momentary ghosts of Andy's prick spreading her open—it was a kind of private beauty, too. Beauty was a kind of pleasure, after all, or pleasure was a kind of beauty.

Lila sighed, and put one hand to her breast, feeling the full round shape of it, the way the flesh gave to her fingers, springy and deliciously firm—beauty. Perhaps sexuality was just the most potent kind of beauty, she thought. And though she was still a little frightened of it, she knew now she was determined to overcome that fear. And she wanted to do that with the people here, the similarly brave and similarly vulnerable people . . . who had just seen her fuck a complete stranger.

She stopped dead, feeling the whole weight of her past descend on her. Then, to her incredible relief, she saw Brandi sitting on a bench by the path, smoking a cigarette and nursing a bottle between her thighs. As Lila walked up, she recognized the bottle as identical to the one they'd just been spinning, and she bet herself that Brandi had stolen it from the Attahoosa before the other students could arrive.

She called out, "Hey, Brandi?"

Brandi looked up at her with a tragic expression on her brightly painted features. When she recognized Lila, her usual good cheer almost broke through; but she conquered it with an obvious effort of will, forcing her face to reassume its mask of melancholy. She said plaintively, "Did you hear what those fascists are doing to me?"

Lila laughed. "Hey. It's just a week."

"*Just* a week. Wow." Brandi shook her head. "Okay. I gotta sit down with myself and think about, what if I was an army wife? I mean, there's people in the world way worse off than me." Then a sly look crept into her eyes and she sized up Lila. But after a minute's thought she shook her head and said, "The worst of it is, I don't even dare proposition anybody, 'cause if they gave in, I'd get them in trouble, too. Then they'd get the punishment, and it'd spread like wildfire. The domino effect. In a week flat, I could turn the whole place as sex free as a Southern Baptist seminary!"

Lila laughed. "Wow. That almost sounds appealing right now," she said.

"Ooh, don't give me your crazy talk. Sit down and tell Aunt Brandi all about it." She patted the bench beside her.

Lila plumped down with a grimace for the sweet soreness she felt in her pussy as she sat. Brandi offered her the bottle. Lila took it, smiling. "Did you steal that?"

"No, no way. Drew from Perkins gave it to me to apologize."

Lila took a swig of wine, and the taste brought back the memory of the circle of watching students, their young faces intently antici-pating, the features indistinct in the dark, and the same circle seen from the floor where she lay while Andy fucked her so desperately, deliciously. She sighed and looked at the bottle. It was identical to the one she'd been drinking from inside, and it almost seemed like a friend now, as if they'd been through a lot together. She said, "I'm sorry, Brandi. And I've got the opposite problem."

"Too much fucking," Brandi said. "Well, I'll try to be sympathetic." She laughed and added, "I'm just kidding. Not everybody's an old veteran like me."

"Oh, I'm just having growing pains, I guess." Lila looked back up at the stars. "It's just that I keep doing things that I don't expect. I feel like I don't know myself anymore." She explained to Brandi what had just happened. She tried to keep the heat from her voice—she didn't want to make Brandi feel left out—but her tone got tender and yearning despite her, and she realized that she was wishing she'd stayed and maybe taken Andy home. They could have done it again, and again . . . woken up in the morning. She finished up by saying: "I don't even know what I'm supposed to feel. Should I want to go home with Andy? With someone else? I don't know what's expected of me."

Brandi shrugged. "I don't know for sure, honey. But I'm the biggest fan that ever lived of Babylona Parris, and if I know anything about her, I'd say you're not *supposed* to feel anything. I mean, it's no good telling someone what they're supposed to feel. It's just that maybe you don't like what you *do* feel. Is that it?"

"Hm. That's totally it. But shouldn't I be able to change what I feel, or what I feel about what . . ." Lila sighed. "Oh, hell. I wish I could just take it slow, but it seems like as soon as I got here, I jumped in the deep end. And now I almost want to leave. I feel like I could change too much, and then I'd never be able to go home again."

She hadn't expected to say that, but now that it was out, she realized it was true. It would be so soothing to be lying at home, in her own bedroom, crying out her sorrow about Tad with a pint of ice cream and a chick flick on DVD like a normal girl.

"Whoa," said someone from the dark. "What are you saying, roomie?"

It was Anna, who strode up with her carefree walk, wearing her usual attire of matching lacy underwear. Tonight's outfit was classic black, with a pattern of openwork roses in the bra, which clearly showed the rosy tint of Anna's nipples. In her lingerie uniform, Anna looked doll-like, her huge brown eyes and porcelain skin making her slight figure look delectably feminine and fragile. She walked up and sat beside Lila with a graceful motion. "Somebody having a bad night?"

"A little bit," said Lila. "Maybe I'm having a crisis."

"She fucked someone she shouldn't," said Brandi. "Or someone she should, only not when she did."

"But why am I here," Lila asked, "if that's what I'm like? The sex was as good as it could be."

Anna clapped her hands. "What are you saying, girlfriend? You know what you just did?"

"What?" Lila frowned at her, caught off balance.

"Well, nothing but your homework for Miss Foré's class! Arousal, peak . . . all you need is a pen! Congratulations! You just lost one thousand dollars!"

Lila laughed. "That's one way of looking at it, I guess."

Anna put an arm around her and squeezed her shoulders. "Hey, don't worry. It gets to be too much sometimes, for almost everyone. I never felt that way at Babylona, but that was because I'd already been through it out in the real world. Take it from me; it's better to go through it here. In fact, that's a good reason to stay."

"Really?" said Lila.

"Absolutely. In fact, I had a really bad experience just before I got here that made me almost not come. I didn't want to think about having sex with anyone, or the fact that human beings have genitals, or anything that brought it back."

"A bad experience?" said Lila cautiously.

"Oh, nothing violent or anything like that," said Anna, smiling. "Looking back, it's actually kind of funny. Now that it all worked out all right. But at the time it scared me half to death. Or it scared me enough that . . . well, the first few nights I was here I didn't leave my room. Finally what happened was that a guy called Brian came

to my room to give me a hard time about it. Well, he ended up licking my pussy for about two hours. I came and came until . . . well, I
think I may have turned inside out at one point. I've never been quite
the same. I mean, I can now do the lotus position."

"What was the bad thing that happened? I mean, before you
came here?" said Lila.

"Oh, well, this was in my groupie days. Not that I was ever a
real groupie. Real groupies care about the music and the fame and
they . . . well, they know the band's name, at least. Let's put it that
way. I cared about fucking musicians. Just something about a man
with a guitar, on a stage. It was something that always worked for me.
I'd be watching the band play, and then I'd be watching the lead guitarist play, and then I'd be watching the lead guitarist's crotch. Next
thing I knew, I was throwing my bra on stage and I ended the night
in the van, drinking beer with a nice guitarist's dick in me, five ways.
I liked to actually drink beer *while* being fucked. By a guitarist. And
every once in a while, to change it up, by a bassist—*and* a guitarist.
So, looking back, it should have gotten predictable and boring. In its
own way, it was vanilla sex.

"So I'd been following this up-and-coming band . . . or the guitarist. He was this really young West Indian guy, almost skinny but
with those gorgeous guitar biceps . . . and his skin was like dark
gold silk. Real serious-looking, and he had tattoos all over his arms,
those black tribal things; they drive me crazy. And on his belly he
had his name, stenciled in big letters: DANTE. He was only about my
age—nineteen.

"But he had this fierce girlfriend, some druggy blond girl, who
used to drag him off with her after their set. Like a guard dog.
She was older than him—I mean, like, older to a faintly creepy
degree—and . . . piggy looking." Anna made a face, and Lila and
Brandi started to laugh.

"Obviously she wasn't good enough for him," said Lila.

"Chick was a cradle robber," Brandi said.

"It was a total rescue mission," said Anna. "I was going to free him from his chains. Well, this night I'm talking about, the pig girl wasn't there. So I was all over that. I'd been preparing my ground for a couple of weeks. And that night I'd brought some preworn panties to throw on the stage, so I was set. I mean, not that I was wearing dirty underpants. I used to carry panties in my pocket. This is a tip: You can look *really* stupid trying to take your panties off in a crowd of people. Plus, I really prefer to dance without any panties on. I like the feeling of the air on my bare pussy. And I'd written a message on the panties: 'I want to taste your cock,' I think."

Anna's eyes went dreamy. She said, "I love the part where you don't know for sure if he's going to sleep with you. I used to chase guys *shamelessly*. I like getting a guitarist cornered, like, if it's a smaller club where they'll drink at the bar . . . you can catch them in the hall sometimes, and just corner them. Pin them against the wall, one arm on either side of their head, and start telling them how amazing their playing was, and your hips just drift—gently forward—until you're pressing against him. Like, feeling the hard-on coming. Pressing it where it's just a little bit . . . spongy, you know, and moving your hips back and forth so that you can feel the shape, where it's stiffening from the base, and arch into the end so he can feel with the tip of his penis where it would go into your cleft . . . I like seducing guys, anyway. I don't get so interested if they're chasing *me*.

"So this night, I was chasing Dante. My boyfriend, Kaz, was with me for backup . . ."

"Your boyfriend was there?" Lila blurted.

Anna grinned. "Yeah . . . we hunted together, you know. We liked sharing."

Brandi nodded approvingly. "Me and my friend Choo-Choo used to go out together, only if he scored with some girl who didn't do three in a bed, he'd blow me off every time."

"And I guess you never blew *him* off?" Anna said.

Brandi looked affronted. "Well, sometimes, if the new guy didn't want . . . I mean, some guys are homophobic. It's not their fault. And you can't just send them home alone. It's like throwing out good food."

Anna laughed and went on. "Okay, so I threw old Dante my panties, he turned bright red and just left them on the floor. I took my shirt off and danced in my bra and miniskirt . . . It was this flame-red bra that was nothing but lace . . . He wouldn't even look. Everybody else looked! And it gets you damned hot when you're dancing around with your tits more or less exposed, and all the guys in the place are staring and starting to circle round . . . I mean, I could have gone home with almost anyone but. Well, hard to get is right up my street, so I'm holding out for Dante.

"When the set was over, he was packing up and leaving, fast as that. Kaz went ahead and he was waiting for me in the car, like pretending not to know me. Finally I caught up to Dante in the parking lot. I cornered him alone. He had his guitar case. When I caught up to him he looked all around for help.

"I'm still holding my shirt in my hand, after all. It was a summer night. I like to feel the breeze on my bare skin. Or I like to feel drivers staring at me, take your pick. Anyway, me in my bra and a miniskirt that shows my butt every time the wind blows. I'm hunting bear.

"So I said, 'Come on, baby, don't keep running away from me. I won't hurt you,' which turned out to be a lie. And I reached out to shake his hand. So he fell for that, and then I wouldn't let go. That's my favorite trick. Well! I've still got one hand free, but he's got one hand holding his guitar, the other is mine, and I start to just touch his chest through his T-shirt. I'm asking him about his tattoos. And Dante, it's delicious, he's a mess, he's saying things like, 'Well, that one, it took, I remember that one, the one you mean, it took a long time, that one . . .' He couldn't make any sense at all. And every now and then he'd give up and look down at my tits, and lose his thread altogether.

"So then I pull out the big gun, you know what I mean. I say 'Is something wrong?' and then I let my hand trace down and find his hard-on. God, it was beautiful. He just froze up like he'd turned to stone. And I got a little bolder—there were people going through the parking lot, but we were in shadow—and began to stroke it, up and down, just gently through his jeans.

"By now, it's all Dante can do to breathe. And his face is all shiny with sweat, his beautiful skin is all glossy and I lean forward and put my mouth on his mouth and first I lick his lips, back and forth. I can hear his breathing, all fast and high-pitched. And I start to lick the sweat off his cheeks, tasting the stubble there . . . and then down his neck, with all the beautiful muscles, and I can feel his pulse going like mad.

"And then I just start leading him back to my car. He comes as quiet as a lamb. But as I'm getting there, I think showing Kaz to him is too great a risk, so I gesture to Kaz to duck down in front. And I get old Dante into the backseat, and I creep on top of him. God, my breasts getting squeezed down on top of his thighs, and then his hard dick. He's so lost to all reason that as soon as I get the door shut, he unzips his fly and he's got his dick out, and I'm ready for him, crouching over him. In he goes, just like that, and I gasped like anything; you know how good a guy's dick can feel when you've been thinking about it for weeks. That sweet, and thick, and hot. And now that the ice is broken, Dante isn't shy at all. He plunging in and out of me, his long slick dick going *all* the way in, and then coming *all* the way out, so his tip catches just slightly on my clit every time it goes back in and it just dives to the bottom and tags me inside on my G-spot until I'm crying, almost, with the pleasure. And I start riding him, coming down on him so his dick is driven even deeper up into my belly, and I can feel his sweet big balls pressing into my ass. He reaches up and he's playing with my tits, tugging the nipples in the red lace, so the scratching of the lace and the pinching is driving me crazy at the same time. And I go on rising way up to feel that poke on my clit before his cock slides past and in and—oh, God. And both of us are moving faster and faster and harder and harder. It's so good I can't see; it's like five kinds of dirty pleasure happening all at once, over and over. And then I bring my hips up especially high and come down—but he's in the slight wrong place and—"

Anna had been getting heated, but now her face went somber and she gulped. She said, "Well, it broke. His penis just snapped at the base. I guess it was so hard, and we caught it at the wrong angle . . ."

Lila and Brandi were staring with their jaws open. Brandi said, "No! That can't happen! Tell me that's not true!"

Anna said, "It can. I didn't know that could happen *either*. I just assumed it couldn't." She hugged herself and went on. "Well, Dante screamed, of course. And there was all this blood then. And I screamed. And then . . . Well, Kaz stuck his head up over the seat and screamed." She made a little guilty face. "So *that* cat was out of *that* bag. But it was good he was there, 'cause he had the presence of mind to drive us to the hospital, *fast*.

"Well, the upshot was, Dante's penis was all right . . . they got it back *on* in plenty of time. So the one thing that can go wrong after that is, sometimes it curls up . . ."

"Like a pig's tail?" said Brandi, horrified.

"No, not so bad as that. No." Anna laughed a little nervously. "But it can be too much to be, um, functional. Useful. Only Dante was okay . . . except for Piggy Woman—no pun intended. It's not like this story has a happy ending where Pig Woman gets a pigtail-penised lover.

"Anyway, so she found out the hard way about Dante's little adventure with me. And what was weird about that was, she sent me a letter afterward, thanking me—*thanking* me, because I'd been the one who taught her Dante was untrustworthy, and so she knew she shouldn't marry him. She needed fidelity as a top priority or something. And now she'd found the right man, a man who would truly love her, and who was a dentist or some noncheating profession that I don't even want to think about. Like, she's finished with no-good dirty cheating musicians.

"Well, I got a bug up my ass about it, that woman drove me nuts. So me and Kaz went to her house and she let us in and before you could say 'big ugly hypocrite,' Kaz was fucking her, dentist or no dentist. She was so full of shit. All that kind of jealous person is just dying to cheat, that's their problem. All you had to do was give her a glass of wine and she started to touch her own tits, you know, surreptitiously. So Kaz says, 'Hey, let me do that for you.' Ten seconds flat, he's *railing* her. Not that that's a bad quality, in anyone who wasn't half pig, but . . .'"

Brandi nodded firmly. "Know thyself," she said. "You got to know thyself, and then it's all cool."

Lila sat back, feeling frustrated with herself. Here she was having trouble with one little instance of public sex. And both of her friends here had been doing it for years. She couldn't even imagine cornering a man and seducing him against his will, never mind cornering a woman and seducing her, *with* someone. "You're both so fearless," she said, sighing.

"I'm not scared of sex." Brandi shrugged. "But I'm deadly afraid of having a real job. Just the thought of waking up at 6 a.m. gives me a cold sweat. I've got to make my fortune young, like Babylona."

"Didn't you make a lot of money in the . . . movie industry?" Lila asked.

"Oh, hell, no! We were a bunch of dumb kids with a camcorder. Only our last film even got distributed. But I made good money stripping." Brandi made a face. "Didn't like it, though."

"Why not?" Lila tried to imagine stripping. Immediately she was horny again; she was beginning to think she must be an exhibitionist. "Isn't it sexy? And . . . well, easy for the money?"

"Well, that all depends." Brandi shook her head sharply, one two. "Even on the sexy, that's partial and uncertain. 'Cause there's days when dancing naked can seem like washing dishes. It's real physical work; the place is always either too hot or too cold, and everybody's screaming all the time till your ears ring. Well, I'm a pretty friendly person, but when it comes to fifty different men you never saw before shoving dollars into your crotch—you know, I start getting scared of all the germs. What if they had poison ivy, even? But sure, I had some days it was sexy. But even that could end in tears. Tears and embarrassment of a monumental order."

"Sweet," said Anna. "Tell us the story."

"*The* story? There's like a dozen stories, all of them enough to make a sensible girl turn into a nun or else move to the moon, or both."

"But you'll tell us one," Anna said, and jabbed Lila with her elbow.

"What?" said Lila. "Oh. Yeah, you should tell us one."

"It'll make Lila feel better," Anna said virtuously.

"It will," said Lila, smiling. "No, honestly, it will."

"Okay, story that's gonna embarrass the hell out of me, what could be easier? They're common as flies. Well, this was the last one, the thing that got me out of stripping.

"This was when I was working in New York, this year, kind of a crazy time. I'm working my usual shift, six to two a.m., and this bunch of kids comes in at seven. Drinking. I mean, everybody's drinking, but they're drinking the way people do when they want an excuse for the lousy behavior they're gonna exhibit. Shouting at each other and heckling. And they're okay kids; they're just kinda spoiled rich kids—they got the idea that because it's a strip club, it doesn't matter how they act. Well, that's my place of work, where I have to spend every day. You start throwing things or chanting insults, you're ruining my quality of life. It's like you come into my neighborhood and litter.

"So, what you do about that, is make friends with them. Then you can get them on your side. So in between my dances, I go and chat with the guys. You know. 'Hi, where you from? I haven't seen you boys before.' Then they get real docile. You know they've decided the stripper's hot for them. But I don't mind what they think. I'm spreading happiness, even if it is to jerks.

"And I'm sitting with them—they bought me a drink—and I'm talking to this one guy who's—just by the way—drop-dead gorgeous. A big guy, like six foot two, and he's got that high school athlete look, like a lacrosse player. The lean, hard muscles, and the glossy hair, the rosy glow in his face. And he's a little shy, too, like nice-boy shy. Well, I can't help it—I put my hand on his thigh at one point and whisper in his ear: 'I'm going to dance just for you.'

"And when I get back up to dance I'm thinking about him watching me. That makes it different; like if Choo-Choo came to watch me dance, I'd always have to fuck him afterward. I'd throw all the other girls out of the dressing room and screw him on the floor. I love that feeling of having my ass ground against a carpet. Mm.

"Anyway, so I know schoolboy's watching me and thinking about me undressing for him. He's wondering if I'm going to sleep with him later, too. Schoolboy's dream, right? So when I'm flashing my boobs, it's not just an automatic gesture; it's flashing them *at* some one, and feeling how he's dying to touch them. And then I'm dying to let him touch them.

"And the same when I'm slipping my panties down and just letting a little peep of my pussy show. I'm thinking about him seeing me and wanting me. And then about his fingers stroking there, up and down the slit. And then when I open my legs to let everyone get a good look at my cunt, it's like I'm opening up to let him shove his sweet cock in. I'm imagining him getting hard in his pants, and by then I've pretty much decided I'm going to screw him. So I'm thinking how I'm going to get to see his dick in just a little while, and how bad he's going to want to shove it home.

"My performance is getting more and more intense, and I'm fucking the pole for real, feeling the rod slide against the wetness in

my pussy until I'm so close to coming . . . Then the music ends. And
I'm too far gone to think . . . I slip on my robe and stumble back out
to the table of drunk kids.

"When I get there, he's staring at me with his eyes glazed over—
staring at my body. Up and down. He's still seeing it naked, I can
tell—and his friends are all silent. I walk right up and put out my
hand and say, 'Take me outside, Tad.'"

Lila gasped. Brandi paused for a second and frowned at her, but
Lila just shook her head and gestured for her to go on. If this was
what she feared it was, she'd rather know once and for all. And if
Brandi found out that Tad was her ex, she might soften the story to
save Lila's feelings. This was her only opportunity to find out the
truth.

Brandi said, "Well, we staggered outside, with his friends whoop-
ing behind us. And in the parking lot out back, there was a little
patch of grass at the back that sloped down so couldn't nobody see
you. I led him back there, and as I got to the grass, I dropped the
robe. Then he went crazy and grabbed me. He was kissing me and
groping my tits and squeezing them hard as he pressed his hard-on
against my naked pussy. Then he grabbed my ass in both his hands
and lifted me against his cock. I was holding on to his strong shoulders and I wrapped my legs around his hips to let him rock against
me. I could feel the whole long shape of his dick in his pants. Then
he crouched down and let me down on my back in the grass.

"But then—just as I feel his hard dick opening me—he comes.
So there's a big splash of come all over the front of my cunt. Drib-
bling down. Good for nothing. He collapses next to me, sighing,
just staring into space, not saying sorry or anything. Just lying in the
grass like a happy little kid resting after a game of tag.

"So I guess I look kind of expectant, or maybe even mad. 'Cause
after a minute, he says, 'Oh, sorry, what do I owe you?'

"What do I owe you! Well, I said, 'No need to pay me, honey,'
still trying to be nice, 'cause I guess I'm just too nice for my own

good, sometimes. This is one of those times, because when he hears that, he doesn't realize he should be down on his knees doing some serious pussy licking—instead he gets a big shit-eating grin on his face, like he's the Great Stud of Studs. And you might think this couldn't get any worse, but he instantly starts to tell me his whole life story!"

"His whole life story?" said Lila breathlessly. "Like what?"

"Oh, how he's getting married, but he doesn't know if he's old enough. And his girlfriend is this *wonderful person*, but he doesn't feel the same *passion* for her as he used to. Basically, he wants to screw around, but he doesn't want to get in any trouble. And he's talking and talking like he's getting paid by the word.

"So in the dark, I start to play with myself. I can't stand it anymore. I let my fingers slip down my clit and get my fingers inside. I'm so horny, it's like all the flesh there is taut and straining, like the orgasm is just on the tip of my tongue. I get all my fingers in and fuck myself, and I'm using my other hand to stroke my clit. So I'm doing this, just quietly, quietly, in the dark. I can feel the dewy grass on my ass and thighs and back, and the fact that I'm sneaking makes it sexier. I'm going to make myself come, and he'll never even know.

"All the time, he's talking about himself, and how he's such a good-looking guy, he knows he could sleep with hundreds of girls, if only he wasn't tied down. I'm half listening, and thinking about him fucking hundreds of girls, while I let my body find its rhythm. And just as I reach the point of no return, he reaches over and starts playing with my breasts again. There was something about the way he's groping them, testing their firmness, teasing the nipples, without realizing that I'm getting off—that sends me over the edge. So I try to control myself, but a long moan gets out. And he says, 'Wow, you have such sensitive breasts,' like he thinks he made me cry out.

"So I had to get back to the club, but when we were walking back, he thanked me for helping him make some decisions. And I said to him, 'Lad, just tell her you slept with a stripper, and she'll boot your ass to kingdom come.' I didn't even mean it. I was only having fun. He said, 'Oh, you don't know my girlfriend. She's so crazy about me, she'd put up with anything.'"

"He *said* that?" Lila exclaimed.

Anna and Brandi squinted at her.

"Yeah, something like that," said Brandi. "Why?"

"And his name was Tad? Do you know what his last name was?"

"No," Brandi said, crossing her arms. "But I know what his fiancée's name was, and I know what she looked like, on account of Tad showed me a picture."

Lila gulped. "What she looked like?"

"That's right. And I've been wanting to tell her this story ever since I saw her walk into Satisfaction class. And to tell her that her no-good boyfriend came back to my club the night after he broke up with her and tried to get me to have more no-good sex with him. He told me how he broke up with her, and I told him if I ever saw him again I'd set his hair on fire." Brandi frowned thoughtfully. "I know that's kind of a funny thing to say, but it was what sprang to mind."

Lila felt her eyes filling with tears. "You mean you knew . . . you . . ."

Anna said, "Wait. You're telling me this is the same guy—Lila's Tad? Asshole Tad who said—"

"He said I was boring in bed!" said Lila. "He said you showed him what sex could really be like!"

Brandi put her arm around Lila. "Shush. Shush. Don't get upset, kid. He was just a kid who had too big an idea of himself. Everybody goes out with some guy like that when they're in high school. At least, I did. He was beautiful-looking, he was just a little—"

"Asshole," Anna said firmly. "I already knew he was an asshole; now it turns out he's a lying asshole."

Lila didn't know how to feel. Part of her felt like Brandi was playing with her feelings to make an impression. Another part of her was still reeling from the full understanding that she'd never known Tad.

She said, "Do you think . . . do you think he loved me?" Now the tears began to well out and drip down her cheeks.

Brandi gave her shoulders a squeeze. "Of course he did, sweetie, in his own way. He wasn't even such an asshole; he was just a little in love with himself. That's okay, I hope. But he was way too young to get married—and so are you, you crazy girl. You were eighteen, silly! You were just too young to know you were too young. You trying to tell me you were ready to marry, when the day after the wedding falls through, uh-oh! Here you are at Babylona!"

"It's not like that," said Lila. "I was traumatized by . . . I wanted to show him . . ." Her mind reeled. Was that the real reason? If it was, there was no point in her being here anymore. Tad had been lying all the time. Brandi had never even given him a blow job. And unless premature ejaculation was his idea of advanced sex technique, his whole story about how Lila was boring in bed had been a total fabrication. This was her green light to leave. She could go home— she already knew how to have sex!

"I think someone needs the champagne hot tub," Anna said.

Lila sniffled and said, "I don't know if that's . . ." Then she thought again, and asked, "But isn't it cold?"

Brandi said, "Kind of luke. Some people don't like it. Too warm to drink, too cold to be a real hot tub, they say. But for my money, it's like the best Jacuzzi in the world. The way the bubbles play around your skin is just crazy good. And I'll drink warm champagne. I'll drink *hot* champagne."

"Okay," said Lila, wiping her eyes. If she was going to leave Babylona, at least she would have done everything. "Let's go. I think I could do with some warm champagne myself."

Chapter Nine

L ila woke the next day with her hair all sticky and her sheets sticking to her champagne-saturated skin. For a moment she lay there breathing in the fragrance and remembering the end of the evening. There had been a few other sleepy students at the hot tub, and they'd all lounged there silently, staring up at the stars, occasionally ducking under to take a mouthful of wine (except for Anna, who said she wasn't normally squeamish, but there was just something about it). By the end, Lila could hardly walk, and while Brandi and Anna both took showers before going back to the dorms, she had staggered straight to her bed and collapsed there, with Anna's friendly, "You're going to be sorry you didn't wash . . ." ringing in her ears. When she peeked, Anna wasn't in bed, but there was a have-a-nice-day note from her on the floor, with two aspirin resting on top of it.

In the shower, with her slightly achy head full of the conversations and events of the night before, she tried to figure out what her next move should be. For a moment last night, the idea of leaving Babylona had seemed like a wonderful escape. She wouldn't have to face her own possibly out-of-control desires; she wouldn't have to feel exposed, uncertain, even—if she was honest with herself—dirty. She could get a job as a secretary, or go back to some normal school. The kind of school where hookups weren't mandatory. She blissfully imagined herself telling a guy that she *wasn't on the market right now* as she worked shampoo through her hair a second time. The champagne was proving a little tricky to get out, and the whole bathroom already smelled like wine. She could major in something normal, something easy. Like English! She could be an English major! And if she wanted to have sex with lots of men, she still could. It was hardly unprecedented. But nobody would be expecting her to write a three-page essay about it, or capture it on film.

She kept lathering herself with soap, over and over, until her skin was tight and squeaky clean. As the wine washed down the drain, she felt more and more that this entire episode with Babylona was crazy. Her fiancé had betrayed her, and she'd lost her mind for a little while. That was all it was. She didn't belong here—she wasn't a tough person like Brandi or Anna. Never in a million years would she go out with her boyfriend to pick up boys—or girls—in order to sleep with them three in a bed. When she'd come here, she'd known there would be sex involved, but the nonstop intensity of it was too challenging for her. She was the kind of person who could get married at nineteen, no matter what Brandi said, and stay faithful for the rest of her life.

Once she was dressed, she went out for a walk around campus, half believing that it was to say good-bye to the place. She even went up to the main parking lot and sat in her car for a while, thinking that she could just drive away. She didn't even have to explain to anyone. Anna and Brandi, well, she could call them or send them a postcard. But a half hour passed and she still hadn't put her key in the ignition.

She remembered arriving here the first day and going to see the adviser—Ben. That was where it all started. As she remembered it, a warmth stole through her. She still didn't understand what had happened that day, why he had broken the rules to have sex with her. But she remembered what he'd said about Babylona, how what you learned there wasn't really about sex; it was about intimacy and accepting people as they were. And suddenly she felt sure that he was the one she should talk to. He would understand what she was going through, and somehow he would know what she should do.

She got out of the car and went up the path to the stately Student

Services building. As she went, she was conscious of how she'd left the dorm with no makeup on, of the jeans she was wearing that tended to make her look thick in the waist. She tried to stand up taller to make her waist elongate. Then she admonished herself: *Come on, Lila, that's not what this is about.*

Still, as she got to his door and saw it ajar, the skin all over her body flushed with mingled excitement and embarrassment. She paused short of the door, her breath coming shallow and fast. For the first time, it occurred to her that he might be busy. Or he might not be there at all. The world didn't revolve around her, after all.

Thinking of interrupting him in a conference, she realized that although there wasn't anything to be ashamed of, she didn't want anyone to know she'd come here. She was halfway to turning tail and fleeing when he suddenly appeared in the doorway, saw her, and froze.

She froze. Then they were staring at each other with their mouths open, looking as startled as if they'd never seen a member of the opposite sex before.

At last Lila said, "I was coming . . . I needed to talk to someone about . . . I don't know what it's about."

"Oh," he said. "I was hoping to see you. I mean, I wanted to apologize, or . . . why don't you come in?"

Then they both smiled awkwardly and didn't move. There was a long minute in which Lila looked at his green eyes and felt all kinds of things she couldn't name, things that exploded gently like the bubbles in the champagne hot tub. Then he took a deep breath and led the way into his office.

He paused as he was about to sit at his desk and said, "Maybe we should just sit on the couch."

Lila colored, thinking about what he'd done to her over that desk the last time she'd been here. The leather couch was reassuringly six feet long—she would be able to sit out of arm's reach of him without it seeming strange.

But somehow, when they were sitting down, she found that she was near the middle of the couch, with her knee just an inch away from his, sitting back in the soft cushions.

She took a deep breath and said, "Okay, I wanted to talk to someone because I think I might not belong at Babylona. I think I came here for the wrong reasons."

Ben looked more shocked than she'd expected. He took a minute to pull himself together enough to say, "What makes you think that?"

Lila made herself tell him the whole shameful story of Tad, of Brandi, of her skewed and mixed-up motives for deciding to pursue a career in sex. As she told it, she was surprised to feel that Tad's betrayal of her didn't hurt her so much anymore. In fact, although she was trying to be as honest and straightforward as possible, the main thing on her mind was actually what Ben was thinking of her. And every now and then, she would pause and find herself thinking about him bending her over the desk and fingering her . . . slipping his cock into her from behind . . . and then it seemed as if his smooth olive skin was itself a drug that she needed more of. She had to force herself to keep talking, just so that her mouth would be occupied; it helped her stop wanting to lick his neck.

When she got to the part about the men in the woods, she found herself saying, "The fact is, Tad only told me I was boring in bed to hurt my feelings, I think, because he was jealous. I mean, it was obvious I was turned on by those men. And he was planning to break up with me, but he probably would have been nice about it, if that hadn't happened. I don't know. I guess sometimes things get a little twisted in the heat of the moment." She smiled ruefully, and found herself feeling sympathy for Tad.

Ben said flatly, "No, that's like the worst thing I ever heard."

Lila started, and then burst out laughing. "You're not supposed to say that."

Ben shrugged. "I don't know. I guess I hate to think of someone deliberately hurting you. And then making you feel insecure sexually . . ."

"But . . . he wasn't like that usually."

"I guess you must have seen something in him." Ben shook his head. "No. I'm sorry. I don't mean to make you feel bad."

"We got together when I was fifteen. I guess we grew up together. Until I came here, I'd never . . ." She stopped herself and looked away from his face fast.

"You'd never . . . ?" he said. His voice was faint and anxious.

"Tad was the only man I'd ever had sex with. Until I came here." Then she made herself meet his eye. He was staring at her in a fixed way she couldn't interpret. She said, "I mean, until you."

"Oh, God."

"But that's a good thing. I mean, it's not a bad thing. That is, I really liked . . . you, and it wasn't bad or even medium; it was good. It was positively good."

"You're sure?" Ben said. "I mean, it wasn't bad?"

"No! It was good."

They both fell silent again, looking into each other's eyes. Then Ben leaned forward and kissed her gently on the lips. She gasped, and her heart began to race immediately. She put her hand to his cheek and shut her eyes, kissing him back. His soft lips sent a chill down the back of her neck. Without intending to, she was touching his chest, feeling the planes of muscle under his shirt. Then he pulled back, saying, "God, Lila. I have to explain . . . I never meant to do that."

She kissed him on the cheek; she couldn't stop kissing him. His hands went to her slender arms and began to stroke them, making her shiver with desire.

"I guess by now the other students have told you what I did was against the rules. And it was the wrong thing to do," he said softly.

"No, it wasn't. It was the right thing."

Then she felt every infinitesimal stage of his hand drifting up her arm, caressing the skin on her neck, and then moving on down to cup her breast. She pressed forward into his hand. Her hands were already pulling his shirt free from his belt, going under to feel the smooth skin there, the thin, soft line of hair that led down his belly toward his penis.

"I don't know what made me do that," he went on. "I didn't mean to do it."

"You don't usually do that?" she said, not knowing what she was saying. And before he could even answer, she had pressed her lips to his again. Her hand came down and found the hard-on in his pants, hot through the cloth. She formed her hand around it and squeezed, making Ben groan. He was unbuttoning her shirt and pulling her heavy breast free from her bra. He pulled away from her kiss to lick his way down her breast to the nipple, which he took gently between his teeth and nibbled. Then his tongue and lips took the place of his teeth, and he was sucking hungrily. Lila arched her back, giving herself to the sensation. He reached behind her and unsnapped her bra, pulling it up off her breasts, which shook as she fell on her back against the soft leather. He kissed each nipple and then moved his mouth down to her belly, snaking his tongue briefly into her navel. It seemed to be directly connected to her clitoris, which twinged in sympathy. Then Ben had opened her jeans and was pulling them down. He caught his breath when he saw that she had no panties on. In a second her jeans had come off, and suddenly Lila felt his lips and his tongue attacking her pussy.

He first kissed her clitoris lingeringly, and the pleasure moved over it and then fell deep into her vagina. Then his tongue came out, going in circles around the sensitive button, faster and faster, while Lila held her breath, the feeling ringing and throbbing in her cunt and making her squeeze her eyes shut. His tongue stabbed into her, and she cried out sharply and moaned sweetly as his tongue began to fuck her, swiping her singing clit with each thrust. Finally, he began to suck her clit, tenderly, expertly; his mouth seemed to ride her pleasure, controlling and directing it. He was sucking harder, bringing her up to the very edge of orgasm, until even her face was tense and tingling with the coming explosion. Then he would soften his mouth, licking ever so lightly around her labia and only tagging the nub of her clitoris in passing, teasing her with the flash of the orgasm to come. Lila finally put her hands down and let her fingers twine into his silky hair, feeling the movement of his head. Now he thrust his fingers into her, fucking her deeply as he licked her clit harder, rapid-fire, the change in action making her readjust before she could approach her orgasm again. But then it was there, and his hand fucking her hard and precisely, his tongue tickling her, all came together in a giant blow of heat and ecstasy.

The bliss held and held; and as it finally began to die away into aftershocks, Lila felt Ben rise up onto her, reaching down to free his cock from his pants. Then he was inside her, fucking her cunt, which now seemed to be a pure ring of coming; she orgasmed again and again as she felt his big cock forcing its way through her spasms. He cupped her breasts in his hands again and began to tease the nipples between his thumb and index finger, making the pleasure leap from her tits to her pussy and back again. She was coming so hard now she felt as if she were fainting. The pleasure had taken complete control of her; she had no memory of what it was like *not* to be coming, *not* to be fucking Ben, *not* to have his sweet long cock driving into her while she thrusted back and gripped it with her spasms.

At last he let go of her breasts and she felt his fingers digging into her buttocks, pulling her up so he could drive that extra inch into her, deep, deep, inside; then he cried out and she felt his cock jerking and shooting his sperm into her. She cried out, too, lost in a world where nothing existed but the feelings racking her body, and the sweet shape of his strong body on hers, racked with the same obliterating bliss.

His body loosened slowly; as her orgasm quieted, she began to register the shape of him, the mounded pectorals and the flat belly still arched forward, as if he were clutching the last moments of his pleasure. She didn't want to open her eyes; she was afraid of leaving this fantasy behind, of letting the real world flood back and change the meaning of what had just happened.

She began to kiss his neck, tasting the sweat and feeling the silky skin against her tongue. And then it was his collarbone, the thick muscle of his chest. His cock had begun to ease out of her as it softened. She pulled him to lie by her side. Then—she couldn't help it—her hand went down and rescued his cock from her. She felt its shape, half hard, let her fingers slip down to his balls. Again her breath caught in her throat. He was kissing her mouth, her cheeks, her forehead. Without opening her eyes, she shifted down, and down, finally slipping off the couch and kneeling on the floor beside him. Only then did she open her eyes.

The sunlight filtering through the blinds startled her. Then it was the beauty of his body that was startling her: the smooth, generous muscles of his chest; the round, taut ass. His penis, still flushed purplish, was rimed with pearly come, both hers and his. She ducked her head forward and pressed her lips to its head. Then she licked slowly, tasting the come and feeling the delicate dimple that led into his penis opening. He gasped and his hand came toward her, but when she stilled her tongue, he relaxed. She could almost feel what he felt, the way his cock was still sensitive from his ejaculation, how each movement of her tongue was painful in a funny-bone way that still had the flavor of pleasure. She let the tip of her tongue rest, moving it slightly from time to time to gauge his response. At first he flinched with every movement, but after a while he remained passive, and she grew bolder, moving her tongue over the velvety tip and exploring under the hood, then licking over the top again. His cock, which had never fully gone limp, began to grow and straighten again, twitching in response to her tongue's teasing. Soon she had the head in her mouth and was sucking gently, flicking her tongue rhythmically against the sensitive underside. Ben, lying on his side, reached down and began to play with her hair, running his fingers through the strands. His cock had become fully hard again, and darting her tongue forward, she felt the veins standing out again on the velvety surface.

Ben's hand closed on a handful of her hair, and he began to thrust gently into her mouth, holding her head in place. The delicious hardness of the shaft gave her a blurry, almost sleepy rekindling of her pleasure; she let one hand go down to her crotch and pressed her fingers into herself, stirring the deep ache of pleasure that remained there. At first she let her lips remain loose, content to attend to the shape of his dick as it passed through her soft mouth again and again. His cock was just slightly bowed, and its shape somehow filled her mouth perfectly. The way he was fucking her mouth was almost like reliving how he'd fucked her pussy; she moved her free hand up his hard thigh, feeling how the muscles pulsed as they tensed, shoving his stiff dick into her throat. Then she moved her hand up to find the delicious weight of his balls, squeezing them teasingly with the memory in her head of how he'd sucked her clit. Soon he was thrusting harder, stretching the back of her throat with his cock's straining tip. Ben was moaning now and gripping her hair. She could still smell their mingled juices, that and the faint musk of his body. She had begun to moan, too, feeling how the sounds vibrated in his cock when it was sunk full length in her mouth. And then he stiffened once more, his hands molding themselves over the back of her head as he ejaculated, shooting his delicious come deep into her throat and filling her mouth with it. Lila swallowed and swallowed, and the hot liquid going down her throat—and dripping out of her cunt and coating her fingers below—made her feel saturated with him.

She held his cock in her mouth gently afterward, feeling the stiffness and urgency ease from it. He was stroking the back of her head, breathing deeply. At last he pulled out of her mouth, and she looked up. She felt so in tune with him physically that she had no doubt he was feeling the same tenderness and fulfillment that she was. And the starry, soft look in his eyes assured her that she was right.

"I'm sorry," she said. "I guess you broke the rules again."

"Don't be sorry," he said. "I don't care what happens."

She slipped up onto the couch again and fitted her body to him. Flattening her pillowy breasts against him gave her the best feeling yet, as if the experience had been wrapped up for her to keep, once and for all. "I guess you've done it before," she said. Immediately she wished she hadn't mentioned it, because it seemed like she was asking to be reassured.

In fact, Ben stiffened. He said, "No, of course I haven't."

Lila looked at him quizzically. She tried for a moment to return to the perfect relaxation and trust of a moment before, but something about his tone . . . "Why of course?" she said, and an edge of sarcasm crept into her voice. "I don't see why you wouldn't."

"Because that was the contract I signed when I took the job."

"Well, but it's not a very serious crime, is it? It's like . . . stealing office supplies or something."

Ben was now actually scowling at her, and he'd drawn back from their embrace. "I don't see it that way. I think in a place like Babylona, there have to be boundaries. Even though it seems like anything goes, there have to be rules and safety zones. It's a matter of respecting the students as people."

Lila's heart had begun to feel hollow. She looked at his face, which was now set in a cold frown of irritation, and realized she didn't know him at all. At that moment, it seemed completely possible to her that he'd been sleeping with freshmen all along—every day—and giving each and every one of them this Boy Scout routine about rules and boundaries. "So what did I do to *not* be respected, then?" she snapped.

"That's not what I meant. That's not how this happened!"

"So how did it happen? The same way it happened with everyone else, or differently?"

"I just told you, there never was anyone else!" He pulled away from her roughly. For a second she was distracted by the sight of his gorgeous body: the clean long lines of muscle and the faint dusting of hair over his chest that was echoed in a thicker fur down below;

the curled, rosy penis that had just . . . but the sting of longing she felt only made her angrier. She wasn't going to be running after some guy just because of his looks.

"Maybe you forget, but I came here because it was getting too much for me. I came for help! I was thinking of leaving . . . because things had happened too fast. And that's at least partly down to you!" Then she felt a wash of shame. The last thing she wanted to do was make Ben feel guilty for fucking her. As if that was a bad thing to do! It was the best thing she'd ever felt in her life. In fact, if she'd ever thought of leaving Babylona, that idea had vanished once and for all when he sank his cock in her again. Not only did she realize that she was—for better or worse—exactly suited to this place, or any place where she could express her sexual desires without fear or shame. But she also didn't think she was ready to leave any place where she could see Ben on a regular basis.

Ben was looking stricken. Lila tore her eyes away from him, feeling desolate. She should take it back, but all she wanted to do was run back to her room and hide. Quickly she refastened her bra, found her panties on the floor. As she put her clothes to rights, Ben stared at her in dismay. At last he said, quietly, "Don't leave like this, Lila. This is crazy. You've slept with other people since I saw you last. Even if I had slept with other students—"

Then a flash of jealousy went through her and the apology that she'd been concocting vanished from her mind. She swallowed and said to him evenly, "Of course you're right. There's no reason at all for me to care. It's just all in a day's work—for both of us." With that, she turned and stumbled out the door. She raced down the hall and found herself out in the parking lot again, scrabbling with her keys to get into her car, where she collapsed over the steering wheel, grateful for the meager privacy in which she could give way to tears.

Chapter Ten

Brandi pulled her convertible into the strip mall parking lot with a mounting feeling of excitement. Ever since she was old enough to understand rules, she'd been happiest when she was breaking them. She wouldn't ever hurt anybody or steal from anybody (except for those underpants, but underpants didn't count). Most rules didn't even bother her; in fact, it was only rules about what kind of sex she should have, and where, and with whom. Even then there were limits, the usual limits. The not-with-Fluffy rules were safe with her. Also the not-with-your-brother, -father, -mother. With or without a rule, those people might as well have been pieces of furniture for all the erotic interest they contained for her. But there was something about a cousin, for instance, or a Baptist minister that made everybody else in the room disappear.

It was that feeling that had nearly turned her into a lesbian when she was eighteen and her neighbor, the girl marine, had lured her into a clinch. The idea that if anyone found out she would be a pariah was so sweet that Brandi began to sneak out to the only gay bar in her small town, looking for pussy. She spent two months in a daydream of forbidden lust. The fun finally waned when she discovered that everyone at school knew about her activities and nobody cared. The very next day she began to have a fearsome longing for a fat stiff dick, and girls had been only a side dish from that day on.

From time to time, she had tried to revive that old idea of being a sexual deviant, a *pervert*, that had been so potent when she was a kid, but queerness had become more and more depressingly prime time. Today, though, Brandi thought, as she got out of her car and approached the storefront of Asian Magic Massage, today she was breaking all kinds of rules. She wasn't even supposed to be having sex for another three long, endless, interminable, impossibly draggingly slow days. She wasn't supposed to be off campus. The massage girls might never have had a female customer, *L Word* or no *L Word*. And paying for sex, she felt instinctively from her years as stripper and porn actress, was just plain *wrong* on every level.

People paid *her* for sex; the other way around was taboo. Going from commodity to customer was like suddenly switching from rooting for the Yankees to supporting the Red Sox. If any of her old friends from the Pink Palace or the Gentleman's Delight knew what she was doing, they would be scandalized to the black roots of their peroxide hair. It was nothing short of depraved. The thought was so wonderful that Brandi couldn't believe she'd never thought of it before.

When she opened the door, an Asian girl in a filmy baby-doll nightie looked up from a computer screen and frowned. The decor was stridently Asian—gold dragons, banners with Chinese ideograms, and shelves filled with a hodgepodge of Thai, Chinese, and Japanese knick-knacks. The air was suffocatingly heavy with a musky, spicy scent of what Brandi supposed—with a shudder of anticipation—was scented oil. Immediately she imagined slender fingers snaking, slipping, over her buttocks. Then the same fingers sliding in between her labia, stroking the slick oil down her clitoris . . . over and over again . . . The girl herself was slender hipped with small breasts whose dark aureoles showed clearly through the gauze of her nightie. Her long hair and clear skin made Brandi whimper inside; this was the girl she wanted, and she wanted something more than a hand job, too. But she would cross that bridge when she came to it.

"Can I help you?" the girl said in a jarringly businesslike Midwestern accent. She narrowed her eyes at Brandi skeptically.

"Oh, I just want a massage," Brandi said. "A sensual massage." She smiled steadily while the girl looked her up and down. Brandi made herself relax her shoulders and look determinedly casual.

At last the girl said, "Are you a transvestite?"

Brandi scowled. "Come on, honey. You know very well I'm not a transvestite."

"Are you a she-male?" the girl said in the same bored tone.

Brandi crossed her arms. She would normally have joined right into the fight—Brandi was never scared of a brawl, and in fact there was nothing she liked better. But right now she had to keep her eye on the prize. So she said sweetly, "Are you trying to make me mad? 'Cause I'm not *going* to get mad, so you're just wasting your breath. I don't want any fight with someone who's *homophobic* or some damn thing from the Victorian century. I want a *sensual massage.*"

There was a pause. The girl continued to stare Brandi down with her mouth set. Finally she shrugged and went back to her computer.

Brandi said, "Hello! Paying customer!"

The girl responded in a bored voice, "Is it possible you think you're the first Babylona student who ever came here? Is that what you're trying to tell me?" The girl hit a key and something began to print out. She turned and watched the page emerge from the printer, saying, "Wait a second. This is for you."

"I'm not a Babylona . . . Well, so what if I am? Is there some reason we can't . . ."

The girl whipped the page from the printer and set it in front of Brandi. It showed a picture of Brandi, with her name underneath, and the phrase: "Quarantine Terms 3b, expires 10/1."

Brandi scowled at it and said, "Who's this girl? Never seen her before in my life."

"Nice try. I got a phone call from Ben at your school three days ago."

Brandi gazed disconsolately at the printout. She muttered, "They *own* this town."

The girl shrugged. "They own this establishment. And even if they didn't, Babylona's my alma mater. Class of 2005."

Brandi bit her lip and considered. Admitting defeat seemed not only cowardly, but just plain morally wrong. But the slightly amused face in front of her showed no trace of weakness. Brandi said bitterly, "Well, if I take desperate measures and end up sleeping with somebody who cuts me up and eats me, it's going to be—"

"Ben's fault," said the girl. "And tell him hi from Madison, when you see him. We were in the same class."

Brandi gritted her teeth, realizing that not only was she getting nowhere with this Madison—but Madison had doubtless slept with the delicious Ben. Life was worse than unfair. It was deliberately aggravating. She said with all the dignity she could muster, "Well, I guess I can't blame you. You're just their pawn."

Back in the parking lot, Brandi stalked along the storefronts, fuming. Normally she liked to think she got along with everybody. Easygoing, sweet, tender-hearted . . . that was the Brandi brand. But just a few days without sex, and she was ready to tear people apart with her teeth. It was spoiling her kindly temperament. Plus, it was giving her a rash on her forehead—stress! Didn't they know stressed people died of heart attacks? This was going to kill her before it was done.

And who came up with all these stupid rules? Her own goddamned role model and former—*former*—favorite person in the world, Babylona. As if Babylona could live without sex for seven days! If that selfish, hypocritical, uncaring woman were here, Brandi would give her a big fat piece of her mind!

She was barreling along, with her high heels flying, and before she knew what was happening, she'd slammed head-on into someone coming in the opposite direction. She rebounded and stumbled a few steps, arms flailing, trying to get her balance. Finally she landed on her knees. It stung like crazy, and she was just about to let loose a string of curses when she looked up at the person she'd run into.

It was a buxom redheaded woman who could have been any age from twenty-eight to forty-eight. She had strikingly large blue eyes and a delicately molded nose and cheekbones. But her powder-pink lips were almost obscenely full, and gathered in a permanent, teasing pout. She was dressed in a full-length black leather coat that hugged her generous curves. From its tight fit, and the way the woman's fine-skinned bare legs and generous cleavage showed under it, Brandi guessed she wasn't wearing anything else.

And Brandi had no difficulty recognizing her as Babylona.

"Oh my God!" she said, pressing her hands to her mouth. In the first instant, she even wondered if she was hallucinating. By the second instant, her face had flushed bright red with mingled embarrassment and anger. Half of her was ready to deliver an angry tirade. The other half was mortified at the thought of it alone. This was Babylona! *The* Babylona! For years, Brandi had been longing to meet her face-to-face. And now that she did, all she could think of to say was *I'd like to see you go without fucking for a week!*

"Are you okay, sugar?" Babylona's rich, husky voice was exactly as Brandi had always imagined it. It had a luxurious sleepiness about it—like the drowsy, grateful sex cries of a girl who had been making love all night with the man she loved . . . and several others.

Brandi tried to speak, but she was paralyzed, her hands folded in front of her open mouth. Even as she was trying to grasp what was happening, another part of her mind was formulating a plan. A low, conniving, sex-driven plot—just the thing, her instinct told her, to earn Babylona's admiration.

Babylona began to laugh. "Are you praying to me?"

Brandi caught her breath. The last piece fell into place. She said, "Well, Miss Babylona, ma'am . . . if I was, would you answer my prayer?"

"That all depends, of course." Babylona put a hand on her hip and half closed her eyes. "What is it that you want?"

"I'm in love," Brandi confessed with a throb in her voice. "With a girl called Madison. She works for you, ma'am, in your massage parlor, right here. But she won't have sex with me because . . ." Brandi paused and, with her hands still clasped to her mouth, turned slightly away. Then she swiftly, surreptitiously, yanked out a few of her own nostril hairs. With a tear already forming in her eye, she continued. "But if I tell you that, you won't help me." Her heart was pounding with the daring of what she was doing.

Babylona's face had already softened. "Hey, get up off your knees, girl. You came to the right place. Are you one of my kids?"

Brandi nodded humbly as she scrambled to her feet. "A freshman," she said pathetically.

"Well, do me a favor and don't tell anyone I'm in town. Sometimes I like to visit *some* people, without seeing *other* people. If you know what I mean."

"You mean you can't fuck everyone every time," Brandi interpreted readily.

"You see the problem! There are people," Babylona said sadly, "I can really only fuck on birthdays and holidays. But they do get their feelings hurt when I fuck certain other ones every week." She opened a white satin purse and extracted a pack of cigarettes. Lighting one, she inhaled luxuriously. "So, why won't she give you any? You broke?"

"Oh, no, ma'am! I offered to pay! It's just that . . ." Brandi blinked and was delighted to feel a fat tear dripping down her cheek. But in the meantime her plucked nostril had begun to sting unbearably, and before she could stop herself, she sneezed so hard she bent nearly double. Then she sneezed again, her eyes watering uncontrollably. When she had recovered, dabbing her tears carefully to keep from detaching an eyelash, Babylona was squinting at her skeptically.

"Gesundheit," Babylona said. "And congratulations. You took me in for real. Was that the nostril hair trick?"

Brandi grimaced. "Well, if it was—"

"And, let me take a wild guess, you're on a quarantine?"

"I was just getting ready to tell you!"

"Well." Babylona shook her head. "I suppose I should have you expelled right now."

Brandi's eyes went wide. "Expelled?"

"That's what most people would do, in my place. You're off the premises, aren't you, sugar? Trying to solicit sex?"

Brandi shut her eyes for a second. Her heart was pounding again: She loved the institute. She loved it so much, she was already scared of graduating in three and three-quarter years. It was the first place she'd truly felt at home. Still honor was honor. So at last she opened her eyes and said boldly, "And then I could go get laid tonight, instead of waiting another three days. Some threat!"

Babylona burst out laughing again. She said, "Do you mean to tell me your quarantine is only for another three days?"

"But I've gone *four* days already," said Brandi bitterly. "I got a whole week, not just three days!"

Babylona shook her head. "You put me to shame. You're that desperate after less than a week? Well, I think a sex drive like that calls for a medical excuse, don't you?"

Brandi caught her breath. "A medical excuse? Do I have to see a doctor?"

"No," said Babylona. "I just have to make a phone call."

Brandi instantly said, "You mean two phone calls. To Madison and to Ben."

"Oh my God, girl. You're quick." Babylona laughed again.

Brandi grinned broadly. "You get there faster with a one-track mind. No local stops, you know."

"Well, if you really can't make it home without . . ." Babylona took a tiny silver phone out of her purse and waved at Brandi with a "scoot!" motion. "Go ahead and see your girlfriend. She'll be on the phone when you get there. Wait—that thing about being in love?"

"Oh, well, it was what I was feeling at the time, or it was a near approximation . . ."

"I thought so. Go on."

Brandi impulsively grabbed Babylona's free hand and kissed it, getting a whiff of her sweet and dizzying perfume, then dashed off back toward the massage parlor. The gravity of what had just happened began to sink in as she arrived at the door. Brandi had always imagined that if she ever met Babylona, her brash manners would fall away, and she would turn into a humble and worshipful acolyte. But apparently, she had only one mode: big-mouthed slut. *Oh hell*, she thought, *it takes all kinds. And Babylona liked me, after all, or else why'd she let me off my leash?*

As promised, Madison was on the phone as Brandi opened the door. Brandi flashed her a gigantic grin. Madison looked a little stunned; she frowned at Brandi and said into the phone, "She's here, all right. I'll . . . I'll help her out." She hung up the phone and shook her head at Brandi. "I don't know if you're lucky or—"

"Magical powers," said Brandi. "And, um . . . can I owe you the money? I'm just—"

"No, you cannot *owe* me the money! You—"

"Kidding!"

After a double take, Madison began laughing. Then Brandi leaned forward over the desk and took a handful of Madison's smooth thick hair, letting it run through her fingers. Then again. With her other hand she reached into her purse and slipped out a few twenties.

Madison said, "One hundred fifty dollars," but her voice was already a little husky, and when she spoke she seemed to be addressing Brandi's cleavage.

Brandi's hand wandered down Madison's smooth collarbone and then to the upper swell of her breast. While one hand counted bills down onto the desk, the other began to toy with the swollen tip of Madison's breast, rolling it between two fingers, then stroking with a fingertip, then pinching gently again. Madison's lips had parted and she was watching Brandi put money down impatiently. When the money was all there, she swept it up in one hand and shoved it into the tip jar, saying, "Let's go."

Brandi followed her down a corridor, admiring the perfectly round cheeks of Madison's ass that switched seductively as she walked. Now that the counter wasn't in the way, Brandi could see that Madison wasn't wearing any panties under the see-through negligee, and so when Madison entered a room and turned around to face her, Brandi could see the dim outlines of her shaved pussy between the gentle swelling of her thighs.

"Lie down," said Madison. She gestured to a padded massage table with a table beside it covered in a variety of bottled oils. It also featured a neatly aligned row of dildos and vibrators.

"Wait." Brandi reached toward Madison's breasts again, but Madison batted her hands away.

"Lie down," she repeated more sharply. "Now."

"Aw, I'm not so into all that," Brandi said. "Sub/dom stuff, I mean, it's okay in—"

"I don't care what you're into," Madison said coldly. "I'm following orders."

Brandi gulped. Clearly this was a double-cross; it only remained to be seen how bad of a double-cross it was. Forcing herself not to ask some pointless question like *But I still get sex, right?*—Brandi crept up on the table and began to undo her blouse. She was half afraid that Madison would stop her, but the other girl just muttered, "Make it fast," and went to the table of oils, where she frowned at the array of dildos, ticking down them with a finger in a sort of "eeny meeny miny mo" gesture.

As Brandi slipped off her bra and panties, her bared skin felt doubly nude, almost raw with uncertainty. She was aware of every inch of her that might be about to be subjected to some cat-o'-nine-tails routine like she'd played with Rooney in *Teen Queen Suck Sluts.* Any Babylona graduate would know how to whip somebody without doing any damage, of course (not like goddamned Rooney—she'd spent the whole next day with an ice bag on her butt). But that might not have been her orders. Who knew what Babylona might come up with to punish someone who had challenged her authority? Not that Brandi was fearing for her life and limb—just for her dignity and for her comfort over the next hour or so.

On the other hand, that uncertainty seemed to stoke Brandi's already raging desire still further. As she lay on her back, she couldn't help but spread her thighs wide apart, and she could already feel the stiff invasion of the dildo. Madison's breasts hanging over her like trembling ripe fruits, or pressing into her own breasts deliciously.

But Madison snapped, barely looking up, "No, get on your stomach."

"Oh . . ." Brandi almost objected, but decided that resistance was useless. She flipped over onto her stomach—and immediately felt Madison grasping her wrists, pulling her arms out from under her so she flopped heavily onto her breasts. "Ow!" Brandi said. She wasn't especially hurt, but more startled. And then she felt the handcuffs going on—old-fashioned heavy metal cuffs that were cold against her skin. When Madison let her go, her wrists fell naturally to her back and the cold metal made her flinch with a complicated pleasure/discomfort.

Then she felt her ankles being spread and each got its own cuff, binding her ankles to either side of the table, holding her now helpless on her stomach, with her pussy open and defenseless. Now the desire overwhelmed everything else, and Brandi was just panting, longing, afraid only that she would not get the fucking she so desperately needed.

There was the faintest, teasing stroke along one buttock that made her squirm with the flames of lust that shot through her. She tried to crane her neck around to see where Madison was, but instantly a stinging smack to her behind stopped her.

"None of that," said Madison in the same cool voice, and spanked Brandi again.

The stinging joined with the aching need in her cunt, making Brandi writhe again, pressing her pubis into the padded table. Meanwhile she heard the slightly scary, but much more enticing sound of Madison pouring grease on her hands and rubbing them together rapidly.

And now those hands came down squarely on Brandi's buttocks, warm and slick. They rested there quietly for a second and then slipped over and down to the beginning of her thighs, squeezing and pulling the flesh apart there so that even more of Brandi's now-wet and eager pussy was exposed to the air. Brandi made a gentle sound and again Madison spanked her, whack! It was just hard enough to make Brandi jump, but soft enough that the singing excitement that went through her ass and pussy overwhelmed all else.

"Quiet," Madison barked. And then there was an excruciating pause while nothing happened. Nonetheless, the sensations continued to run through Brandi's pussy on their own, surges of electricity and expectation that had her reeling. Maybe she had dismissed the whole sub/dom thing too lightly. She didn't remember the last time she'd been so aroused. On the other hand, not getting laid in four days . . .

Then Madison walked in front of her, and Brandi saw what she'd been doing. She was now wearing an enormous strap-on dildo, with a leather harness that fit like a G-string, separating the lush cheeks of her ass and the now-bared lips of her shaved pussy. The dildo was black, and, apart from the delicate ribs that ran all along its length—and its size—was shaped lovingly like a real cock. A real cock two times life size. Madison smiled down at Brandi, running an oiled hand up and down the dildo like a man readying his stiff dick for entry. Then she had walked around the other side and out of sight.

And now Madison was touching Brandi's ass again, gently pulling at the cheeks to open Brandi's pussy and anus to the air. And a finger tickled up along the tender lips of Brandi's cunt, and ringed her anus lightly, making her catch her breath with desire. Then she felt Madison slipping a knee up onto the table and rising up ready to mount her. Brandi involuntarily arched her back, and spread her thighs as far as her restraints would allow, her pussy throbbing with expectation.

The first thing was Madison pressing down on top of her, now completely naked. Brandi felt that Madison had oiled not only her hands, but her whole body, and the effect of the soft, springy pressure of her breasts was intensified by the slippery, elusive quality of the contact. Meanwhile, Madison had reached under Brandi's belly and found her clitoris, so that while the slender girl's body arched on top of Brandi, she simultaneously felt two fingers scissoring onto her clit and rapidly, lightly, flicking it between them in a way that made Brandi cry out and then catch herself, waiting for the spanking.

But this time what happened was that Madison growled, "Bad girl," and plunged the enormous dildo into Brandi's needy pussy. She had an immediate sensation of panic; it was too much, too much all at once! She wasn't going to be able . . . but then the wave of relief hit her, and Brandi bit her lip to keep from screaming with the pleasure.

Madison pulled back and fucked into her again, filling her up so completely that Brandi felt utterly helpless before the attack. Then it was a steady barrage, stretching her cunt as far as it would go, while from the outside, Madison continued her two-fingered manipulation, making Brandi almost weep with delight.

Soon she was having orgasm after orgasm, one for every stroke of the dildo into her. Her eyes were squeezed shut, and she only dimly felt Madison's hands moving rapidly now between her nipples and her clit. Her breasts began to tingle to the same rhythm of the dildo spearing into her, until she could swear her tits were coming.

And then, shockingly, the huge dick slid entirely out of her, the vacancy a blow as extreme as its initial entry. Brandi waited, her pussy still caught on the edge of coming again, her whole body tense, as Madison slipped off of her and again the pause came. Then she felt, to her dismay, the deft fingers at her anus, oiling the opening, preparing it to be fucked. Brandi bit her tongue, wanting to protest. She could take that enormous dildo anally—she knew it was possible. People did it; hell, she'd seen it on film! But she'd never *done* it without anything bigger than—well, a penis. Not on film, not anywhere, and she wasn't really dying to try it out. She supposed this was Babylona's idea of a joke. You want to get laid? Well, take that!

Then Madison had leaped back on top of her with one swift motion, and Brandi could swear the girl was quietly laughing. Her hands spread Brandi's ass cheeks . . . then let them go. Spread them . . . let them go. Despite herself, Brandi was beginning to ache in anticipation, her pussy preparing for another series of orgasms, her ass waking to a nostalgic memory of buggeries past.

And then it came: the delicate pressure at her little nub, the slickness there making it impossible to resist. And the dildo slid in just a bit, spreading and invading her. Brandi caught her breath, and then it was sliding all the way in, making her cry out helplessly now. There was nothing more Madison could do to her, anyway. She yelped as the dildo thrust deep within her, splitting her almost unbearably, pleasuring her almost unbearably. And again she was coming, but coming with that deeper, stranger pleasure that anal always gave her. She found herself straining at her handcuffs, her body instinctively trying to escape even as the pleasure deepened and spread. Soon she was only half conscious, struggling and taking it at the same time, her mind and body focused only on the violation that was occurring, the thrill of being taken more completely than ever before.

When Madison finally slipped out of her and off of her, Brandi had no idea how long it had gone on. She was as weak as a kitten, and she felt as if she must be glowing all over with the force of the orgasms she'd just had. She barely registered the faint click of the handcuffs being unlocked. But when one ankle and then the other was freed, her body again instinctively wanted to escape, and she found herself sitting up on the edge of the massage table, facing a grinning Madison.

Brandi said, "No fair!"

Madison, who had already divested herself of the dildo, and was shaking out the little baby-doll nightie, said, "Hey, orders are orders."

"Oh, hell. What if she ordered you to jump off the Empire State Building, would you—"

"No," Madison said coolly. "But she only ordered me to do something I wanted to do." Then she winked at Brandi and tossed her her panties from the table. "To someone who wanted it. And what absolutely clinches the deal—I got paid."

Brandi sighed, pondering her panties with a hangdog feeling. Though her body felt absolutely wrung out from the pleasure she'd experienced, and the nagging need for sex had gone . . . she couldn't help feeling in some part of her heart that she'd been had.

Chapter Eleven

As autumn's chill began to intensify, Lila found herself set-
tling in to the life at Babylona. Although at first the thought
of Ben's stricken face haunted her, with time she accepted
that she wasn't ready to deal with the complications attached to her
affair with him. If it carried on, it would become a degree of rule
breaking that would cost him his job—and maybe get her thrown
out of the school. But the risk that really mattered to her was the
risk of getting hurt again. She wasn't sure she wanted to get seriously involved again while she was at Babylona, anyway. And she
was absolutely sure that she wasn't ready for it. She was just beginning to feel safe again; she'd stopped waking up in the middle of
the night realizing, as if for the first time, that her wedding wasn't
going to happen. But the wounded part of her still insisted that
she shouldn't trust Ben. Somehow, he was lying to her. It was hard
to believe that he was a liar who used his position only to screw all
the girls (which, in the context of Babylona, was hardly a shooting
offense—all the girls would have been very gratified if Ben *did* use
his position for that). But he must be lying somehow. He couldn't
be as perfect as he seemed. And the best way to stop from finding
that out, and feeling the sick sense of betrayal that would follow,
was to simply avoid him.

In the meantime, she herself had been sleeping with three different men. She and Andy had replayed their spin-the-bottle scene,
this time in private with time to spare. They'd found a hammock
at the edge of campus, and she'd perched on top of him, controlling
the penetration of his dick as he swung the hammock gently with

one foot, creating a deliciously unpredictable tilt to his thrust. She'd had a wonderful sixty-nine session with a boy called Ralph; it was a night when she'd already come three times (courtesy of Anna, who'd decided that Lila needed further "adjustment"—this time to make her less "screamingly, deafeningly, hetero") and the sex became more playful than urgent. Lila used it as an opportunity to pay attention to the idiosyncrasies, the twists and turns, of her sexual response. Ralph probably got less of a careful blow job—but he wasn't complaining. Finally, there was the night Miguel had convinced her to let him fuck her between her breasts, promising to show her how she could have an orgasm by having her breasts alone stimulated. As she'd suspected, that last part was an exaggeration—but not by much. He did in fact have an amazing way of coaxing sensations out of her breasts, and of making her see them through his eyes—his intense appreciation of their size and shape and texture, which came across in the devoted attention he gave to sucking and stroking them, made her feel something of the same when, at the end, she shaped them around his big bowed dick, lubricated with some apricot-scented oil whose scent clung to her for days afterward, reminding her of his athletic thrusting, and the explosion of sperm whose scent, mingled with the apricot, smelled like apple pie. She made a comment to that effect, making Miguel retort that her pussy was all the apple pie he wanted—so she had her orgasm the old-fashioned way, with Miguel expertly tonguing her into relief. After all that, she could hardly feel uncomfortable about Ben sleeping with other girls . . . except that she did, and she didn't want to think about it. Consequently, she didn't want to think about him.

One day, she went into town with Anna to shop. That day she created the basis for her new Babylona look: tight sweaters with V-necks cut dangerously low, worn without a bra. Sometimes she let a nipple creep up over the neckline; it always gave her a baseline excitement to sit at her desk, or walk through campus, with that nipple bare, acting as if she had no idea. She would notice men sneaking looks at it, and smile inside.

At first she wore miniskirts she'd brought from home, but as the weather got colder, she began to favor a pair of jeans she'd found that were full of holes, including one in a strategic part of the crotch; there was always a snippet of lace on view, and sometimes a glimpse of pink beneath it.

Other people were more daring. In the second week of school, there had been a vogue for nudity, pure and simple. Within two days, it had already been transformed into nudity overdecorated; girls wandered around with complicated patterns drawn on their flesh, nipples painted every color under the sun and adorned with glitter. Crotchless underwear of every color and design appeared, and there was a brief arms race among the cock rings worn by the male students. A few of the penile adornments took on the dimensions and elaborateness of Mardi Gras masks.

As the weather cooled, there was a backlash: some of the men began to wear suits, which, in the context of Babylona, seemed particularly pervy, almost like fetish gear. Girls appeared in suits, too, though these usually had short skirts that allowed said suit to be transformed into a porn costume by the easy expedient of sitting knees apart, to reveal a bare cunt or one merely traversed by a whisker of silk. But there were also schoolmarm dresses and elaborate gowns—it seemed that as soon as the rule had been established that clothing was to be regarded as a sexual prop, anything whatsoever could become absorbingly filthy.

There were always some people, like Brandi, who only felt comfortable in pasties, crotchless hot pants, leather bustiers. Or people like Anna and Lila, who were too lazy to make a hobby of devising new costumes. Ginny, the blond girl who had made such a big deal of finding spin the bottle too elementary for her taste, announced early on that the cold was going to be the death of her (she was from

Alabama), and thereafter only appeared in an ankle-length white fur coat, with nothing underneath.

Since Babylona had only one hundred twenty students altogether, the seniors, juniors, and sophomores all knew each other intimately already—in the clear-cut sense that they had all slept with one another, often numerous times. They had woken up in each other's beds and gone into drunken crying fits on one another's shoulders. Some of them had changed sexual orientation; a few had changed sexual orientation multiple times. They had gone on vacations together on which they had love-bombed unsuspecting locals and taken them into an alternate hotel-room reality they would never forget.

In some ways, that meant that the freshmen were facing a tight group of friends who were looking at them suspiciously, not sure whether the new kids would fit in. But it also meant that they were facing a group that was looking at them hungrily, as new conquests, playmates, or even—for those who were that way inclined—serious love interests. Lila had been approached a number of times in the student bar by older boys and girls who asked her a seemingly endless series of questions before more or less subtly inviting her to the back room.

The bar had quickly become her favorite place. It was a labyrinth on several levels, with bunk beds, water beds, and just plain beds scattered among the more customary bar furniture. Cushions were strewn haphazardly over the carpet, as well, so that in the evening, when it was full, there were students lounging at every level, from those who were splayed on the floor with a drowsy companion, to those who were perched overhead. Unless there was a special party, public sex was not allowed there—for that you had to go into the back room, which was an actual back room with broken furniture and janitorial supplies—opinions were divided on whether this was intended to be a new wrinkle of sensuality, or whether it was because the powers that be had overlooked this one room in their general luxury drive. Either way, it *did* provide the tirelessly inventive Babylonans with new wrinkles of sensuality; some people swore by the chilly unfinished concrete floor, and others the broken chair that tilted at a forty-five degree angle . . . quite apart from the uses the more persevering found for cleaning equipment of the most surprising kinds.

But Lila had seen it only in passing, through a hastily closing door—she still hadn't entered fully into the promiscuity that surrounded her. Anna and Brandi considered it normal to sleep with two or three different guys in the course of a day—encounters often sparked by something as slight as a conversation in a hallway in which a toothsome male student innocently mentioned the presence of a certain sling of a certain kind in a certain room that happened to be conveniently empty . . . cue Anna and said toothsome student spending two hours developing a contortionist, death-defying sex routine and appearing for their last class sticky, fragrant, and pink in the face. But then at least half of the students would be in the same condition. Even after the frost had begun to dull the emerald shade of the lawns, couples would sometimes be seen writhing together in the grass in plain view. A teacher arriving in the classroom might interrupt four or five hasty couplings—girls and boys on their knees under school desks who were forced to leave their partner halfway through . . . until the class ended, when the couplings would re-form instantly.

It wasn't that Lila didn't want to be part of it all. She fully intended to—soon. But even Brandi supported her in taking it slowly. "Don't want you freaking out again. Don't worry, you'll be the biggest slut of them all by the time you graduate. Plus, you're the one everyone *wants* to fuck worst. What fun would it be if the horn dogs didn't have to wait? Crank up the suspense, sweetie." Most nights Lila would be tucked up alone in the dorm room, watching TV while Anna was out learning how to screw in a handstand position while appearing to be unconscious, or the no-hands vibrator technique, or any of a hundred pieces of Babylona lore that she then went home and described to Lila in hilarious detail.

In the comfort and safety of her fluffy white bed, Lila spent the mornings she had no classes reading all the way through *A Life on All Fours*, following the escapades of Babylona from her early days in porn films to the exclusive sex show she opened with her friend Friselle Belesci, the Corsican celebrity prostitute whose game show had become a phenomenon throughout Europe. People who wanted to see the sex show had to join a drinking club, the Callisto, whose dues were thousands of dollars a year. They also needed to be nominated by a member and be approved by a board (which, Babylona confessed in the book, consisted of herself, Friselle, and James Parris drinking cognac in a sunken bathtub). The lucky members of the Callisto were then introduced into an atmosphere that was much like Babylona Institute's, except that there was a nominal boundary between the spectators and performers. The performers *began* the night on stages throughout the club—though they might end the night in a couch with one or more spectators. And the spectators began the night in the audience, though they might end up on stage before closing time. The group of performers who worked at the Callisto became a kind of extended family for Babylona; later they would travel through the world together, performing for royalty, rock stars, and—in strict secrecy—politicians.

It was during one of those tours that Babylona had met John Banks. She and Friselle had been relaxing after a long night at the one bar that was open at six a.m. in Oklahoma City—or possibly in the entire state of Oklahoma. Babylona got it into her head to play pool. She had been a pretty good pool player when she was a kid; her brothers had taught her. She wanted to see if she would still be able to play. Since Friselle swore she was too tired to stand (her part in the act required her to be on her feet the whole time, mostly tied to a pole while various men screwed her from various angles), Babylona asked the only other customer to play with her.

That was John Banks. He played pool for half an hour with the then-twenty-seven-year-old Babylona, who was a voluptuous creature with luminous white skin, long bright red hair, and a dress that was almost, but not quite, the length of her torso. But Banks seemed not to notice; he won every game, conversing quietly and politely about his time in the army, his financial problems, and his current job with a traveling carnival.

"Well, I'm a carny," Babylona said. "Or my parents were, you know. I'm lapsed."

They traded a few stories about life in the carnival, mostly stories about drunken fights and grisly accidents due to drunken stunts by carnies after hours—climbing the Ferris wheel, jumping from seat to seat on the speeding roller coaster. Banks told Babylona that his current job was running the pirate ship—a huge mock ship that swung forward and backward massively on a swing. She sighed and said, "Well, I certainly would love to go see it . . ."

As she put it in *A Life on All Fours:*

> I couldn't get sure he was interested in me. Every now and then I meet a man who simply seems to lack any sex drive whatsoever, and at first I mistook John for one of those. But when I invited myself home with him, he looked me deep in the eye for the first time, and I began to grasp the scale of my error. Just looking at me steadily was enough to turn me into mush. I was hypnotized, and by the time he looked away I was breathing heavy. He said, "Do you want to take my car?" and when I said, "Sure," my voice was hoarse as hell. I was just like a teenage girl!

They fucked for the first time in his car, and for Babylona, it was a revelation. ("For John, too, I flatter myself, though he never would admit it. Still, it speaks for itself that he started to pack his suitcase to leave with me as soon as we got to his tent.") It wasn't that the man was especially beautiful. He was attractive, and in formidably good shape, the kind of person who could look startlingly agile just crossing the room or pulling up a chair. But he wasn't anything like the model-gorgeous men Babylona employed in her act. He wasn't anything like her James Parris, who had blond quarterback looks that had always seemed a little out of place in the owner of a topless-bottomless bar. Banks was a man with a plain-looking face and a skinny frame.

Babylona wrote five pages just about his sexual technique. The main thing, she emphasized over and over again, was that for Banks, it wasn't a technique—it was nothing he'd studied or reasoned out. It was just that he instinctively knew what to do, from second to second, without ever thinking about it, without ever making a mistake. It was as if he could feel what she was feeling. Every touch built on the last exactly, every sensation dovetailed with the last seamlessly; there wasn't a single thing out of place. And when his dick went into you, it felt—well, it felt like something better than a dick. As if all other dicks were just plastic imitations of the One True Dick, which only Banks possessed. Her pussy *recognized* it. And every split second of its course in and out of her was its own distinct pleasure. Although Babylona hadn't had any complaints about sex before, this gave her the feeling that all her life she'd been craving something, and here it was: Banks' dick fucking her the exact way Banks did.

And the final thing about him was, he had stamina and endurance that beggared imagination.

They fucked again in the tent—that was when Banks decided to pack his bags and accept Babylona's invitation to travel the world with *her* kind of carnival. "The sleeping arrangements are better, if you don't mind Hiltons," she had said. "And if you don't mind girls."

Then, as the sun was beginning to rise, but before the other people began to wake up, he took her up onto his ride. Babylona described it in detail; he was sitting in the seat, and she sitting on his lap, facing forward. With each downward swing of the gaudily painted ship, she was first lifted free of gravity, up nearly to the tip of his dick—and then as the ship fell, she was agonizingly slowly let down, down. At last the speed picked up and she was plunged, skewered, and pressed down on him, his dick coming up deep inside her as she was flattened to his chest, unable to move away as his hands roamed under her shirt, playing with her breasts. And then again. And at a certain point, when she was getting close to coming for the umpteenth time that night, she was being lifted up from her seat on his cock at the upper extent of the ship's swing, and he lifted her with his hands a little extra way, so for a moment she was soaring free of anything but his hands; and when she came down, she was just displaced enough that his cock found its way not into her cunt but her asshole. Again, she slowly was skewered by the force of gravity, a little more and a little more, until they reached the lowest point and his cock sliced deep into her, making her come again, the nearly unbearable filling of her anus mingling with all the punishment her pussy had had all night and morning to make her scream out loud as the wind whipped her hair back from her face, and Banks came in her one more time.

Well, after that, of course they were the best of friends.

Lila would sometimes masturbate while she read the book; and even that seemed different, less furtive, in a place where sex was the given, and *not* having sex was the special case. Sometimes she went to the window and spied on other people having sex—on the grass, in the bushes, in the windows opposite—and masturbated there, standing up, letting herself be excited by the fear of getting caught. Though, if anyone had caught her, the most she would have got was a friendly—but not very welcome, in the circumstances—wave.

Mr. Banks was the only person mentioned in the book whom she'd met. And it was impossible not to speculate about him, as he taught the class in an absolutely dry manner, apparently without a dirty thought in his head, though he was typically talking about double penetration, daisy chains, and gang bangs. All of the kids, male and female, had a crush on Mr. Banks (though Ginny swore she "completely saw through his superior routine").

He also, frustratingly, wasn't sleeping with any of them. He lived somewhere off campus, and no one had any idea of his private life. He never drank in the bar, and though he was invited to almost every party, he never appeared. But there were still a few of the older students who claimed to have slept with him—though they had to admit he was in disguise at the time.

This was because the highlight of Groups and Growth every year was the compulsory Halloween party, which was really a compulsory orgy. The rules were very simple; you had to come in a costume that made it impossible to discern your identity. Those insufficiently disguised were turned away at the door. Once inside, you were not allowed to speak. Your costume was also meant to be a carefully kept secret—no one should know who you were until they actually tore enough of your clothes away to recognize you—or recognized your cock or pussy by feel.

Everyone liked to say that there were always a few extra people, outsiders who had snuck in somehow, or who were old alumni, or (this was the most scurrilous rumor) who had paid off members of staff to obtain entry. The final rumor was that Mr. Banks himself appeared at every Halloween party in disguise, had sex with all the students who appealed to him, whom he could recognize even through their disguises, and left again without removing his mask. It was under these circumstances that some people claimed to have slept with him—they claimed they had had the same experience Babylona described, and that it was unmistakable.

The greatest challenge was to find or contrive a costume that sufficiently disguised you—but didn't make you look ridiculous. While there were always a few people who gave up and came in full bunny rabbit costume or the equivalent, most of the students were still doggedly trying to look sexy when they had to hide everything that would give away their identity. On a campus where everyone had become intimately familiar with one another's breasts, butts, and genitalia, as well as every other inch of their naked bodies, this was a challenge. Even a distinctive shape could give you away. Therefore corsets of various kinds were a classic ploy; almost everyone also wore some kind of padding. The results tended to be cartoonishly exaggerated feminine and masculine bodies, some with an outer coating of feathers, some finished with historical dress, and some simply zipped into a superhero costume. Wigs were almost necessary. The masks had to cover the entire face.

There was a costume room at Babylona for this purpose and for general use in classwork or performances. And throughout October, the room was overrun with people consulting and squabbling. The first things to get snatched up were the few burkas; then the best prefabricated costumes went to the people who fit into them. Lila had found a loose, gauzy, full-length nightgown whose sheer fabric and lacy inserts gave glimpses of nipple and buttocks without giving a clear idea of what exactly they were like. She wore it with a four-layered bridal veil and a blond wig. Anna was wearing a heavily padded Wonder Woman costume, taking advantage of the opportunity to have big boobs for once; and Brandi, who could not bear the idea of going to a party covered up, had found a corset that distorted her shape enough that she considered herself unrecognizable—with the addition of a Minnie Mouse head. "I don't mind if nobody's looking at my *face*," she said. "And I could do with a whole night where I *can't* give anybody head. I mean, my jaw muscles are getting like biceps, no joke. I think I could bench two hundred with my mouth."

The day before the party, Lila had no classes, and after her usual long morning in bed, this time writing a particularly boring essay for her Porn Perspectives class about legal definitions of obscenity, she went to the bar to waste time. At that hour of the day, there were only a few people there. She had been hoping to see one of her friends, but to her disappointment, all the people there were seniors or juniors, mostly people she hadn't ever met at all. What was worse, a crew-cut guy at the bar who'd once tried to lure her into the back room, looked up at her and then looked pointedly away without saying hello. She tried not to take it personally: everyone said that guy,

Mark, had been having a hard time because his Babylona girlfriend had broken up with him when he arrived back for the new semester. She'd left him for two other men, and the rumor was that when she'd broken the news to Mark, she said, "I think I can only be in love with *two* men." And that he'd said, "I can be two men!" But she apparently specifically wanted two men that weren't half Mark.

Lila went to the opposite end of the bar, giving him his privacy. The girl tending bar saw her and smiled. Her name was Hannah, and she was in Satisfaction with Lila; she had been the first one daring enough to demonstrate masturbation in front of the class. Lila could still remember her air of terror and concentration as she perched on the teacher's desk and spread her legs. She had spread her labia for a moment before doing anything, as if to let everyone see exactly what there was to work with. Then she just licked the tip of her index finger, and the whole class held its breath, watching her stroke herself up and down with the tip of that finger, until she stretched her legs out straight, pincering her own hand between her thighs. Her body tensed, then tensed again . . . and that was all there was to it. She stood up, rearranged her skirt, and said in a perfectly normal voice, "Of course, that wasn't a *porno* come." Then everyone laughed, relieved that the ice was broken, and gave her a round of applause.

Lila asked her for a beer and settled down at a table near the bar.

As soon as she'd sat down, a man detached himself from a group that was curled up on a water bed and came slinking toward her. He was a tall Latino guy whom Lila immediately recognized with a sinking in her stomach as the man she'd first seen in a video Ben had shown her, having sex with a thin blond girl in a man's shirt. For some reason, the memory made her feel both shy and anxiously turned on. She took a sip of her beer, hoping that he only wanted to talk, or that at least he wouldn't be pushy about getting her into the back room. Some people thought she was playing a game when she said no and that she would be disappointed if they didn't actually try to drag her.

"Hi, I'm Victor," the man said.

"Hey," said Lila. "Sit down if you want, but I'm not here to fool around today."

He shrugged and sat with her. "I'm not here to be a pain in the ass today. Don't worry."

He asked her the usual array of questions: Where are you from? What brought you here? Do you like it so far? What do you think you'll do with your degree? Do you have a boy/girlfriend? Which do you like best, anal, oral, or vaginal? Do you like spanking? Are you into sex toys? Exhibitionism? Lila had gotten used to it, though she was always a little worried she was answering the questions wrong. Did she like spanking? Sometimes yes, sometimes not at all. Could you choose between anal, oral, and vaginal? Apparently some people could, because when she was with a group during the Q&A, a few people always volunteered strong opinions. But as far as Lila was concerned, it was like asking which she liked better: ice cream or going to the beach.

All the while, she was remembering Victor fucking that blond girl on the edge of a school desk, his cock moving in and out of her. While Ben fingered Lila from behind and gently pulled her panties down, getting ready to . . .

"Victor?" she said suddenly, in a soft, tentative voice. "Do you want to . . . I know I said I wasn't here to fool around, but."

"But?" His voice caught a bit. He stole a glance at her breasts, on display as usual in her low-cut sweater.

Lila bit her lip and tugged slightly at her sweater, letting her nipple appear just over the fabric. Victor's hand immediately rose toward it, but then he caught himself, looking guiltily at Hannah. He said, "I've been watching you since you first came. I've been wanting to touch your tits for weeks. You're *so* beautiful. I keep thinking about it."

She said, "I want you to."

They both got up, and the eyes of everyone in the room followed them as they went to the unmarked door to one side of the bar. Lila went in first, and as soon as she got in, Victor had her up against the wall, pushing the door shut hastily as his free hand closed immediately on her breast. Then he freed the other breast and grasped it similarly roughly. He let out a low groan and was already shoving his hard-on against her. She opened her legs so she could feel his jean-covered bulge against the hole in her own jeans, the rough fabric pressing into the soaked lace.

Then he unzipped his jeans and she was feeling his bare cock nosing against her, pushing into the wet fabric, trying to force its way into the hole. She shifted herself slightly, holding on to his shoulders for balance, and he tugged the panties clear of her pussy. Still his cock was only pushing into her clit, making her gasp with pleasure but unable to make room in the hole there. She was gazing, panting at his finely chiseled features, remembering the video, Ben's strong hands on her ass . . . how she had shamelessly given herself.

Then his fingers were hooked on both sides of the hole in her jeans. He whispered, "Can I tear it?"

She said, "Yes! Yes, tear it . . ."

He ripped the hole open and the next second his cock was tearing into her, making her yelp and clutch his shoulders to keep from falling. He fucked her with all his strength, making her tits bob and tremble where they had been pulled free of her clothes. Her cunt was so grateful, she was ready to come almost as soon as he began to fuck her. But just as she felt the crescendo that was leading to a blinding orgasm, the door flung open.

Both of them froze momentarily. It was Mark, standing in the doorway, looking at them with a slightly lost and embarrassed expression. She could tell Victor was trying to hold still, but his cock had a mind of its own, and he kept fucking her, evenly and deeply, as he said in a choked voice, "What's up? What's going on, Mark?"

Mark said quietly, "Can't I . . ." He looked at Lila imploringly, and then looked away.

Then Lila suddenly wanted him—wanted both of them at once—desperately. All it took was for another man to appear. Once again she was out of control of her own desires, and she said, "Yes, please."

Victor pulled out of her and Lila, without thinking, got down on her knees on the floor. Turning her back to Mark, she took Victor's dick in her mouth and began to suck. She put one hand on his hip to guide him into her throat, and with the other, she ringed the base of his long thin cock with her fingers, squeezing it deliciously and pressing into his balls as she brought him forward. He groaned again and she began to maneuver her ass back and up, putting her knees wide apart to show Mark where her jeans had been ripped wide to allow easy access to her dripping cunt. All the while she was thinking of Ben approaching her from behind, fingering her from behind, fucking her from behind.

When Mark's touch came, it was just as gentle, but more hasty. He tweaked her left nipple as he played with her clit and thrust one finger in and out of her cunt, making her seize up with the new beginning of the orgasm she'd been cheated of. And then it was his cock dancing over her clit and dipping teasingly into her opening; he was using his cock's head to stroke her slippery clit, and the pressure made her moan as she swallowed Victor's now greedily thrusting dick. The idea of the two dicks enjoying her body excited her more than she expected; now she was remembering the two men who'd seen her naked in the clearing when she was with Tad, the night he'd broken up with her. This was what she'd wanted to do with them. She just hadn't had the nerve to fully realize it.

And now Mark had pressed into her, his dick separated her tingling lips and splitting her deeply. That moment, she began to come, and he fucked her through it, his dick spearing her deeply as it rang new depths of pleasure from her body. And just as he arched into her still more and came, so did Victor, the hot come spurting over her tongue and down her throat as his cock leaped in her mouth.

She swallowed it all, feeling the last few thrusts of Mark behind as he milked the last of his orgasm. His hands were gripping her hips with the intensity of it. Victor had pulled out of her mouth and was standing with his eyes shut, breathing shallowly through his mouth. At last he opened his eyes, and smiled at her, saying, "Oh, God. That was unbelievable. I tell you, that was like the first time I ever—"

Mark laughed from behind her. "Whoa, flattery will get you everywhere."

"Not flattery." Victor shook his head, offended.

Mark pulled out of her from behind, a shocking feeling of cold that was immediately relieved as he bent down to hug her and pull her up against him. She turned her head and saw him grinning. He kissed her on the cheek. "I'm just kidding him, Lila," he said. "If what you did for him was *anything* like what you did for me, it wasn't flattery. God, girl, you got it going on."

Lila said, "I can't talk right now. I just fainted from pleasure." She let herself relax against Mark, smiling drowsily at Victor. Her beer was still waiting for her. It was still only noon. She'd just had her first back room sex, with not one but two strangers—and she felt fine. She felt better than fine, in fact; she felt like she understood exactly what everyone else had been feeling all this time. They'd been feeling *good*.

So she knew exactly what they would do in her shoes, and suddenly it was the right thing for her, too. She said, "Hey . . . you want to go have a few drinks and then come back and do it again?"

Chapter Twelve

The Halloween party took place in the Belesci Ballroom, a huge glass structure on the edge of campus. It was filled with flowering trees, palm trees, and a complicated system of fountains. The actual dance floor was relatively small. Among the trees were various tents, made of silk and velvet with embroidered flowers and birds, that had cushioned mats on the bottoms—for the usual purpose. Some of the tents were as much as twenty feet long, and all of them were dripping with tassels. Inside they were lit with strings of Christmas lights.

By eight o'clock, the room was packed with Spider-men, Vikings, big-bosomed fairies, and versions of every other costume that permitted the wearer to remain completely hidden. Some of the students were dancing to the loud techno music with a glass of punch in one hand, but most had immediately paired off, in tents, under trees, or just up against a glass wall. Some were on their second or third pairing. It was bizarre to see a girl in a princess mask and Elizabethan gown being hammered at both ends by a robot and a ghost; or a huge chipmunk being sucked off by a geisha whose mask was shoved round onto the side of her head.

Lila had been there for an hour, dancing and watching the scene. The time she had spent with Mark and Victor the day before had somewhat drained her libido, although the wine and the atmosphere were waking it up again. Still, twelve hours of screwing and sucking and drinking and then starting it all over again—in the grass, in her bed, on the rowing machine at the gym—had taken their toll. By the time the sun had gone down last night, she'd been thoroughly raw, and almost rubber legged with exhaustion. They'd ended the night by going out to the hot tub down by the river, which was *not* filled with champagne, and therefore sometimes could be empty. It was empty, and they lounged there drinking a bottle of Calvados Mark had and talking about all their troubles as if they'd known each other all their lives. Victor's Catholic family had stopped talking to him when they found out he was coming here, though his little sister still corresponded with him secretly. He thought they would come around, but he was afraid he was going to have to spend the rest of his life pretending to be a Realtor at large family gatherings. Lila confessed all her problems with Tad, her growing pains on arrival at Babylona, but kept back the experience with Ben (after all, he could get in trouble). Mark discussed his ex-girlfriend, Celinda, who'd left Babylona recently after deciding that in fact she only wanted *one* man, and for that one man to only ever sleep with her. Her whole "I can only love two men" speech had been part of a bad reaction to their open relationship, to Babylona, and possibly to sex in general.

"Wow, I hope that doesn't happen to me," said Lila.

Mark and Victor laughed.

"You didn't know Celinda," said Victor. "She was a little high-strung."

"She was impossible," Mark sighed. "But wonderful in her own screwed-up, tantrum-throwing, blow-hot-and-cold way."

"Matter of taste," said Victor.

Lila argued half seriously that she was high-strung herself. Sometimes she thought throwing a tantrum would feel great. And just weeks ago, she'd been ready a few times to give up all this for monogamy . . . but the boys remained skeptical—so skeptical that soon she was in a tangle of limbs again, remembering why she'd changed her mind.

Now the party was tugging her back into that state of mind again, where she felt her body taking over and glowing with a pure physical joy that made all other people seem like part of her. Being completely anonymous made things seem possible that she never would have considered. Snaking through the dancers to get another glass of wine, she let her hand play over asses and crotches, and felt other people reciprocating, molding their hands to her breasts in the filmy fabric of her nightgown, squeezing her ass and pressing fingers forward to feel her cunt. The pressure there on her raw vulva was half stinging, half thrilling. A man in a bull mask who had painted his bare chest gold and strung it all around with gold chains caught her by the waist and pressed her up against him. The cold pressure of the chains on her tits was surprisingly sexy. She immediately put her hands to his hard buttocks and rode the contact, feeling his half-erect penis curled against her mound. She didn't even try to guess who it was; she just smelled the masculine smell of him, combined with some wearing-off cologne and the fragrance of wine on his breath. He was wearing leather pants, and even through the gauze of her nightgown, the slickness of the leather aroused her. Soon her hand was exploring the growing bulge, trying to find his balls under the leather, and her cunt was blazing with longing again.

He ran his fingernails over the front of her nightgown, finding the tight points of her breasts and teasing them by flicking past them again and again. She was cupping her palm over him and pressing her cunt against her own knuckles now. At last she found his zipper and freed his now straining, hard cock from his pants, letting the hard hot length of it press into her palm.

Then she turned impulsively and went on. The hands kept brushing past her, igniting the desire already smoldering in her sore nipples and cunt. When she reached the line at the wine table, there was a man dressed as a priest who had his dick out and was unselfconsciously stroking it. Lila, getting in line, noticed that, without anything having been said, every girl was pausing after pouring her drink, crouching, and sucking the man's dick for a few seconds, before passing on with her drink. One of the guys—the man in the spectacular chipmunk suit—also did it, and the priest stiffened in a particular way, looking down to watch the bobbing chipmunk head intently. As soon as the chipmunk rose and turned away, the priest rapidly milked his cock to orgasm, spurting streams of milky fluid onto his hands and his already spattered black robe. Lila wanted to laugh—was it a telltale of the priest's sexual orientation? Was it a chipmunk fetish? Or perhaps—somehow this was the funniest idea of all—the chipmunk was the mysterious Mr. Banks and he had conquered the Priest of the Wine Table by sheer transcendent sexual technique.

Lila decided to take her wine into a tent and get some peace. She might even masturbate—carefully—to let off steam without putting her pussy into even worse condition. And as she stole around the outskirts of the dance floor, carefully avoiding further contact, the idea came to her that she wanted to be as ready as she could be for sex—in case she ran into Ben again. Then she felt flustered and leaned against a tree trunk for a moment, wondering if he was here. Of course he *shouldn't* be—the hallowed rules and all that—but if no one ever knew who it was . . .

He might be fucking other women right in front of her right now. He might be—oh, God!—the chipmunk!

Suddenly Lila was chilled to the bone. She forgot all about her new body connection to all the universe. All she could think about was Ben's cock thrusting into some other girl, some other girl who had been here for three years, knew everything, and would make Lila look . . . boring. Ben kissing that girl, comparing her with Lila. Of course this was all insane, and contrary to everything she'd learned since she got here. Still, Lila was half blind with distress as she wove through the many lurching tents, lit inside just enough to betray the faint outlines of squirming couples. She was now desperately looking for one that might be unoccupied, a private place to gather her thoughts. She remembered Celinda, and felt a passionate rush of sympathy with her. It would be so easy to slip from needing more and more men to only being comfortable in some straitlaced, faithful, *Little House on the Prairie* type of marriage to a man, forsaking all others, till death do us part. It would be so easy to construct your sex life around avoiding pain.

At last she saw a tent that was still and dark. It was a purple velvet thing, a bit smaller than the others. It actually looked as if it were designed for people to sit alone in. For people to gather their thoughts, away from the crowd. For highly strung girls to throw tantrums where no one would see them. Lila swooped on it and ducked into the flap, tripping on her skirt and then getting one arm entangled in her veil as she fell awkwardly onto a man.

She gasped and rolled off of him. At the same time, the tent flap closed, so that she could barely make out the man's features in the dark. From what she saw, however, she was shocked to find that he wasn't wearing a costume. In fact, he was dressed in what looked like an absolutely ordinary sweatshirt and jeans, clothes that would have been unusual on a Babylona student even on an ordinary day. No strategic holes, no codpiece, nothing. In the dark and through her veil, she couldn't see his expression, but his posture seemed perfectly comfortable, as if he'd been expecting someone to appear.

And in fact, why wouldn't he? That was probably exactly what he was expecting. He might even be one of the outsiders that everyone talked about. He'd snuck in before the party started, secreted himself in a tent, and waited. Now that she was here, he would take advantage of the dark to have sex with her without being recognized as an interloper. And Lila would—well, Lila would have had sex with a stranger stranger. A more strange stranger than before.

That would normally be all in good fun, but right now she just wasn't in the right frame of mind. She gestured with her palms out: *Don't touch me.* Realizing he probably couldn't see in the dark, she waved her hands more violently. She was feeling the weary inevitability that she would have to break the rules and talk. And those few Babylona rules seemed very important now that they were the only thing stopping Ben from sleeping with all of her friends.

"Are you asking to be left alone?"

His voice was baritone and calm; with the music going on outside, she couldn't tell if the voice was familiar. She said softly, "We aren't supposed to talk," and then blushed in the dark. Of course he must already know that. Unless he was a homeless guy who'd snuck in here to get out of the cold. That would have been a lucky night for some guy down on his luck. However, the general look of the man made that an unlikely conclusion.

"We can talk in here," he said. "Do you want some whiskey?"

She saw the gleam of the bottle as he handed it over; she caught it by the neck and felt the slight touch of his hand on the side of hers, dry and slightly rough. It gave her an odd sensation. And she knew immediately, instinctively, that it was Mr. Banks. She froze inside, thinking about it. Did that mean the stories about him skulking around at the party, sleeping with chosen people, were true? But then why would he be in this tent and out of disguise? Perhaps he didn't choose the people; he just waited and let them come to him by chance. "What are you doing here?" she said, somehow certain he would know he'd been recognized.

"It was a whim. I thought I'd sit in here until someone flushed me out. Then I'd walk out among the students like a god." She heard his dry laugh. Now his deep voice and Midwestern accent were unmistakable. Lila couldn't help feeling a particular girlish thrill: The heartthrob teacher was talking to her as if she was a real grown-up!

"So you should be walking out there like a god about now."

"You took too long, darling," he said. "I had too much to drink, and I had too many thoughts."

"Oh, thoughts," she said. She took a swig of whiskey, and her own thoughts reappeared to her. Ben, sex with strangers, Ben having sex with strangers . . . Thoughts were sticky. "I came in here to have thoughts," she said. "Too tired for acts, I guess."

He didn't reply, and for a long time they sat across from each other in the dark, with the throbbing music and the squeals and

groans of intercourse—Babylona's typical soundtrack—dimmed by
the velvet of the tent so that the hedonistic sounds seemed almost
like insulation from the real world. Lila decided to let herself be
sad; there was no way she was going to be happy about Ben screwing
other girls. And the fact was that even if he wasn't doing it here on
campus, he was almost certainly doing it somewhere. Just like Tad,
except that she wasn't allowed to feel bad about it. Or if she did feel
bad about it, she had to pretend she didn't. Or . . . she could run
away and find a nice faithful God-fearing sort of man to marry and
that was that. Except she didn't want that, and she was back at the
beginning of the vicious circle.

Suddenly Mr. Banks said, "Is it a love problem?"

She started and felt almost unjustly treated. She had decided that
they were in agreement about *not* talking. They were both there to
have thoughts. But the flattered feeling won, and she said, "Jealousy.
I can't help it. I'm only a freshman, so I'm not . . ."

"When you're a sophomore, and a junior, and an old woman,
you'll still get jealous," he said. "I promise."

Lila gulped. "But then, how can all this work? Babylona? Having
a career in sex? Won't it make us all miserable?"

Mr. Banks laughed and his hand reached forward. For a paralyzed
second Lila thought he was reaching for her. Then she understood,
and handed him back the whiskey bottle. He took a drink and said,
"Listen, darling, if you try to avoid being miserable, you're going to
waste a lot of time and—be miserable."

"I'm going to be miserable?"

"I guarantee it. But I'm hoping you haven't been miserable your
entire time with us?"

Lila digested this, and finally said, "So it's okay to feel jealous?"

"It's inevitable. Don't go running away from the one rational
place in the world to chase something that never was."

Lila sighed. "And it's okay to make other people jealous."

"It's inevitable. And it's a hell of a lot more fun."

Then she felt his hand on her foot, a light, sure touch that seemed to radiate warmth, energy, some nameless fire, into her skin. She thought of healing touches and caught her breath. The warmth spread into her foot and made her whole body relax into a state of quiescence and expectancy. "Can't we ever make each other happy?" she said, and her voice came out husky and helpless.

"Now, that's a silly question, Lila," he said. And his hand traveled up her shin, sending the same overwhelming glow up her leg. She was breathing hard already, and she felt as if her blood had been infused with some incredible drug. She wanted him to touch her more, but she couldn't speak or move. She was frozen.

Nothing had ever been a greater relief to her than seeing him move forward in the dark. He quietly ran his hands over her, feeling her shape under the nightgown. Then he matter-of-factly lifted the veil from her face and she could see his features. It gave her another chill to see him; it made it real for the first time. "You're a very beautiful woman. You can make a lot of men happy."

Then he bent down gracefully and kissed her. Again, she felt connected to some profound force; and his hand playing with her breast seemed to be turning it into something else, like a breast made of light. She felt ridiculous to be reacting this way, but she felt tears coming to her eyes. And when he pulled up the skirt of her nightgown and stroked her thighs, there was a moment when she thought she could have fainted; there was a twinge of darkness in her mind that led that way. But then she just moaned desperately, and said in a whisper, "Help me . . . do it."

The next thing she knew was the sure pressure of his hard-on against her belly, the weight of him arched over her. His thighs were parting hers, and she felt the thrilling cold against her wet cunt, all the sensitivity there. She could feel each individual part of her pussy exposed; it too was suffused with the hyperawareness that flowed from Mr. Banks' skin. He had pulled her costume up over her breasts, and as he gently, rhythmically pressed his hard dick into her belly, he craned his head down to suck one of her nipples. That was a different, keener kind of electricity, and she cried out sharply, feeling her nipple harden immediately to such a crunching intensity that it almost made her come. She thought of Miguel claiming that he could make her come by touching her breasts. She had no doubt that Mr. Banks actually could.

And then he lifted his hips lightly off her and she felt his cock sliding into her. The sensation was so intense that she didn't even come; her mind was too profoundly intent on comprehending and following the feelings that were coming from her clitoris, her vagina, her whole belly. His hands were on her ass, lightly kneading, and there, too, waves of electrifying pleasure flew into her.

Then she was coming, while he fucked her in a way that was absolutely simple, but was . . . as if she'd only ever had a toy version of fucking before, and this was the real thing. As if she'd only ever had artificial sex before, just as Babylona had said. She was having the sex she'd imagined when she was first beginning puberty, when sex was a mystical and unfathomable wonderland. She came and came, but her orgasms were only decoration; it was the fucking itself that felt so good, it was the shape and the exact size, the twisting motion of his dick. Her orgasms almost seemed like something going on at a distance. She couldn't stop herself from trying to capture the feeling, to remember it in all its detail. He was fucking her from all different angles, each thrust finding a different pleasure to call from her. And the effortless strength of it made her feel impossibly vulnerable, as if she might be killed with pleasure, and be unable to do anything about it.

And then he had thrust into her in that final way, his hands pulling her ass up to take his semen. She cried out in disappointment, she almost begged him to wait, but it was too late. He was coming, his dick kicking inside her with an extra jolt that swept her into a moment of actual blackness. She was half in a dream about being in the middle of the ocean, but it was an ocean that was also somehow

an orgasm. And in the dream, she knew she was in the exact middle
of the ocean, so there was no danger of ever having to go back to
shore. But all the while, she knew that she was there and that Mr.
Banks was incredibly coming inside her.

Then she was fully awake and lying in Mr. Banks' arms. His
cheek was against her hair and he was holding her gently. They lay
like that for a long time, holding each other close as if consoling
each other. At last she said, "You shouldn't do that to people, should
you? Won't . . . won't I be jealous of *you*, now?" And she tried to
laugh, but it came out a little broken.

"No, don't worry," he said. "No one's ever jealous of me." And
he gripped her still closer to him. Now it seemed as if he was seeking comfort from her, and Lila relaxed, feeling her selfhood coming
back. The helplessness was receding, though his arms still felt warm
in a way that wasn't exactly physical. That wasn't, she would have
thought, exactly possible.

"I mean, any woman would pine for you. Wouldn't they?"

"Women don't fall in love with me, darling."

She could feel him smiling, his cheek shifting against her cheek.
"All the girls are in love with you," she said flatly, stating an undeni-
able fact.

"No. Don't worry, beautiful one, you won't pine for me. You'll see."

"Are you sad?" Lila tried to pull away enough to see his face. But
he held her tight; she couldn't get free. At last she relaxed again and
said, "Maybe you should try running away from your misery."

"No, that's another thing you'll see. When I was your age, I
thought I could fight my misery, or run away from my misery, or
outsmart it. Now I understand that everyone's miserable just as
much as they can be. And when they can't stand it, they make someone else miserable. Take Babylona. She has no strength for putting
up with pain. So . . ." Now he'd let her go. She looked at him finally
and it was astonishing again; Mr. Banks, this close to her, lying on
his side and casually zipping up his jeans. And he'd just fucked her.

And it had felt—like *that*. But her memory of the feeling was already receding.

"Babylona?" she said, having almost forgotten what he was saying. "She has no strength for pain?"

"She's a pleasure girl. That's a good thing," he added, with a wry note in his voice.

Lila had caught a momentary sense memory of what the sex was like, and she blurted, "Why did she let you go?"

"Oh, she hasn't let me go. She doesn't let people go, exactly," said Mr. Banks. "In fact, she's going to visit very soon, partly to make sure I'm *not* let go."

"And then she'll make everyone miserable?"

He laughed again, with an edge in his voice that she didn't understand. He said, "She'll make *me* miserable. She'll make me miserable by making everyone else in the whole place happy." Then he had ducked out of the tent, and Lila was left lying on her back on a slightly damp velvet coverlet, her body humming and glowing and telling her that life was a wonderful thing—while her mind tangled with the idea that Mr. Banks was dying of jealousy, just like she was, and life was a terrible, miserable thing!

Chapter Thirteen

Brandi stalked away from the raucous sounds of the party, carrying the Minnie Mouse head under her arm. Okay, granted someone *could* have recognized her by her body, which was mainly on display in the waist-crushing corset and boots, which were all she wore. But she'd goddamn well gone to the lengths of putting on a mouse head—she'd played ball. Of course, the Halloween party rules said she had to be totally unrecognizable. That could be interpreted as meaning that if the door guy could tell who she was from her bare breasts, she was out. And sure, her breasts were the part of her body that people knew best at Babylona. But that was the letter of the law, not the spirit. It seemed like it would just be good manners for the door guy to look the other way. Instead of which, he'd looked her right in her beady mouse eye and said, "Brandi, who do you think you're kidding?"

And barred her. Now her personal party was over, unless she could come up with some costume that *would* absolutely mask her identity . . . but what were the chances of that, when every possible scrap of disguise had been seized by greedy Babylonans over the past few weeks? No, she'd gambled and lost. And now she'd just have to find some other miserable, doomed, unhappy, nonpartygoer to fuck away her sorrows.

As the sound of hip-hop dwindled behind her, she couldn't help but be struck by the darkness and silence that reigned everywhere else on campus. Usually there would be lit windows all around her, and the sounds of laughter and conversation coming from a dozen half-open windows and a dozen dark nooks in the woods and grass.

Mingled with the stray whimpers of sexual bliss, of course, that made this her spiritual home. Now only the Belesci was lit, and the dorms, the school buildings, and the lawns and woods were all abandoned, bereft. Apparently Brandi was the only one who had been thrown out.

But then, as she came past the Student Services building, she saw a dim light on in one of the second-story windows. She slowed down, not really thinking about it yet, and gradually came to a stop. After a minute, she realized she was just staring up like a dog begging at a dinner table.

That light meant someone was there—probably. And that someone was a Babylonan—certainly. And if it was a Babylonan, it was fuckable—very.

But if it was Student Services, it was staff—off-limits.

But—and this "but" made her perk up again with a surge of renewed energy—it might be *Ben.* And with Ben, alone of all people in the world, she had a score to settle. A score that involved him fucking her until he begged for mercy. Which was her favorite kind of score.

She tried a side door and was relieved to find that it was open. Of course, theft was hardly a problem at Babylona. Everyone was too preoccupied with delinquency of a different kind. She sat down on the stairs to take off her boots—she didn't want Ben (or whomever it might be) hearing her approach. Ideally she could sneak up and be ready for them by the time they realized she was there.

She left her boots and Minnie Mouse head by the door and crept up the stairs barefoot, the cool marble already giving her a wonderful sensual feeling. She began to think about men licking her toes . . . licking men's toes . . . then the toe suddenly vanishes and the man is pressing a fat engorged dick at her lips . . . yes . . . and her lips part and her tongue—

She almost tripped and grabbed the banister hastily. Thank God marble didn't creak when you tripped. She continued up, trying to

concentrate only on the progress of her feet. As she reached the
second floor, she could have sworn she smelled sex . . . the fragrance
of seafoody goodness that had perfumed her so-far-happy life. She
sighed as she tiptoed up to the door with the crack of light under it
and pressed her ear against it.

She heard nothing. For long seconds she stood, holding her
breath. Still she heard nothing. At last, she mustered all her resolve
and knocked.

A minute passed. Nothing happened.

She knocked again. Deciding he might have fallen asleep, she
pounded on the door three times with all her might and then held
still, her heart pounding with all its might in sympathy.

Nothing.

This is just foolishness, Brandi told herself. *There's no one in there, and
anyway, that no one isn't Ben.* But just in case, she tried the doorknob,
ready to interrupt a private scene of forbidden sex, a private scene
of just-embarrassing masturbation, or a private scene of furniture
all alone.

The door was locked. Brandi almost walked away. But then she
could have sworn she heard something. A soft, soft something that
could have been a cough, a stifled laugh, or even a chair being shoved
back over a wooden floor. What it couldn't have been was a chair
shoving itself. Her heart began to pound again, and she raised her
fist, ready to pound along—but stopped.

Whoever was in there didn't want to be found. They weren't going
to open the door, and no amount of knocking was going to change
that. If she called out her name, well, it could only get worse. Either
it wasn't Ben, in which case, they didn't know her at all. Or it was Ben,
who wouldn't open up to Brandi outside of office hours for anything.
Ben, she had to sourly admit to herself, had her number pretty good.

Then she had a brilliant idea.

Dashing downstairs, Brandi rushed outside, leaving the boots
and Minnie Mouse head where they lay, and ran barefoot around

the building past the lit window she'd first seen to the side of Student Services that was flanked by woods. Sure enough, there was a second lit window there—at the corner. It was a corner office, and this window—handily near the thick branch of a big oak tree—led to the same room as the other. Brandi paused to catch her breath and congratulate herself. Then she approached the oak tree gingerly, careful of the acorns under her bare feet.

Tree climbing in a corset was no joke. Brandi had to summon up all her memories of being a naughty eight-year-old to grit her teeth as the bark scuffed her tender inner thighs, dirtied her hands, legs, belly, and even cheek, and shed a little sap on her palm that wouldn't come off for love or money. But at last she was shimmying, possibly a little bloodied (she couldn't be 100 percent sure), but unbowed (now that was for sure) down the branch to the lit window.

Long before she got there, the branch began to thrash noisily, shaking all its pretty green, orange, and yellow autumn leaves in a near-deafening rush. It was as loud, Brandi thought, as standing next to Niagara Falls. But she carried on, figuring that it was equivalent to knocking—except that this time, when she got to the end of the branch, whoever it was wouldn't be able to exactly hide. He might be able to lock her out, but he wouldn't be able to pretend he wasn't doing it.

When she was within a meter of the window, she saw that it had been left open by just a few inches. And as she took her next careful shimmy toward it, she spotted a shadow inside racing to meet her. Inspired suddenly, she shot forward and crammed her bare foot in the open window just as Ben appeared and raised both arms to slam it shut.

"Ouch!" Brandi cried out—though he'd seen her foot in time and checked his motion.

Ben squinted at the glass, which obviously was too covered in glare on the inside for him to see her properly. Then his squint turned into wonder and amusement. "Tell me I'm hallucinating," he said.

"You're hallucinating someone who's going to fall and break her neck if you don't help her." Brandi smiled winningly and slightly arched her back, hoping he could see the way her nipples peeped provocatively over the lace trimming on the corset.

"Oh, I think that branch is pretty sturdy," said Ben.

Brandi sighed. "Nobody ever wants to reward initiative in this place. I don't know how you want to send us out into the world, when we're all institutionalized. For serious."

"Wouldn't let you into the party, huh?"

"Oh, some people know everything!" Brandi said irritably. "Goddamn, if it's so obvious, then you know why I'm here."

"Yes, and I should have been escaping down the tree when I heard you pounding on the door."

Ben laughed, and Brandi found herself laughing with him. She said, "Well, hell with you, the only reason you can even outsmart me is that you're so pretty I can't think straight when you're around. Which is all the more reason you ought to stop being a pain and sleep with me. I'd never ever tell. *And* I'd tell you a secret you might be interested in, too."

"So you're going to tell me someone else's secret, and that's supposed to make me believe you would keep my secret?" Ben raised his eyebrows.

"Oh, hell, the other secret isn't really a secret. I mean, it's not that kind of secret. It's more something nobody knows."

Ben considered. Then he leaned down and produced a bottle from behind his desk. To Brandi's delight, he then pulled the window wide open. But when she moved to come in, he blocked her way. "No, I'm coming out. I feel like sitting in my tree. You know, I sit there all the time and watch people go by. So you're invading my private place, on top of everything else." He reached the bottle out toward her.

"How am I supposed to seduce you in a *tree?*" Brandi complained.

"Exactly," Ben said. "Now scooch back or else we'll snap this branch and both of us are going to break our necks."

* * *

Brandi and Ben ended up sitting on adjacent branches near the trunk, drinking wine while Brandi told her story of meeting Babylona in the massage parlor parking lot. "I *would* have kept her secret, of course. Except for her playing games with my head like that. That's just throwing the red rag at the bull."

Ben was shaking his head. "Brandi, you really like being in trouble, don't you?"

"You know it." She shifted uncomfortably on the branch. "Ouch. And anyway, you didn't say whether you slept with that Madison. *Not* that I'm judging you, because I liked her in the end. No pun intended."

Ben was staring disconsolately at the lawn below. "Well, back in the day we fooled around. Just like everyone at the institute. But I haven't been sleeping with anyone in a while. If you want to hear my secret . . ."

"Of course," Brandi said.

"I think I fell in love." He sighed heavily. "And now I think I'm at your mercy."

"Ha!" said Brandi. "You mean you're in love with *me*."

Ben's mouth fell open. Brandi went on cheerfully. "Which is a good thing actually, because I'm in love with you, too. That's why I'm chasing you all over the place, and the only thing in the world that's going to cure me of my love is if you fuck me right now. Do it in the tree if you must." Brandi's eyes shut languorously and she leaned back, calculating how Ben would have to balance on the branch . . . would it break? How much would it hurt if . . .

"Okay, you had me going for a second."

Brandi's eyes flew open. "No, make it five minutes. That's all I need."

"Five minutes?" Ben laughed. "Is that what you think of me?"

"Beggars can't be choosers." Brandi sighed. "But okay, what's the story? Who's the lucky girl?"

Ben grimaced and opened his mouth to tell her, when he was interrupted by a shriek below. A girl in a feathery Mardi Gras mask and nothing else came running under the tree, her breasts bouncing frantically. She was pursued by two burly football players in full regalia. As Brandi and Ben looked on, one of the football players leaped forward and tackled the girl, who screamed with all her might and sprawled on her stomach in the grass. The second football player, trying to stop before colliding with the other two, skidded and fell flat on his ass. All three burst into hysterical laughter as football player number one sat up and pinned the girl to the grass.

"No fair!" she cried out. "I just want to go home and sleep."

The football player was fondling the girl's ass, squeezing the plump cheeks as the girl kicked, trying to get him with her bare heels. The second football player got to his knees and grabbed the girl's feet, spreading them to position himself between her thighs. Then he was pulling down his pants. In a second, he was fucking her from behind. The girl ably twisted her torso around and soon the first football player was angled over her face, fucking her in the mouth. From the tree the details weren't clear; all that could be made out were the rhythmic movements of the men's asses thrusting into the girl from both ends.

The girl's cries had changed to muffled moans of pleasure. Brandi wanted to leap right out of the tree and join them. If only she could change places right now. But then she caught a glimpse of Ben out of the corner of her eye; he was staring down as if stricken.

"So," she whispered to him, "what if you got caught in a tree with a naked student?"

"Don't even think about it," he whispered back fiercely.

"You know what I'm thinking about."

He continued to scowl down at the people in the grass.

Brandi said, "Well, I'll try this. Suppose you don't want me to tell everybody at school you're in love with Lila?"

Ben jumped and almost lost his balance. The branch he was sitting on flailed noisily in the air as he caught at the trunk to keep from falling. He whispered, "How the hell . . . Did she tell you?"

Brandi grinned. "Educated guess."

"But you never . . . I've never even been with her in public!"

"You've never really been with any of us in public, dummy. And—double dummy! Every guy on campus has a crush on Lila."

Ben stared at her. "You mean you didn't know? So I just gave it away . . ." He swallowed. "Well, I guess I can only beg you not to get me fired."

Brandi shook her head. "My friend, you're *way* too easy. Till you said that, I only thought you were in love with her. Now I know you slept with her, too. And that means something else."

"Oh God."

"You see I already knew you slept with a freshman, from our first little tête-à-tête when you wouldn't sleep with *me.* But what didn't occur to me at that time is that you must have done it when you had your orientation meeting. That little meeting I didn't go to. Which I sorely wish I had now that I know . . ."

"How could you know that was when . . . You couldn't! Really, did she tell you?"

"Wow, what a reaction. Hmm. I say the case is closed." Brandi winked. "Now that's what I call being at my mercy."

Ben shook his head. "I'm going inside. This isn't even funny anymore, Brandi."

He began to climb back down the branch to his office window, the wine bottle tucked underneath his arm. Below them, the first football player was arching his back, coming with a long groan. Brandi scrambled to follow Ben, barely pausing when she felt one of her nipples scratched painfully by a branch. "Ben, hell—can't you tell when somebody's kidding you?"

Ben was already climbing through the window. Brandi managed to get her head in the window before he could close it. For a second she had his hand in her face, shoving. Then he had let her go and she tumbled in headfirst, catching herself with her hands and falling sideways onto the rug. Then she was staring up at him with her corset on sideways, and the breath knocked out of her.

"Sorry," said Ben, looking down with a contrite expression. "Are you okay? I guess I lost my temper."

"Oh, I'm okay. I could lie, but I guess I gave you a hard enough time." Brandi patted her hair back into place and tugged her corset, peering down to try to measure the effect on her boobs. "And in case you were wondering, no, I would never tell on you. Even if you resist my charms."

Ben said, "But I'm not going to resist your charms anymore."

"What?" Brandi let go of her corset and stared. "You're—"

"Shut up."

Ben grabbed her by the hands and pulled her up to her feet. The next thing she knew she was pressed against the wall with Ben's hands at her breasts. His lips came down on hers fiercely, his tongue pressing into her mouth. Her whole body seemed to melt with the relief of being touched inappropriately again. The strong hands fondling her breasts made her pussy instantly respond.

Then his hands moved to her shoulders, pushing her down. She resisted instinctively for a second before going down on her knees. Then she was nuzzling the crotch of his jeans, feeling the erection that was forming there. She felt for its shape with her teeth, smelling its delicious musk through the cloth. She remembered how she'd said that the Minnie Mouse costume would stop her from giving head for one night and smiled. Well, it always did seem kind of unnatural. Then Ben's hands appeared, opening his belt and freeing his cock. It was already stiff enough to spring up as he pulled his jeans and briefs down. Brandi's mouth found it instantly, her tongue curling around the smooth knob at its end, sucking on its luscious hardness.

Ben's hands went to the back of her head, and then he was thrusting into her mouth, filling it with his big, perfectly formed cock. She shut her eyes to savor it; Brandi was a connoisseur of dicks, and this one was beautiful, even its taste faintly sweet. Brandi's pussy was on fire. Her clit was stiff and swollen in sympathy with his cock, and it thrilled with every thrust of Ben's hips.

At last she felt his dick throbbing and swelling to an extra pitch of hardness, preparing to spurt; gracefully, Brandi slipped her mouth free and ducked out from his constraining hands. "No," she said throatily, her tongue still tasting his precome. "You *have* to fuck me. I mean, or else I'll die on the floor here crying."

"Didn't anyone ever tell you about playing hard to get?" said Ben.

In response, Brandi threw herself down on her back on the floor. Her hand went to her pussy and found the lush wetness there. With the first touch, her whole body felt a chill as her cunt spasmed. She looked up at Ben piteously.

He smiled, cradling his hard, gently curved cock in one hand while he stroked it with the other. His eyes were half lidded, languid. He said, "What if I just get myself off all over you?"

Brandi whimpered, spreading her thighs wider, pressing her hand almost viciously down to crush her singing clitoris. "No . . . not this time."

"This time?" Ben smiled. "When did I do it before?"

Brandi looked at him desperately, stroking her aching pussy faster and faster. "You can't tell me you didn't jerk off after that last time. You know you did."

Ben's jaw set. Then he was looking at Brandi's recumbent form, letting his eyes sweep up and down over her until his gaze came to rest on her open pussy. The narrow landing strip of blond fur she'd left unshaved there was glistening with damp, her pink lips were open to her playing fingers. "Goddammit," he said. Then he was on his knees, pulling her hand away to make room for his hungry cock. In a second he was thrusting into her angrily. She gasped and began to cry out, but his palm pressed over her mouth.

Then he was pounding her powerfully, his cock spearing her with a thousand precise gestures of lust. Brandi felt herself gathering and gathering to orgasm, each sweet stab of pleasure lifting her a notch. Her pussy was gripping his cock, getting tighter and wetter as her excitement mounted. Then Ben thrust into her hard, and his cock began to jerk, pouring come deep inside her. Brandi let herself come at the exact same moment, her screams of pleasure muffled in his strong hand. The room was spinning around; the world went black for a split second. Then Brandi was back, panting; Ben had taken his hand away from her mouth and she stared up into his green eyes with an irrepressible smile.

"Oh, sweet Jesus," she said. "The earth moved, all right."

Ben smiled. "I'll take that as a promise not to tell anyone."

Brandi shut one eye, considering. The devil on her left shoulder was whispering that she ought to secure a promise of sex—maybe every other day. But the angel on her other shoulder shook its head firmly. She owed Ben something for giving her such a wild, sweet ride at the moment when she needed it most. She sighed. The battle was going to the angels this time—damn them. "Well, I won't tell anyone, all right. But could you—if you want—ever see your way clear to doing it —"

Ben grinned. "Now, why did I see that coming?" He smiled and pressed his cock, still half hard, into her one final time. He said, "I'll see what I can do. But you have to help me out with Lila."

"Well, that goes without saying," Brandi said. "Just call me Cupid. After all, none of my mother's children was ever selfish."

"Just oversexed, sneaky, and unscrupulous in getting what they want?"

Brandi glared at him with as much dignity as she could muster with her hair mussed, lying on the floor in a mess of sex juices. "That," she said seriously, "is near as dammit our family motto."

Chapter Fourteen

Lila lay on her stomach on the sheepskin rug in front of the roaring fire. Her naked body was pleasantly overheated on one side, equally pleasantly cool on the other. On the gleaming hardwood floor in front of her she'd spread her sister's letter, and she was idly reading it while waiting for Jim and Andy to get their cameras and lights set up.

The fireplace surround was white marble, carved to show a pair of lovely nymphs embracing each other on either side of the fire. The mantelpiece was black marble, and on it lay a small bronze sculpture that suspiciously resembled Babylona. It lay on its back with its legs cunningly tucked up so that its rump was slightly raised in the air. On the walls were various paintings of naked men: asleep on a lawn, on horseback, intertwined with an equally ravishing naked girl. The arched windows all had their dark green velvet curtains tightly closed, and the firelight bathed the scene in a comforting, ever-flowing rosy glow.

This was Babylona's private office, which usually was used only on her visits to the school. But it was also the only private room that was big enough to accommodate the scene that Jim and Andy had written into their film project, a sci-fi epic with the working title *The Horny Alien Movie Thing*. This scene called for two maiden warrioresses to wrestle in the slime of a swamp planet (actually lime Jell-O) until surprised by a furious alien lizard creature, which has been summoned by Warrioress #1 to punish her archenemy; the alien, predictably, energetically has its way with Warrioress #2 before turning on his mistress and . . . etc. Lila had been cast in the role

of Warrioress #2 across from Carola, a slinky Guatemalan sophomore, and Andy himself as the Alien Swamp Thing. Right now he
was still buck naked, fiddling with equipment. He couldn't do much
of anything in his lizard costume, he'd said, except fuck.

Nick, a tall, absurdly good-looking guy with long black hair, who
was tragically (or so Brandi always said, and her voice would actually
crack with the tragedy of it) resolutely gay, paused to peer over Lila's
shoulder at the letter. "Anything good?" he said.

Lila looked up, half asleep from the heat of the fire and the
general well-being she was feeling. "My sister. She's the only person
I know who still writes letters. It's 'cause she likes to draw people
for me."

"That's sweet. That's *really* sweet." Nick booted Lila gently in the
butt.

Lila laughed and caught unsuccessfully at his foot with her hand.
"What's that for?"

"*That's* for having a cooler sister than me," Nick said. "My sister
joined the marines, and she tells everybody her brother died in a car
accident."

"She doesn't."

Nick sniffed. "Does. And you know if she would only tell the
truth . . ." Nick drifted off, staring into space blissfully. At last he
sighed. "Marines."

Lila said, "The Cannon Cockers."

"The what?"

"That's the Eleventh Marine Regiment. One of Brandi's girl-
friends was in it. I thought you'd appreciate that. *And* I thought all
girl marines were queer."

"She is, but that doesn't stop her being uptight as anything.
Queer's okay, but porn school is 'unworthy of me.' Cannon Cockers,
ouch. Now you're just breaking my heart." Nick shook his head and
went back to his chore, hauling huge Tupperware bowls of Jell-O up
from the kitchen and upending them onto a huge plastic drop cloth

on the floor. There were already several gallons of the green glistening stuff on the blue plastic, and the effect was distinctly gross—just a little bit too much like real alien swamp slime. Lila was perversely looking forward to getting it mushed up into her hair. It sounded like fun; like getting buried in the sand, or getting caught in the rain. She had always liked getting dirty.

Her sister had written:

> *Maybe you inspired me, Lila, because I've been sleeping around—in a modest, Bethany kind of way. I mean, I don't think I could ever really sleep with two people in one day. (I'm trying to say, you're brave. Not that I'm too good for that. Oh—never mind. I'm just going to trust you not to take things the wrong way.)*
>
> *Anyway, the main thing I have to trust you about is what happened with Tad. Your Tad.*

Here Lila caught her breath. She looked around the room, suddenly feeling exposed. But everyone was still occupied with other things: Now Carola had joined Jim in hauling Jell-O, while Andy was apparently trying to figure out which end of his lizard suit was up.

She read on:

> *I was waiting for my friend Joanna in that dive bar in town, when someone suddenly put his arm around me from behind. It was Tad. I was pretty cold to him, but he wouldn't take the hint. He sat down next to me and started talking about how he was doing, like I was interested. (He got into Yale. Final, conclusive, total proof that life isn't fair.) Anyway, to make a long story short, just as I was getting ready to go wait for Joanna in the parking lot, he said, "Hey, you know I always thought you were hot?" I wanted to pour my drink over his head.*
>
> *But I just said, "No, I didn't know, and I didn't want to know." Then Joanna came, and I got rid of him. But the moral of the story is, you were really lucky to get rid of him And*

"Lila!" Nick was standing in front of her with his hands on his hips.

Lila blinked at him, nervously crumpling the letter in her hand.

"Lila, I've been calling you and calling you," Nick said. "We're ready."

"Oh . . . sorry. I got distracted." Lila hurriedly tucked the letter in the bag with her clothes and hurried over to the Jell-O pit. Andy had spread drop cloths over all the surrounding furniture and set up a backdrop with an alien landscape crudely depicted in house paint. The painting featured a cactus forest against a red sky with a green moon. Or so Andy said; from the painting you would never guess. The competing smells of Jell-O and house paint cheered Lila up somehow. She always seemed to be doing something cheerfully silly at Babylona; it was hard to stay in a bad mood. Especially when the silliness turned obscene, as it would again within not very many minutes. And she found that in the warm, opulent room, preparing for a naked Jell-O fight/fuck, any interest she might have had in Tad's future, character, or sexual exploits was so tiny and distant that the idea of him going to Yale and hitting on her sister felt cheerfully silly, too. She *was* lucky to get rid of him. And it all seemed so long ago that it was like remembering something embarrassing she'd done in primary school.

"Okay!" Nick said. "Take your places, girls!"

"Where's Andy?" Carola asked.

"Here!" Andy called from behind the backdrop. "I'll be out when the time comes."

"I want to see what I'm fucking!" Carola whined. She tossed her long black hair petulantly.

"You just want to laugh at me," Andy diagnosed.

"Well, duh!" Carola and Lila laughed.

"Come on, take your places. We have to get out of here in a timely fashion," Jim said. "That means, before we get caught. And *don't splash.*"

Carola and Lila ventured gingerly onto the plain of Jell-O. Their feet slipped treacherously with every step. Carola whispered, "We've got to do a controlled fall, first off. I don't want to go down hard."

"Agreed," said Lila.

"Okay—action!"

Lila and Carola crouched down, sneering at each other.

"So it is you—you who killed my lover!" Carola cried. "Prepare to be punished!"

"Ha-ha! You are the one who will taste my wrath!" Lila snarled.

Then they leaped on each other, wrestling frenetically. Carola pulled Lila off to the right, and they fell in a not-entirely-controlled way, causing chunks of Jell-O to fly in every direction. Then they did their planned roll, wrestling from one side of the plastic to the other until their naked bodies were both coated with shiny green goo.

In no time they were both grappling all over each other's bodies, the slickness of Jell-O making every contact obscene. Lila felt Carola's hands slipping over her butt; their breasts slid over each other. Then they began to kiss—the script called for them to be overcome by sexual desire in the midst of their fighting. The grappling turned into groping. Lila felt one Jell-O-ey hand probing between her legs, while another toyed with her nipple. All the time, she was aware of the film rolling, capturing the entire filthy, ridiculous scene.

With a graceful slither, Carola flipped around and buried her slippery head between Lila's thighs. She gripped Lila's buttocks and began to lap hungrily at Lila's pussy.

"Rrrrrr!" Andy leaped out from behind the backdrop. Both girls froze and stared.

Then they burst into helpless giggles.

There was nothing wrong with the costume. It was actually bizarrely convincing—a straightforward *Creature from the Black Lagoon* outfit. But a hole had been cut out where the crotch was, and from the center of the lizard-man costume protruded a fat red hard-on.

Lila laughed so hard tears ran down her face, clutching Carola's slippery thighs. Nick was gesturing at them madly to carry on. Andy stalked forward, menacing with his claws. At the first step onto the Jell-O surface, though, he slipped and fell headlong, landing on top of Lila and Carola in a rubbery heap. He managed to pull himself to one side and caught both girls in a rough embrace, pressing his hard-on blindly against slippery flesh.

Carola had begun to get control of her laughter; her tongue again probed Lila's cunt expertly. Lila caught her breath and found Andy's lizard head staring at her from between Carola's thighs. And suddenly a strange idea flashed through her head. What if the whole scenario was real? What if she were *in fact* about to be sexually abused by a lizard creature from the planet Zog?

The funniest thing yet was—the idea turned her on! And what turned her on still more, improbably, was the idea that the entire scene would be captured on camera. But hey, why couldn't they have home video on the planet Zog? No reason at all.

While one hand dutifully continued to play with Carola's pussy, using the Jell-O as a lubricant to tease her swelling clit—Lila's other hand sought out the giant lizard's penis. It was fat and still impressively hard, with a first drop of precome at its smooth tip. With the Jell-O all over her, her hand slipped deliciously up and down his hard dick. She tightened her grip, taking advantage of the lubrication to apply pressure. The lizard growled with appreciation.

At Nick's hand signal, Carola slipped out from in between Lila and Andy, saying, "Now, my lizard minion will take his pleasure of you, she-bitch!"

And the lizard pinned her to the Jell-O-ey plastic, plunging his huge dick deep inside her. For a moment, Lila shut out the unmistakable sight of the chandelier overhead, the velvet curtains—all the evidence that she was *not* on planet Zog and this was *not* a real alien lizard rapist. She lay back with a creeping feeling of horror, shame, and delight as the alien creature violated her. The sheer size of Andy's dick did its usual work, making her feel overwhelmed and stretched dizzyingly open. As he thrust into her, the slippery rubber slapped against her inner thighs, and against her clitoris, which tingled at the unfamiliar sensation. She began to come almost instantly, and Andy groaned in a very unlizardlike fashion as he felt the gripping spasms of her climax. Lila let herself go and shrieked with the pleasure. Her orgasm peaked and then came back to the rhythm of Andy's increasingly frenzied thrusts. Then Andy was coming, his cock buried deep inside her, his hips still shoving forward, deeper, deeper, as he moaned in ecstasy.

Then suddenly the door was flung open and a hysterical voice cried out, "Oh my God! No! No!"

Lila opened her eyes and saw Anna standing in the doorway with both hands pressed to her mouth.

There was a moment of shocked silence. Then Nick said, "Um, it's not real."

"Goddammit, I know it's not real, asshole!" said Anna. "What's real is, Babylona's just downstairs and she's *on her way up!*"

"Oh, no!" cried Nick, Carola, Lila, and Andy.

"Oh, yes," said Anna.

"Shit shit shit shit shit!" said Nick. "Oh, God, well, I guess we've got to try. Guys! Up!" He began frantically to roll up drop cloths. "And—nice take!"

Carola ran to the backdrop; Anna began to help with the drop cloths.

Andy shook his lizard head and said, "Oh, well. Might as well be hung for a sheep as a lamb."

"What?"

"I think I can fuck you again."

"Andy, we've got to get up." But Lila's head was already back in Zog, where her alien, bestial ravisher was capable of fucking for hours! Hours at a time! Her hips tilted up eagerly, and she felt Andy's cock respond, jerking inside her.

"Yes, you've got to get up," said Nick. "What are you doing there? Come on, people!"

"Oh, okay," said Andy. "Damn."

But then the door flew open again. Everyone froze for a second time.

There in the doorway stood Babylona. She cocked her head to one side and scowled, taking in the whole scene: the Jell-O, the half-rolled drop cloths, the crudely painted alien landscape, and finally, the Jell-O-smothered girl in flagrante with the *Creature from the Black Lagoon.*

"Well," she said. "I can't wait to hear your excuses."

"Ma'am," Nick said stoutly, "the fact is, this is our homework."

Chapter Fifteen

It turned out Babylona wasn't even angry. Once they'd cleaned up the mess and shown that no damage had been done (though there was an anxious moment when Lila discovered a glob of Jell-O clinging to the painting of the naked horseman—luckily it came off the man's face without leaving a stain)—Babylona decided the episode could be considered concluded with no harm done.

"I like your ingenuity," she drawled as she closely observed Andy struggling out of his lizard costume. "Though I don't get where the abstract art fits in," she added, gesturing at the backdrop.

Lila and Carola ended up taking their clothes in plastic bags and dashing across the lawn naked, smeared green. It had snowed for the first time the night before, and by the time Lila burst into her dorm, her teeth were chattering. While she was in the shower, gradually washing the Jell-O and the cold off herself, she heard Anna come in. Immediately she realized that she was still horny. There was something about being walked in on by Babylona that had made her hot all over again.

"Anna!" she called. "Want to come shower?" Her voice sounded absurdly, childishly hopeful. She heard Anna's wild peal of laughter in response, and added sheepishly, "I mean, if you want to. If you need a shower. I mean—"

Anna appeared in the bathroom, busily shedding her clothes. "I think I heard a cry for help."

In a few seconds, she was in the shower, busily soaping Lila's breasts. Lila reciprocated, and her fingers instantly found Anna's cleft. One part of her watched what she was doing, quietly amazed that this already felt like second nature. Her whole body was ready for sex, again and again, and it took only the slightest cues to get her into the flow of it, the ballet of pleasure.

The bathrooms at Babylona were ideally suited for this purpose; the baths were a good six feet long, with two different showerheads and a variety of curious ledges and even a post coming out of one wall that Anna swore was meant as a dildo. (Lila had tried it, fore and aft, but had ended up supposing that it was meant only for girls who were six feet tall. Or it was a washcloth hook. One or the other.)

Anna's pussy was already wet, and Lila worked the moisture up around her clit, running two fingers back and forth over the hot little nub rapidly, the fingertips crisscrossing over each other until Anna gasped and let go of Lila's tits to brace herself against the shower wall. "God, girl," Anna said. "You got yourself some technique."

Lila moved forward and pressed her soapy breasts up against Anna's, deliciously crushing their two chests together. She tilted her hips forward and let her mound press against Anna's, and her busy hand in between the two. She grouped together three fingers and thrust them into Anna's vagina, feeling the contractions already beginning inside there. Then she began to slide down, pausing to suck Anna's nipples, going from one to the other to the rhythm of her fucking hand. In a minute she was on her knees, licking Anna's pussy energetically. And in another minute, Anna had grabbed two wet handfuls of Lila's long black hair and was coming, her knees trembling as she cried out.

Anna slowly pulled away and slid down into the bottom of the tub with Lila, smiling dreamily. Then she was pressing Lila down, forcing her onto her back, so she was lying in the inch of warm streaming water in the tub. For a minute Anna just lay on top of her and kissed her, Anna's muscular body squirming against Lila's softer form. Then Anna reached over the edge of the bath and produced an already buzzing vibrator. "Don't worry," she said. "It's waterproof." It was an elaborate model with a little spur for anal stimulation, and a curved, ribbed body that was just slightly bigger than any penis in real life.

"I wasn't—ooh," Lila said. And her train of thought fell apart as Anna thrust the vibrator into her, twisting it slightly with the movement so that Lila's pussy felt a hundred different wonderful things at once. Anna fucked it in and out of her gently, all the while squeezing Lila's breasts and licking her hard nipples. Then she thrust it all the way in, hooking the spur into Lila's tender asshole, and dove down to attend to her clitoris.

Anna's expert tongue was soon making Lila squirm. The rushing water and the waves of pleasure coming from the vibrator were like an ocean of feeling; on top of it was the intense, close thrill of Anna's mouth, sucking, teasing, and tickling her clitoris. Soon Lila had exploded into a fierce orgasm, her cunt clutching at the unyielding surface of the vibrator. Then she had to pull it out as the post-orgasm sensitivity turned to oversensitivity. Anna laughed at her haste and said, "Lightweight."

Lila frowned. "Am not!"

"Come on, I was only teasing you. Let's get you washed up for real and crack a bottle of wine. I've got some news."

Anna and Lila went down to the main restaurant, the Odalisque, wearing their college bathrobes: fluffy, hypersoft robes with the school's initials, BI, embroidered on the lapel. Of course, there were always jokes about how descriptive that word was of most of the students on campus.

They got their usual postsex meal of a triple order of french fries and settled down on the big sofa nearest to the heater. Only then did Anna begin to tell Lila what was going on.

"Two words: Babylona TV." Anna looked at Lila significantly.

"Oh. For real?"

"Launching next year. With, like, ninety percent original content. A porn channel with a difference."

"What difference?" Lila smiled. "I mean, I'm sure it would be great and all that, but film of people—"

"The difference is that we get in on the ground floor and become international sex stars!" Anna crossed her arms. "I mean, what other difference could there be?"

"Oh. Yes, I guess that's different. If you're us."

"And you are," Anna said.

"Technically I'm only half of us."

"Well, all for one and one for all." Anna pointed at Lila with a french fry. "If we play our cards right, this could be the beginning of great things. All we have to do is convince Babylona to hire us. Then we move out to Los Angeles—it's in Los Angeles—get a little house on the beach. Then get a big house on the beach. Then get—I don't know—a lighthouse on the beach."

Lila looked skeptical. "I'm sure if she's starting a TV channel, she can hire all the most famous porn stars in the business. She doesn't have to hire us."

"But we're young, we're beautiful, and we're her kids. She's hiring Ben."

"She's—what do you mean?" Lila froze with a french fry halfway to her mouth.

"You know Ben in Advising? He's going to be her recruitment consultant or something. Now, that's a casting couch I want to try out."

"So . . . Ben's leaving? But we're not even graduated yet! I'm only a freshman."

"That doesn't matter. That's what Babylona came to visit for; she's secretly auditioning people. Listen, I only know this because her driver told me." Anna shrugged.

Lila sat for a moment with the french fry in her hand, trying to process it all. The only thing that she could really concentrate on was the fact that Ben was leaving. Getting a job on TV, leaving Babylona, none of that seemed real to her. Ben leaving, though—mingled with the not-entirely-pleasant idea of the casting couch he was going to be running—felt all too real. Not that it ought to matter to her. The truth was she hardly knew him. She couldn't be in love with him, anyway, because she was a sex professional, and that wasn't professional. Not that she would *never* fall in love again, but not with someone who was going to have a casting couch, because she couldn't. And anyway, she wasn't over Tad. Or she might be, because she hadn't even finished reading her sister's letter and . . .

"Oh, I'm so screwed up," Lila said finally. "I don't know what I want to do."

"Hold on. Where did that come from?"

Lila sighed. She couldn't tell anyone about her . . . whatever it was . . . with Ben. So she quickly told Anna about the information in her sister's letter about her ex-fiancé. She wrapped up with: "I mean, I don't think I could have gotten into Yale. But I could have gone to . . . I don't know. The University of Massachusetts, something like that. I could have been a lawyer or a doctor."

"Oh, spare me," said Anna. "For one thing, the very thought of it is plain embarrassing. If you were a doctor, all your patients would be stalking you. You're about five times too sexy to live in the real world. Just get over yourself. I could pass as a normal person 'cause I don't have the body of Lara Croft, like you. But that's *if* I had any interest in doing that, which brings us to point two. Which is that in our world, all we do all day long is have amazing sex, and then rest so that we have enough energy to work up to ecstasy again. And we have a warm, loving community of like minds, friends that will last for the rest of our lives and—oh, did I mention the ecstasy? What if you *couldn't* stay? What if you had gotten thrown out for your little escapade in Babylona's office?"

"Well." Lila did feel an inner shrinking at the idea. "But now I'm ruined. I'll never be able to live in the outside world again."

"Oh, come on. I don't really have to start all over again, do I? You're like a princess whining that you'll never be able to be a real maid. Plus, you're going to make me think you don't love me."

"That's just crazy talk."

"Well, then. Think about this. If we *don't* get jobs at Babylona's TV station, we'll have to go back into the real world when we graduate. Oh, we could get jobs in the porn industry or something. But it would never be like this. I mean, honestly, this could be our last chance to avoid the real world *forever!*"

Lila laughed. At last she put the french fry in her mouth. It was delicious; exactly the right crispiness, exactly the right amount of salt, not too greasy. And she realized she had come to take it for granted that everything would be like that. The robe would always be luxuriously soft, the sofa would always be soft and big enough for two people to lounge on. In the real world, though, she would have to *pay* for her sofa.

She gulped. Anna had a definite point.

"Okay. What do we do?"

Chapter Sixteen

When they were finished planning, Anna went straight out to try to recruit men for the effort. Lila had been sent back to the dorm to recuperate after what Anna persisted in calling her "nervous breakdown."

"I don't want you to strain yourself after all that insanity about law school," said Anna. "I prescribe that you go home and read *A Life on All Fours* in a hot bubble bath. And don't come out until the thought of law school inspires a healthy fear."

So Lila was hurrying across the parking lot, huddled against the cold, cursing herself for not having worn a coat, when she saw Ben. He had stopped in the act of opening his car door, staring straight at her.

Suddenly she forgot the cold completely. Straightening her back, she walked on more slowly, trying to decide what she should do.

She should wave and go straight past him back to her room.

She should pretend not to have seen him and go straight past him back to her room.

She should go up to him, engage him in conversation, get into his car with him, and spend the night making love.

She veered sharply and started to walk directly to Ben. Her face melted into a smile that she was sure looked completely goofy. But a second later Ben began to smile goofily, too. So by the time she walked up to him, her resistance was completely gone, and she said, breathless, "Hi. Could you take me for a ride?"

"Where do you need to go?" His voice sounded desperately casual, and he smoothed his hair with one hand self-consciously.

"Oh, I don't know. I mean, I don't need to go anywhere. It's just . . ."

"Oh. Of course." Ben smiled a little awkwardly. "That would be . . . great. It's unlocked." Then, while she got in, she noticed him looking around to check whether anyone could see them. It gave her a little thrill that—for a change—wasn't sexual. What it was was purely romantic. Ben was taking a risk for her. All of her suspicions and fears about him disappeared; now that she had been at Babylona for a while, she understood him better. It had always been crazy to think he would take advantage of her innocence. A Babylona graduate was well beyond having to take advantage of anyone's innocence.

As they drove out, snow began to fall. For a long time, neither of them spoke, and she just watched him drive, admiring his beautiful profile and the swell of his bicep as he turned the wheel. Today she was noticing his thick black eyelashes and the way they set off his eyes. He had the kind of good looks that came partly from the character that showed in his expression—a combination of sensitivity and confidence that was the most attractive thing about him. Lila felt uncannily blissful shut away with him in the warm car.

All she wanted to do was run her hands over him as he drove. In her mind, she could already feel the smooth skin; she could imagine how his lips would meet hers. The landscape outside passed, white and hushed; the heater blowing against her bare leg was soothing her into a drowsy quiescence. It was seductively, wonderfully, like being his girlfriend, driving home from work together at the end of a long day. And somehow being close to him in this ordinary way was sexier than any of the energetic sex she had been through today.

Finally he cleared his throat and said, "I've missed you. I mean, I haven't seen you in a while." His voice was soft but rough, as if he were struggling with some passion she couldn't interpret.

"I *wanted* to see you," she said.

"I know. I wanted to see you, too."

Then they both fell silent again, but now it was a fraught silence. Lila was staring at Ben——the stubble on his cheeks was especially driving her crazy. All she wanted was to stroke it, feel the roughness of it against her palm. Then to feel the muscles in his neck, in his chest . . .

He said, "So how are you doing now at Babylona?" There was something strange in the way he said it; he sounded almost wary.

Taken aback by his tone, she answered cautiously, politely. "I'm doing great now. I mean, I feel much better. You were a big help, too."

"You're not scared about anything anymore?"

"No, I guess I decided I didn't have to be scared."

They drove a little longer in silence. Lila was trying to read his expression, but there was nothing on his face except tension, and what might have been a wounded look in his eyes. Finally he said, "I guess in some ways I liked it better when you were scared."

"You did?" Lila swallowed. "How come?"

"I don't know. I guess the thought of you comfortably having sex with dozens of men makes *me* scared." He smiled at her for a second. "I know that's not very sensible."

"Well," Lila said, her heart pounding. "I think it's nice. I mean, it's nice for me because the thought of you having sex with dozens of girls has been driving me crazy since I first met you."

Ben laughed. "But the difference is that I haven't been doing it. So it's only a thought."

Lila sat back into the car upholstery, which now felt like the most comfortable thing in the world. She had to sit and breathe for a moment, digesting the heavenly news that Ben was only sleeping with her. Then she said, a little giddily, "Well, even for me, dozens . . . It's more like threes, maybe."

"How many threes?"

They both laughed, and Lila said, "Well, maybe two threes at this point."

Ben sighed. "I guess that's not bad at all, considering." He was pulling into a parking lot, and Lila's head started to spin again at the realization that this must be the parking lot of his apartment building. Meaning that he was taking her to his apartment! And everything he'd been saying, everything about his manner, suggested that he was thinking of her not just as a casual fling, but as a girlfriend, or at least a potential girlfriend.

But then she remembered. "But you're leaving! You're leaving the institute."

"No, Lila. I've already left."

She was dumbstruck. He parked the car while she went over it all in her head as best she could. She wasn't going to be his girlfriend. She was going back to school, and he was going to California. No matter what Anna said, she would never get hired by the TV station. (Now that it was important to her, it was obvious she'd never get that job.) And the only reason he had brought her here was that he wanted to screw her again, now that it didn't threaten his job. And once he'd done that, it would be good-bye for good.

She carefully didn't look at him as she got out of the car. Somehow she knew that seeing his intensely handsome face again would be too painful. She tried to tell herself that he'd as good as confessed to being jealous, but it didn't help at all. So what if he was jealous? There was a huge, yawning gap between being jealous and being there. He wasn't going to be there for her—he was going to be on some casting couch somewhere drowning his jealousy in the pussies of a series of eager wannabe porn stars.

But then Ben had come around the car and before she knew it, his arms were around her. He held her close, tenderly, and pressed his lips to the top of her head, his warm breath stirring her hair blissfully. Then he kissed her hair, her ear, her cheek; his hands came around to her face and he was tilting her head back and kissing her on the lips.

Again, Lila's heart began to pound out of control. She went hot and cold as their mouths joined. His kiss was like a downpour of love, of passion, of everything she'd imagined he could give her. Her arms went around him and they kissed seemingly forever, while somewhere very far away snow continued to fall, tiny sharp flakes that faintly stung on her bare hands and forehead.

At last he pulled back and said in a hoarse voice that broke with desire, "Come inside. Sweet Lila."

She said, "Yes. Please, yes."

As soon as she got into the apartment building, she realized that this was a further outpost of Babylona's empire. Again, all the furnishings were opulent and tasteful, down to the art-deco light fixtures and the framed prints on the walls. But she had only a moment to notice this before he had pulled her onto the couch and was kissing her again.

They were lying on their sides together on the couch, facing each other, and Lila let her hands run all over Ben's body, feeling shocked at how much she had missed the feeling of him against her. Every inch of his body felt right to her; it was like having a cool drink after being thirsty for a long time. And when he pulled her robe open and his hot palm ran up her belly to cup her breast, she shut her eyes tight with the pleasure of it. He murmured into her ear, "I've never felt like this about anyone before, Lila. There's something about you, or something about us."

"I know," she said, and her body relaxed into him even more. She opened her eyes, and his face struck her keenly; the green eyes seemed alight with a painful need. She said, "I can't stand it that you're leaving."

Then he smiled. "But it's your fault, Lila."

"How? That's ridiculous." Then she stiffened in shock. "You mean, someone found out?"

"No, no. No one found out. But if I hadn't left, I wouldn't be able to be with you right now."

Lila relaxed again, and as she did, his hand began to move on her breast again, squeezing it, and Ben's hips moved forward instinctively; Lila's moved instinctively to match their force. Both of them moaned, and then they were kissing again while Lila feverishly unbuttoned Ben's shirt, rushing to feel his hot smooth skin again, the muscles over his chest and stomach. She could already feel his cock stiff against her thigh, and her whole body sang with the thrill of really being here, alone with him. They could take all the time they wanted. She could stay all night, and fuck him over and over again, taste every inch of his body.

He pulled the robe off her shoulders, and ducked down to her breasts, sucking hard on her nipples and then releasing them so that his gentle tongue could flick them teasingly. The sensation seemed to spread over her skin in waves, and her pussy responded, her clit stiffening, feeling as if it was concentrating into a point of sensuous need as he continued to suck on her breasts hungrily, his mouth moving now from one to the other, again and again.

Then he was pulling his pants off, taking the underpants off with them so that she could feel his naked cock pressing into her belly, hard and hot. She whimpered with delight and for a moment she was satisfied with pressing her body against his fully nude body; the pressure of her breasts against his chest and the digging of his long dick into her soft belly made her shiver with contentment. But then he was pulling her thigh over him, pressing in between her legs urgently. His dick began to test her opening, probing gently at the wetness there, forward and back. Ben's eyes were shut tight, and she felt him concentrating on the moment, prolonging the act of penetration as long as possible, savoring it.

At last he slowly, deliberately, sank his cock into her pussy, letting it move into her impossibly slowly so she felt it spreading her, opening her. She shut her eyes against the groundswell of feeling, and even though she'd had him inside her before, the pleasure of it struck her as incredible; she wanted to scream, or faint, or fight him—it was too much to feel all at once.

He rolled on top of her, in that gesture sinking his cock all the way home. She cried out and opened her eyes again, reaching for his face. But she was startled to see that his face was angry. In a rough whisper, he said, "You've already fucked someone else today, haven't you?"

She stared at him, her mind still confused by the incredible feeling in her pussy. She couldn't even remember whether she'd fucked anyone—what did it matter? At last she just said, "I'm sorry. I didn't know I'd see you."

"Of course you didn't know," he said fiercely. And then he was fucking her, but this time violently, angrily, tearing into her with all the force of his fury. He was pounding into her so hard that she couldn't move, she almost couldn't breathe. Her body felt completely overwhelmed; it was as if he'd coaxed her out to a point of complete vulnerability and then attacked her. She wanted to cry out, to tell him to stop. But at the same time it was the best feeling she'd ever had. Her mind went black; she was barely aware of herself stroking his back, holding on to him as if she were trying to prevent herself from being swept away completely. She came, and for the first time ever, she screamed as the climax hit. Then Ben was coming, too, crushing her to his chest so hard her breasts hurt deliciously; the aching intensity of the pleasure in her cunt was all mixed up with the pain. As the feeling subsided, she realized she was crying freely, tears flowing down both cheeks as she clung to him.

"Lila," he murmured. "Lila, I'm sorry. I'm so sorry." His eyes were wet, too, and he kissed her gently.

"No," she said. "Don't be sorry. I understand. I know what it's like."

They lay like that for a long time, his dick still half hard inside her, and talked about all the things they'd been through since they last saw each other. It was the strangest conversation Lila had ever had, because they were talking as if they were boyfriend and girlfriend of years' standing who'd just been apart for a few weeks, as if they were just catching up. Everything was understood between them; everything seemed completely simple and natural. And all the time, she was aware that this was the first conversation they'd ever had that lasted for more than a few minutes.

She told him about how she'd felt when she first found out that fucking her had been against the rules, about all her doubts and worries. When she talked about the other men she'd been with, and what it had been like, he gritted his teeth, but nodded at her to go on. He smiled when she told him about Mr. Banks, and his remarks about misery and jealousy, commenting, "Well, at least it's not just me who's completely unreasonable on that count."

Ben, in turn, told Lila about how he'd thought about her constantly ever since the first time she'd come into his office; how he'd *wanted* to feel guilty about having sex with her, but he'd found that whenever he thought about it, he just felt wonderful. He kept expecting her to come back. Every time someone came to his door, his heart leaped, and he had to restrain himself from being cross with whatever disappointing not-Lila person was there. Then she *had* come back, and he'd realized that his feelings weren't just a pleasant crush. They were something beyond his control, something that would make him break all the rules without even thinking about it.

"I love the institute," he said. "I've always been happy there; I think there's something about it that draws really sweet, exceptional people. But hey, if I had to give it up to sleep with you—absolutely no problem making that decision." And as he said that, his penis began to thicken again.

Lila whimpered and tipped her hips forward to take him deeper. She said, "I would make the same decision. Absolutely."

At first he was just moving his cock inside her, shifting it from side to side as he thrusted, as if he were trying to study every fold of her. But then his desire seemed to take hold of him and again he was fucking her, reawakening the sensations of before. But now Lila felt as if the desire she felt for him had settled deep, deep within her, as if he were calling sensation out of her bones and her heart. She moved with him without thinking; it seemed to her as if fucking him were more natural than not fucking him.

Just as she began to feel a new orgasm building, he pulled out of her, saying, "This time I want to lick you." He kissed his way down her breasts and her belly, then moved to kneel on the floor beside the couch and began to kiss and lick her inner thighs, making her squirm.

"No fair," she said. "I want to suck you."

"No, you got to last time," he said, before addressing himself to her pussy itself.

Then she was too absorbed by what he was doing to protest anymore. At first he was concentrating on her clit, toying with the soft little nub in a thousand subtly different ways; she could swear it felt better than any oral sex she had ever had. It wasn't just the expertise—though she did have the fleeting thought that the extra few years of college had made a difference—but the fact that with every slight pressure, lick, or kiss, he seemed to be expressing the real tenderness he had for her, in the same way he might if he were kissing her on the mouth. Lila melted under it, and by the time he began to lick her more aggressively, sinking his tongue into her pussy and letting his fingers play over her clitoris along with his tongue, she was in an almost dreamlike state of passive experience, following the passing changes in sensation as if she were watching beautiful colors flow over a screen. When she came, it seemed like just another color at first. But then it intensified and continued—and still continued. And while she began to gasp at the way it continued and continued to grow, Ben was lying on top of her again, and while his fingers continued to play over her clit, slipping back and forth too fast to follow, his cock was inside her, riding the last waves of the most incredible orgasm she had ever had. He came almost instantly, too, and once more she felt the luscious wetness of their mingled juices dripping from her as they held each other and waited for reality to reassert itself.

At last Lila kissed his cheek reverently and when she opened her eyes, his sleepy smile greeted her. She said, "Can I sleep here?"

Ben laughed. "Well, that would be the best thing that ever happened to me. So I guess that's yes."

Chapter Seventeen

L ila arrived late for Groups and Growth, having been dropped off by Ben after a prolonged and steamy good-bye. After a night in which they'd woken up twice to make love again, and a morning in which they couldn't stop having sex long enough to eat breakfast, she was feeling weak, ethereal, and weirdly blissful, as if the sex had converted her entirely into a spiritual essence. However, it wasn't clear how a spirit could be quite so sore.

At some point they'd found time to talk for hours. They'd agreed that they were both inclined to be jealous, and that it was ridiculous to be jealous, and that they weren't going to stop being jealous, but that it was ridiculous . . . and, the bottom line was, Ben didn't want Lila to quit the institute any more than Lila wanted to quit. Meanwhile, though Ben was going to be working in California in just a few months, he wouldn't be there full time. He was actually going to be spending half his time at the institute still. But while he was away . . . well, it didn't make sense for Lila to expect him to be faithful when he knew she was sleeping with different men every day. On the other hand, that immediately made her blind with furious jealousy. But that was ridiculous.

In short, they had taken a long time getting back to what Mr. Banks had told Lila at the Halloween party: No matter what they did, they were going to be miserable half of the time.

Once Lila had pointed that out, they both laughed and relaxed a little bit. It turned out that if you said to yourself, "I'm just going to be miserable, and there's nothing I can do," you felt a lot better immediately.

*   *   *

When Lila arrived at the Attahoosa Lounge, she was already ten minutes late, and she was surprised to find that Mr. Banks wasn't there, and the Groups and Growth class was scattered around the room, arguing and laughing and very obviously not working. Andy saw her come in and waved her over with a big grin.

"What's up?" she said, smoothing down her hair and wondering if it was obvious what she'd been doing. Of course her worry was ridiculous. Everyone else had been doing exactly the same thing every night . . . but this seemed so different.

Andy grinned. "Mr. Banks has gone AWOL and left us with a field trip."

"A field trip?"

Ginny joined them. "Yeah, it happens whenever Babylona's here. Banks dumps all his classes, and we go on a field trip. Out in the normal world."

They all three looked at the window and shuddered slightly.

Lila said, "Wow. So that means we're supposed to do something with—"

"Civilians," said Andy.

"Well, but *how many* civilians?" Lila said. "And what if one of them hurts us?"

"Don't worry," said Ginny with her usual know-it-all air. "We go out in twos and threes and find some poor innocent waiting to be corrupted."

"Over eighteen," Andy put in.

"Sure, over eighteen," Ginny said. "Come on."

"Can't be an animal," Andy added.

"Now you're just trying to annoy me." Ginny made a face at him.

"Hey," Andy said. "If it could be an animal, that would be pretty easy. Just molest somebody's Labrador, and back to base."

Ginny rolled her eyes. "I'll take human, thanks."

"Well, if you go out in threes, though," Lila said, "does that mean—I mean, if we three go out, and you two screw someone in front of me, can I get credit?"

"You guys are such lightweights," Ginny said. "No way."

"No," said Andy. "But what I want to know is what Mr. Banks is doing right now."

He and Ginny began to make up stories about the interplay between Mr. Banks and Babylona, piling on hyperbole. At that moment, Ginny proposed, Babylona was staggering around in a state of total amnesia brought on by the mind-blowing fuck Banks had given her. Andy's rival hypothesis was that the two had unwittingly levitated and now did not know how to get down.

Lila stared at them, glassy-eyed, smiling vaguely. The thought of having sex with a random pedestrian was not working for her on any level. She was busily forming an excuse—a sudden flu possibly, or a fainting spell—when Brandi suddenly wrapped her arms around Lila from behind, hugging her fiercely and half lifting her off the ground.

"Hey!" Lila protested, giggling and struggling.

After a brief tussle, Brandi let go and Lila whirled around to confront her. "Hey! What was that?"

"Not much," said Brandi. "Except that I found the best vacation package in the history of dirty vacation packages and I need a dirty vacation partner. So . . . who better?"

Lila looked dubious. "I don't know. A guy, maybe?"

"No." Brandi shook her head authoritatively. "If I take a guy, that cuts down on the number of new guys I can screw. It's just not economical. If I take you . . ." Brandi spread her hands, and said, "QED. Christmas, sweetie, in the Virgin Islands. It's cheap, it's paradise, and it's a new resort for sexually liberated eighteen- to thirty-year-olds. Now *there's* an offer you can't refuse!"

"Except, I'm going to have to refuse," said Lila. In fact, all she could think of while Brandi was talking was the kind of Christmas she might spend with Ben. She shook her head happily, "It sounds great, but I just can't."

"Can't? Don't you mean, must? Don't you mean, thank you, Brandi, for offering me the mother of all sex holidays?"

"Sorry."

"Goddammit!" Brandi said. "You'll come to your senses! What's wrong with everybody in the world except me?"

Andy shrugged. "I don't know, but we'd better get going. I have to be back by seven to do party decorations for Babylona's reception. *If* she ever emerges from Mr. Banks' bed again, of course."

"What I don't get," said Ginny, "is what the big deal is about that woman. She's not all that good-looking—"

Brandi, Lila, and Andy said in scandalized unison, "Ginny!"

"That's all I'm listening to," said Brandi haughtily. "I'll see you later. I'm going to go wash my ears out with soap."

They watched her huff off, a little awkwardly on spindly high heels. Lila was laughing, and Ginny was looking contrite. She muttered under her breath, "Just an opinion . . ."

"Okay, girls," Andy said. "Now, before we lose anyone else—you want to come in my car?"

The Lindstrom Mall was crowded at midday with early Christmas shoppers. Children threw tantrums; teenagers lurked in packs, sullen or giggling; adults trudged from store to store with multiple shopping bags in each hand. Meanwhile, Andy, Lila, and Ginny drew stares wherever they went. Lila was wearing her usual low-cut sweater, with her nipples carefully *not* exposed, and Ginny was wearing a see-through shirt over a see-through bra. Both girls wore miniskirts without panties, in this case a practical precaution. Speed might well be of the essence. Andy was dressed fairly normally, in jeans and a T-shirt—but his ostentatiously perfect body, with the massive NFL shoulders, nonetheless made teenaged girls stare and whisper among themselves. After Babylona, where they blended in, it was something of an ego boost, and at first Lila and Ginny had congratulated Andy on his choice of venue. Surely with all this attention, they would score in no time. Piece of cake!

The next thing they knew, they had wasted an hour shopping. Somehow it had just happened; Ginny picked up a little electronic dog that wagged its tail and barked the words "I like you!" and an hour later they came to their senses, each a few hundred dollars poorer, with multiple bags. Then Andy insisted that they go into Harway's, a clothing store for elderly rich ladies, to make sure the shopping fever didn't strike again.

Of course there was a down side to that. Ginny was now standing by a rack of muumuus, disconsolately scanning the shoppers. In an undertone, she said, "Some grandmother is going to have an afternoon to remember."

Lila whispered, "Is that so terrible? We'll be old, too, someday."

"Aargh," Ginny said. "Yes, it is so terrible. Someday will be soon enough."

"I don't see what's wrong with it," Andy said high-mindedly. "I think you're just being shallow. We could learn something really worthwhile from—"

"Wait! Look! At ten o'clock!" Ginny said excitedly. She was pointing brazenly, and the object of her attention, a teenaged stock boy with a heap of coats over one arm, was squinting at her in alarm, apparently worried he was being laughed at. He was the image of a skateboard kid, with long floppy hair and a profoundly desultory air as he hooked coats onto an already overstuffed circular rack. Lila acknowledged to herself that screwing him was immediately appealing; he was exactly the kind of stoner kid she'd had crushes on all through high school.

"Not bad." Andy nodded. "Follow him into the back room. No need to drag him out to the car."

"Yes, yes, yes," said Ginny. "And he'll have sex with all of us at once. We'll be in and out in twenty minutes."

"How do you figure?" Andy said skeptically. "He's going to do what with me?"

"By the time me and Lila get started, he'll have sex with a telephone pole, and thank us for it," said Ginny. "Now, come on! Follow my lead!"

Andy and Lila trailed behind her, trying to look nonchalant. Ginny, however, marched straight up to the boy and said, "Excuse me—me and my friends had a bet. Are you eighteen?"

"I'm nineteen," the guy said uncertainly. His eyes strayed to Lila's chest, and then skittered away guiltily, only to find Ginny's chest, and skitter away guiltily again.

"Wow," Ginny purred. "You look older." She put her hand to his cheek and stroked gently, feeling the stubble on his face. "And you're just my type."

Lila and Andy exchanged glances. Andy surreptitiously mouthed the word "Barf."

But the guy was in seventh heaven. He stared at Ginny as if he were seeing a vision of paradise. She reached down and took his name tag gently in her hand. "Hi, Jared," she said, letting her eyes half close. "Have you got a minute free to help me with something?"

"Sure." Jared immediately dumped the coats he was carrying on top of a rack and smiled eagerly. "Anything you want."

"I'm so glad you say that. What I'd really like"—Ginny seemed to consider whether she had the nerve to say this, and at last whispered daringly—"is to suck your dick."

The guy stared at her, obviously unwilling to believe his ears. *How likely was that?* he seemed to ask himself. And when he said, "Excuse me?" his voice had a pathetic, strained note of hope in it.

"You heard right," Ginny said. Her hand moved from his chest to her own, and one finger drew a teasing circle around her right nipple. "I know this may seem corny, but—I need to get off."

As the dream became real, Lila was fascinated to see the reactions that flashed over Jared's face. Most of them were versions of fear. It was something she had read about in her Satisfaction textbook. When offered the thing they've always wanted sexually, 63 percent of people refused it the first time, running away instinctively as if from a nightmare.

But then she noticed that Jared was stealing glances at her and Andy with some trepidation, and she realized this wasn't such a textbook case. Ginny might be exactly what Jared wanted sexually. Ginny plus two—one of them a big muscle-bound male—probably wasn't.

She took Andy by the elbow and pulled him away gently. He got the hint quickly and moved with her to pretend to inspect some evening dresses. From there they watched Ginny work her charms with the much-relieved Jared. After a minute, though, the boy suddenly turned and walked off, leaving Ginny standing unconcerned by the heap of coats.

"What's up?" Lila said, sneaking over to her.

"He's checking the back room," Ginny said. "If it's clear, we'll go in, and then you guys . . . give me five minutes, then follow."

Lila considered. It seemed like a mean trick. But then again, how many mean tricks of exactly that kind had been sprung on her since she first came to Babylona? And how many of them did she wish had not been sprung afterward? Zero.

"Sounds like a plan," she said, and went back to join Andy.

Two minutes later, Jared reappeared from the back room, looking flustered and upset. When he came up to Ginny, he adopted a conspiratorial air. He already had a more masterful bearing, the enhanced macho of the guy who's about to get laid. Whatever he said to Ginny must have been pretty funny, because she laughed out loud, making several ladies of a certain age look over speculatively.

Then, as Lila and Andy watched in consternation, Jared ducked deftly and shoved himself in between the hanging coats on the circular rack at his side. Ginny, with an air of don't-care-what-anyone-thinks, began to pull the loose coats he'd left draped there over the gap in the middle of the rack to conceal the center from view. If any of the shoppers realized what was going on, they gave no sign; they had gone back into their shopping trance.

Andy said to Lila, "God. She can be a pain in the ass, but Ginny really has something. I would never dare to do that. Never."

Lila cleared her throat. "I think you're missing the fact that Ginny just volunteered you to do that."

"But that feels different." Andy cocked his head. "I mean, I wouldn't bother using it as an excuse to the cops if we get busted. But in my heart, I'll blame Ginny. You know what I mean?"

"No," Lila said hopelessly. "Look, how long do we give them? Still five minutes?"

"Two minutes," Andy said. "This can't take long."

"Gulp."

Andy kept an eye on his watch while Lila stared, mesmerized, at the rack of coats. Once she saw a coat shift, but there was none of the comical jigging that she feared. In fact, if she hadn't known what was going on, she wouldn't have suspected anything.

"Two minutes," Andy said suddenly.

"Okay," Lila sighed. "But I think you should give it another two minutes after me."

She walked forward, trying to feel confident. Her pussy was reminding her already of the hours of sex she'd had last night with Ben, and her conscience was reminding her of all their long conversations about jealousy. But as long as she was at Babylona, she was going to have to live both with the complications of jealousy, and the trials of pussy-burn. So she advanced stalwartly on the coatrack, and when she reached it, she made herself duck and push through the coats.

Inside the rack, it was roomier than she'd expected—and darker. It took a second for her eyes to adjust enough even to see the horrified stare that Jared was fixing her with. Then she saw Ginny's figure crouched over his crotch, her head moving up and down. And Jared's eyes shut again; she could hear his panting clearly in the enclosed space.

Then Ginny sat back, revealing that her blouse was open and her breasts on display. How she had managed to get rid of her bra under those conditions Lila couldn't imagine. Ginny really did have something. And in the dimness, she could make out the boy's red, stiff cock rearing out of his opened jeans in a state of such delirious hardness that it was poking up into his belly. Without thinking, Lila reached forward and stroked her fingers up its length, savoring the smoothness of the skin, the wetness left by Ginny's mouth . . .

Lila pulled her sweater down and let her breasts spill out, a gesture that was becoming second nature to her. Jared, who had opened his eyes again to see what was happening, groaned faintly. Then Lila was crawling forward, posing over him. After a moment's hesitation, he grasped one of her breasts and groaned again. He murmured, "God, I'm dreaming."

There was something about that that set Lila off. She straddled him adroitly, taking care not to jostle the coats, and pressed her crotch against his beautiful dick. As he felt her bare, wet pussy slide along his prick, Jared caught his breath. His cock was so hard, she could clearly feel the ridge along the underside, and it jumped slightly against her cunt, as if it were trying to leap up and insert itself in her.

She took care of that herself. Grasping his hot cock in her hand, she directed it up into her slit and bore down, slowly, driving the stranger's dick all the way in with a force and steadiness that made him gasp. Then she held still, letting him feel the shock of suddenly being in a girl's pussy, in the middle of the day, in the middle of a store.

But he couldn't stand that for long, and he began to buck under her. She gave in and rode up his dick, gasping herself as she felt the mingled pleasure and pain of being penetrated again in her raw cunt.

The soreness made his cock feel huge, and her pussy already began to reach for its orgasm, as if it had never strayed far from coming and needed only the slightest nudge to return to a state of constant climax. Lila forgot everything but the feelings the fuck was giving her, and took turns riding up and down on the boy's dick and then suddenly holding still to let him rut into her from below, the wild piercing motions of his hips making her ring with pleasure.

Then suddenly a shaft of light appeared, and there was Andy creeping in. Ginny shoved over best she could, but Lila still had to press herself flat onto Jared's chest to make room for Andy's big bulk. Now Jared began to mutter protests and struggle. Lila was whispering something witless like, "No, don't worry. It's okay." But Ginny just clapped her hand over the boy's mouth.

All four of them froze for a moment. Ginny had her head up, listening for anyone who might have heard. Andy and Lila were frowning at Jared's face, worried that they had unwittingly strayed into the realm of shopping-mall rape. But Jared was gradually relaxing; his face took on the fatalistic sleepiness of someone abandoning himself to the whims of the gods. When Ginny took her hand away at last, he whispered, "It's okay, whatever you want. Just—don't stop fucking me. Please."

With that, Lila rose again onto the tip of his dick, letting it slip out slightly to tag her raw clitoris, which seemed to glow with the intensity of the sensations. The reminder that they were in the middle of a store had given her a renewed lust; the forbidden, as always, was an aphrodisiac. And as she moved, she felt her back pressing again and again into Andy's chest. Andy was posed behind her, crouching halfway over Jared's knees.

Ginny, who had been watching all this with the scowl of a kid whose toy has been stolen, now grabbed one of Jared's hands and guided it to her bare pussy under her miniskirt. He willingly began to stroke her and play with her cunt, his fingers diving in avidly. Again he gently groaned as the dream got better and better. Ginny was biting her lip with the pleasure, and she reached forward to fondle Lila's nearest breast. Lila gasped as much with the idea of what they were doing as with the fresh sensation. The feeling of Ginny's slender fingers playing with her breast, flicking her nipple— somehow it reawakened in her the idea that she was being obscenely touched, exposed, fucked, just a few feet away from people casually shopping.

And then Andy moved forward and his arm went around her. Now his hand was cupping the breast that Ginny wasn't touching. The different sensations from the two hands, one so slight and soft, the other so huge, while a third person fucked her steadily from below, made Lila gasp. And then Andy was holding her still against his powerful chest, letting Jared fuck her from below as he fiddled with the fly of his jeans.

It took Lila a minute to realize what Andy had in mind. There was even a second when it began to seem too impossible and surreal— what could he do? If he tried anything with Jared, the kid would probably fight his way to freedom. But then Lila's consciousness was wiped out by a particularly deep and telling stroke of Jared's cock. She let Andy take her weight as she dissolved in ecstasy again, the keen painful pleasure of an orgasm gripping her sore pussy, setting off afterimages of all the orgasms she'd had had the night before.

Then she felt Andy's cock nosing at her from behind. She caught her breath sharply, and instinctively tried to move away, but he held her fast. He gently pressed the head of his cock against the tight nub of her asshole, and she felt it begin to sink in, overfilling her. Jared's dick shoving into her again and again joined the almost intolerable sensation of Andy's, and she was coming uncontrollably again as Andy's cock penetrated her anus completely, filling her to bursting. At that moment, Jared also came, fucking her convulsively as he did, and letting out a muffled yelp. She was panting, desperately trying to suppress the wails of pleasure that were fighting to escape. Then the orgasm was subsiding, leaving her helpless in Andy's arms as he continued to gently sodomize her, the feeling of it easing into a deep, deep pleasure as Jared's cock slid out of her in front.

Then there was suddenly a blinding light, and a squeal of shock from above. Jared, Andy, Lila, and Ginny all looked up in alarm as a startled, wrinkled face scowled down at them. A woman looking for a coat in her size was staring at them in complete befuddlement.

For a long moment they confronted the woman, their faces all masks of horror. Lila's heart was pounding as she imagined being hauled out, confronting the store police, and then the real police. But then the woman cleared her throat, shook her head, and firmly closed the gap in the coats. Andy sighed and had already begun to grip Lila again when they heard a clear soprano voice calling out, "Martha! Come and take a look at this!"

Then they were all scrambling to get their clothes back on properly and scattering out from under the coatrack in all directions. Andy, Ginny, and Lila were soon striding purposefully out of the store. As they made it to the entrance with as much dignity as they could muster, Lila glanced back and saw Jared still standing beside the coatrack, staring after them with a distant, dreamy expression on his face.

Chapter Eighteen

The reception for Babylona's visit was held in the Belesci Ballroom. For the occasion, all the tents and even some of the potted trees were removed and the space was filled with long dining tables. The catering was elaborate; all morning, vans were arriving with food, wine, and floral arrangements.

Of the students, only seniors were invited to the party. Nonetheless, every last person at the institute was dressed with special care in the knowledge that Babylona was on campus. At any moment she might walk by, take an interest in some lucky student, and sweep him or her up into her orbit for a couple of years. This had happened—so the legend went—to two different students, one of whom was still in Babylona's entourage, traveling around the world, performing in secret for tycoons and rock stars, and then relaxing at one of Babylona's opulent mansions in Paris, Hawaii, and Rio. Members of Babylona's entourage had been cast in Hollywood movies, married minor royalty, caused sex scandals that brought down governments. Just having the chance to meet them made the seniors bitterly envied whenever Babylona came to visit. To become one of them—it was all they dreamed of.

Except for Lila. All she dreamed of was being able to live with Ben, but to still stay at the institute. She was increasingly certain she was falling in love with him. On the other hand, the idea of leaving Babylona and all the new friends she had made there made her shrink inside.

On the way home from the mall, she, Ginny, and Andy had gotten into a fight about gas money, and for some reason that made her feel even closer to them. She'd only ever had fights with her family, and once or twice with Tad, before. Now she was close enough to Ginny, Andy, Brandi, Anna, Miguel . . . And close enough meant she could snipe at them about gas money without worrying that it would make any difference to the way they felt about her. She'd never felt as safe in her life as she did at Babylona.

Now she was about to do something that could get her thrown out—or give her a place in the Babylona universe for the rest of her life.

As the last party guests drifted into the ballroom, Lila, Anna, Miguel, and Drew crouched in the woods, watching. The elegant glass structure was suffused with a golden light. Although the figures inside were indistinct, the twinkling glass gave an impression of chandeliers, champagne, and laughter. Music wafted down the hill from the string quartet that was playing inside.

Lila had borrowed Ginny's fur coat, but she was still shivering, her feet woefully thinly clad in bathroom slippers. The others had also thrown winter coats over the skimpy clothes in which they were going to do an impromptu performance for Babylona and her guests.

Anna kept saying it was a matter of "fucking for your life." But Lila couldn't help feeling that their success would depend much more on luck than on anything else. They might be stopped at any point. Babylona might realize that their performance wasn't part of the planned festivities, and be so angry at having her dinner interrupted that instead of paying attention she'd have them thrown out. One of the seniors who was going to help with the show could change his mind at the last minute. Or—and right now this seemed most likely of all—Lila could chicken out and run back to her dorm room to drink half a bottle of wine and forget all about it.

But now Anna was giving the signal for the attack. Lila swallowed and looked at Miguel, who gave her a reassuring grin. "I can't do this," she whispered, although she was already getting to her feet.

"You'll be great," he whispered back, shoving her forward playfully.

And then they were all walking up the hill.

As they got to the entrance, Lila was relieved to see that Anna had been right about one thing; there was no one on the door. They would be able to walk right in without anyone questioning their right to be there. As they got to the door, all of them hastily threw off their coats and kicked off their shoes. Then the girls ran in, and two beats later, the men gave chase.

The girls were dressed in what appeared to be normal summer dresses, in navy blue cloth that looked like light cotton. But the cloth was really a particular featherlight fabric they called "tissue" because it was intended to be easy to tear. The guys were dressed in normal street clothes, though they both wore tank tops despite the bitter winter weather.

In unison, Anna and Lila dashed in and ran in between the long dining tables, swerving around waiters carrying trays. Lila spotted Babylona, recognizing her immediately by her bright red hair, and headed toward her instinctively. Anna peeled off to the right somewhere. Now Lila was close enough to see Babylona look up with the same air of casual amusement she'd had when she walked in on the alien porn scene. And close enough to see, to her utter horror, that the man sitting to Babylona's right, currently frozen in the act of raising a wineglass to his mouth, was Ben. Ben, staring at her with a mixture of mortification and concern. She had just enough time to register all this before Miguel caught up to her and swept her off her feet with one powerful lunge.

Then she was struggling with him—struggling a little harder than he'd anticipated. For a moment she was fighting with the strength of desperation, her whole being focused on slipping free and running back into the peaceful night before things got any worse. Inwardly she was cursing herself and Ben in turns. She was such an idiot for not knowing he would be here! But, then, why hadn't he mentioned it? *Anyone* would have mentioned it! Was he trying to hide something?

Her thoughts were racing as she wrestled with Miguel, who took her vehemence as a joke and began to snigger as he fought her. He had swooped down onto the floor, bringing her with him, and the battle was joined there—an undignified scuffle that even involved him pulling her hair at one point, causing her to cry out in absolutely heartfelt dismay. But at last he forced her arms around behind her back by brute force, and pulled out the faux-rope he had stashed in his pocket. This faux-rope, like the dress cloth, was a product sold in the bookstore for the Sex in Performance class. It looked exactly like rope, but it didn't give rope burn, and was, as the packaging promised, "TEN TIMES easier to tie under pressure!" Miguel now gave a good demonstration of how easy it was to use, tethering Lila's hands behind her back before she fully realized the fight was over.

Now Miguel tore a strip of cloth from her skirt and used it to blindfold her. She was privately grateful for the blindfold, because it prevented her from trying to see whether Ben was among the people who had risen from their seats and were gathering around to watch more closely. In the meantime, Miguel pushed her onto her side and rapidly hog-tied her ankles to her wrists. Then he pushed her onto her back again, so that she was lying with her knees bent, her shins under her, her back arched, and her knees naturally forced open to allow easy entry.

Then he tore her dress open with one motion. A cheer came from the crowd, and she was painfully aware of her exposure; her nipples immediately clenching into hardness as they were exposed to the dozens of people she couldn't even see. She could feel the gentle jiggling of her breasts, and in her mind, she could feel all the men in the room getting excited by watching them shake. Then she felt Miguel's hot breath on her breast, followed by his mouth closing on her nipple and sucking, his tongue flicking its tender tip rapid-fire, making her involuntarily squirm in response. The combination of the close, intimate feeling, which seemed all the more private in the darkness that had been imposed on her, and the presence of the crowd standing over her, watching, made her pussy instantly wet.

Now, as if reacting to that fact, Miguel's mouth moved rapidly down her sensitive belly and for a long, tormenting moment, she felt his breath gently brushing over her clitoris, leaving her to anticipate his mouth. He let her wait for another breath, and another, until the crowd was urging him on, telling him in various ways to lick her, to put her out of her misery, to eat her . . . all the voices adding fuel to the fire that was raging in her hungry pussy. As he hovered, making her wait, she suddenly imagined Ben standing there, watching in disgust as a rowdy gang of men leered at her and shouted out encouragement. Once more she instinctively tried to escape, tugging at her bonds and squirming until she could force her knees shut.

But Miguel easily caught her and held her helplessly in place, and even with her knees shut, most of her pussy was easily available to his invading tongue. Even as his strong hands forced her back into quiescence, his hot mouth fastened on her clitoris, and he was tonguing her. Her pussy responded violently, despite her willing herself to remain still, and she found her knees opening, her hips tilting up to offer her naked cunt to Miguel's mouth and to the eyes of the spectators. His tongue first flicked back and forth over her swelling clit, sending a current of response through her thighs and making her pussy a tight burning focus of tormenting heat. Then he suddenly tightened his focus, sucking mercilessly on the tortured nub until she cried out involuntarily. At last he let go and it was his fingers that touched the lips of her cunt, delicately tickling them, letting her wait once again for penetration. He finally slipped two fingers inside, wriggling them deliciously around in an exploration of the folds inside, and at the same time he was rising over her, preparing to enter her with his cock. In the blindfold, Lila was keenly focused on the slightest movements of his fingers, and aware too of the slightest sounds from the crowd, the caught breaths and the muttered comments that seemed to come from all around. Through it all, she realized that when Miguel was through with her, two more men would come out of the audience to use her body in front of everyone. They would be seniors, they would be men she'd never fucked before. And that was all she knew; Anna had decided that it would be sexier if she didn't know who they were at all. When they'd discussed it, it had seemed like a cool idea—nothing special, just a neat twist. Now that it was happening—in public, and with Ben among that public—it seemed like the most profound violation Lila could imagine. The worst of it was that, just as when she had walked out into that clearing months ago and exposed herself deliberately to the two surfer guys—the act that had indirectly brought her here—she was unbearably aroused by the idea of that violation. The fact that there was a crowd of witnesses to it made it even more powerful, and her pussy was streaming with wetness when Miguel's cock found it and pierced her easily, filling her with an overwhelming shaft of pleasure. She moaned, and the crowd around her groaned in appreciation. Miguel drew his cock back slowly, slowly, letting her feel the length of it, the shape of it as it retreated from her, a release that was at once the promise of another assault. And then that assault came; he plunged into her again, and then he was fucking her eagerly, each thrust a deep stab into her resistance, a singing, dizzying opening of her body. It was as if he were carving a space into her that would allow everyone standing around to look in and see all the desperate lust of her real self, the desire to be fucked and fucked again by any man who wanted her. She could feel the orgasm building already, the abandonment of all control gathering deep in her belly, tingles of electricity rising in her buttocks.

But then Miguel pulled out of her, cheating her of her release, and he was instead pressing the length of his dick up against her slick clitoris and vulva, sliding up and down there so that she yelped again with helpless response. Soon he was bearing down hard, the long shaft of his dick slipping along her whole clit and making her gasp again and again with the different pleasure. Just as a new, sharper orgasm was about to tear through her, he pulled away yet again and drove his cock deep into her pussy, fucking her hard and fast, a pounding rhythm that built to a peak as he dug his dick as far into her as it could go, coming and coming with his hands suddenly clutching her ass, the fingertips digging in painfully. Lila cried out again, partly from the intensity of the attack, and partly from the frustration of seeing her orgasm escape her for a third time. As her cry died away, Miguel pulled his dick out of her. Lila's heart thrilled with fear as she realized that the time had come; she was going to be rudely fucked by a complete stranger.

Miguel rose from her all too fast, the loss of his warmth and his comforting weight leaving her alone with her panic. It seemed impossibly dark, and she felt more helpless and naked than she could ever remember feeling. She had no idea from which direction the next assault would come; no idea what to expect from the darkness and the crowd of lustful onlookers. Her breasts and pussy shrank from the air, which suddenly seemed as if it was itself an enveloping gaze, as if every inch of her were coated in the concentrated, pure voyeurism of the watching partygoers.

And then, to her shock, a hand touched her cheek, a gentle caress that moved slowly along her skin and ended with one finger drawn across her lower lip. The finger returned to tease her lower lip, then her upper lip, the adroit, slight touch of the fingertip and fingernail alternating to make her mouth tingle with pleasure as if it were a second pussy. The next thing she knew there was a firmer, broader pressure, and she realized that this was the stranger's dick pressing against her lips for entrance. Her lips parted automatically, and before she knew what she was doing, she was sucking the tip of the cock lovingly, her tongue circling it, finding the ridge under the glans and tickling it with a sense of hungry delight. When the stranger plunged his cock deeper, she didn't see it coming, and the shock of the penetration was so much like an unexpected penetration of her cunt that her cunt in fact spasmed in response. And she sucked hard, feeling every inch of the cock's hardness in her mouth as the simplest, most uncomplicated sexual pleasure she had ever had. It was as if the man were pure sex, a person who existed only to fuck her mouth, to come into her throat. Her head began to rise to try to swallow more of him, and he obliged by beginning to thrust forward into her mouth, the end of his dick forcing its way gently against her throat, just enough to make her feel filled without choking her. In the intensity of her response, she had almost forgotten that there was anyone else in the room when she suddenly felt a hand at her pussy. But it wasn't just a hand; it was a hand that was testing her pussy before, a second later, it was followed by a cock that plunged hungrily into her. At the same time the other cock continued to thrust into her mouth, faster and faster.

Then for a second she lost all control. She forgot about everything except that she was tied up, helpless in a room full of people who could do anything they wanted to her. Her mind cried out against the situation, screaming that it was impossible, that she had to escape, that she couldn't let a stranger do this to her—as the new stranger fucked her mercilessly, his dick pressing into her from every direction. As she felt with razor clarity the pleasure he was taking from her body, and the other cock hammered into her mouth above, she spun into an overwhelming, helpless, abandoned orgasm. In the throes of it, her mouth sucked desperately at the prick of the first stranger while her pussy gripped and released, gripped and released, feeling as if it were screaming its pleasure as the second stranger pummeled it into orgasm after orgasm. Her hips bucked up against him, instinctively meeting his rhythm as she rode her pleasure out to the point where darkness overwhelmed her senses, and she felt the sweet tease of unconsciousness. Then she was back, feeling the pangs of orgasm all too keenly again, her eyes fluttering open under the blindfold as if trying to *see* the pleasure as it hit her again and again.

The second stranger came first; apparently the unrestrained response of her cunt was too much for him. She felt him spurting into her as the waves of her orgasm died down enough to allow her to feel anything outside of herself. And a moment later the first stranger drove his dick painfully deeply into her throat. She twisted her head, trying to escape the pressure, but at the same time she was sucking gratefully, and her whole body relaxed with the satisfaction of it when she tasted the first hot spurts of his come in her mouth. She swallowed it as if it were the affirmation of the whole experience, the sweet proof of the danger and perfection she had undergone.

Both men rose from her at once, and she lay there, feeling completely opened to the gaze of the spectators, at their mercy. She was breathing heavily through her mouth, waiting for Miguel to return and release her. She was privately hoping that he would leave the blindfold on as he led her out into the night. She didn't know whether she wanted to see the faces of the people who had just witnessed the public violation that had taken her so far beyond her own powers of resistance.

But instead of Miguel's hands fumbling at her bonds, she felt a different hand stroking her belly and then moving up to cup her breast. The hand was just as warm as Miguel's, just as strong and sure. But somehow she knew it wasn't his—it was the hand of a third stranger who had decided to take advantage of her helplessness. And of all the people there, only Miguel would know that it shouldn't be happening. Or only Miguel, Anna, and Drew—but Anna and Drew would be occupied at the other end of the room, with no idea of what was happening to Lila. As the stranger fondled her breast appreciatively and then began to stroke her pussy, apparently savoring the soaking openness of it, she waited for Miguel to intervene. But nothing happened, and still nothing happened. Or all that happened was that the stranger was now moving over her. She felt the closeness of his body, and heard the crisp sound of an opening fly. Without thinking, she said, "No! You can't—" But his hand immediately pressed to her mouth, cutting off her cries.

Then his erection was pressed against her cunt, almost lost in the lush wetness there. She gritted her teeth, wanting to struggle, but knowing that it would achieve nothing. There was nothing she could do. And she was beginning to respond again, her body rising to the challenge, seeming to relax even more deeply as she ceded all control.

But when his cock sank into her all too easily, her mind froze with a sudden realization. It was Ben. It was Ben who was taking advantage of her helplessness in front of everyone. Ben who was fucking her with the same sweetness she had enjoyed the night before, in the sweet privacy of their growing feelings for each other. And while her mind resisted the knowledge, and her emotions ran through shame, gratitude, trust, fear—her body went one step further into abandon, letting the perfect pleasure that his cock gave her turn into a further, flowering orgasm that lasted and lasted as he took possession of her again. Because that was what her body insisted it was; her man asserting his rights to her over all others. And the orgasm she had delivered her into a moment of the blackness that had tickled the edge of her consciousness before, a momentary sleep so sweet and satisfying that when she returned from it, the world felt raw and unnatural.

In that space of time he had started to come. With the blindfold on, and her sense heightened by the long intense arousal, she felt the jerks of his cock with intense clarity. When his orgasm finished, it left her feeling as if her cunt was melted into him, as if they had fallen together into the same sleep, the same erotic dream. And when he leaned down to her ear, she opened up to him completely, ready to accept him completely. Some part of her was certain he was going to whisper, "I love you," and she was so ready for that as the culmination of it all that she felt a keen shock of disappointment when he just kissed her cheek tenderly. And then he was gone, and Miguel was there at last, fumbling at her bonds.

Chapter Nineteen

The morning after was like all mornings-after. Lila woke up with the sense that she was doomed, utterly doomed, and that she deserved to be still more doomed. Then she resolutely, vehemently, didn't get out of bed. For the best part of an hour she lay with the covers pulled over her head, dreading the moment that Anna would wake up and want to talk about how *well* everything had gone.

Lila had no idea how well it had gone. It all depended on how well it had gone for Ben. And in the cold light of morning, she had a growing premonition that it hadn't gone well for Ben at all. In fact, it was the clearest sense of dread she'd had since—well, since Tad had broken up with her.

She and Miguel had escaped from the party successfully, racing away through the snow barefoot with their coats bundled in their arms. They hadn't stopped until they'd come to Lila's dorm building, where they'd instantly run a hot bath and defrosted their achingly cold hands and feet. Miguel had kept trying to tell her that she'd been fantastic, and Lila had kept stopping him. "Just talk about anything else, please. *Please* talk about anything else." But every attempt to talk about what Miguel was doing for Christmas, or what was his favorite band, eventually led somehow back to him reminiscing about Lila's performance at the party, the crowd's response, and the shocked moment when Ben had joined the show.

"I guess he must have been dying to sleep with a student all this time," Miguel said, as they were drying themselves off. "I mean, now that he's not subject to the Parris Rule, he seized his chance. I hope you didn't mind." He wrinkled his nose apologetically, and she had to insist once again that she didn't mind, before suggesting gently that he let her have some time alone.

As soon as he was gone, though, Anna appeared, flushed with success. She'd had the job of slipping a letter to Babylona after the show—a straightforward letter asking humbly for a job at her TV station, signed by all four of them, and with their (admittedly skimpy) résumés attached. Babylona had pulled her in, given her a big kiss on the lips, and thanked her—*thanked her!* Well, they were bound for glory, Anna was convinced. Forget the TV station; they were going to be taken into Babylona's entourage. This time next week they would be in some castle in Zanzibar eating caviar from a bucket and counting money while gorgeous men massaged their feet.

Lila was so unable to match Anna's excitement that she finally retreated to the bathtub again for some privacy. She didn't come out for an hour. By then, Anna had fallen asleep. But even in her sleep she was smiling, apparently seeing visions of caviar and glory. Lila had fallen asleep soon after, but her dreams had been a confused jumble of sex, Tad, and a furious Ben, who threw her out of his apartment over and over again, making her leave naked in the snow . . .

Now she sat up in bed, deciding that there was only one thing she could do. If she ever wanted to shake the unbearable feeling of doom that had settled over her, she would have to go and see Ben. Then it would be settled one way or the other. And this was her best chance to see him, because she knew he was in his office today, packing his things.

She put on her baggiest jeans and her oldest sweatshirt, the feeling of her body being hidden from view an incredible luxury. At the last minute she decided that washing her face again would be too much. She'd washed her face about five times the night before, and it was feeling almost as raw as her pussy.

Crossing the lawn to Student Services, she kept looking around paranoically, sure that people would be staring contemptuously at her. *That's the girl who broke up Babylona's reception! Who does she think she is?* But the only students she saw passed by her with the usual desultory wave, looking as sleepy as she did. She gradually relaxed, realizing once again that at Babylona, everyone had a morning after of some kind, every morning. There was never any room to feel more ashamed than anyone else, with the result that there was no point being ashamed at all.

That feeling bolstered her as she climbed the stairs to Ben's office. Ben wasn't going to judge her. He'd been here for six years; there was no way he could judge her. Even if he was jealous, he wouldn't let that affect his feelings for her. They'd already discussed this and decided that she should continue at the institute. That meant sex with other men.

As she came down the hallway, she heard music coming from his office. Then she saw him in the open doorway, and her heart leaped. He was more beautiful than she'd remembered, and her mind immediately returned to the blindfolded sex she'd had with him last night. She felt weak all over. Immediately she wanted him again.

But as she came forward to stand in the doorway, he looked up at her with a coldness she'd never seen on his face before. She caught her breath and said, "Hi, Ben," her voice faltering.

He looked at her without speaking for a minute, and finally said, "Why are you here?"

"What do you mean?" Lila felt her eyes already pricking with the tears that were forming there. "I—I don't know. I wanted to see you."

"Listen, you've got your job at the TV station, okay? You don't have to chase me around anymore."

Lila stared at him, stunned. At last she managed to say, "Oh, God, Ben, you don't really believe that, do you?"

His eyes narrowed, and for a moment he seemed torn between hurt and suspicion. At last he shut his eyes and said, "I'm sorry, Lila. I'm sorry."

She went to him immediately, putting her arms around him, but he broke away and went to sit on the couch. The rest of the couch's surface was taken up with cartons that he'd been filling with books and papers, and Lila was left standing over him, feeling awkward and rejected.

He looked up at her from the couch with a defeated expression. "Listen, Lila, I know this is unfair of me. I know I'm supposed to be more advanced than this. It's almost my job. But I . . . I can't look at you after last night. And I honestly don't know if I'm going to get over it."

Her heart began to pound, and she felt cold all over. All she could think of to say was, "Don't do this."

He shook his head. "It's not something I'm doing. It's something that's happening to me." But then his eyes met hers and his face softened. With a sudden movement, he pulled the carton off the seat next to him and gestured for her to sit. She fell into his arms gratefully, letting her head rest on his strong shoulder, inhaling his fragrance. At the same time, the tears that were filling her eyes had begun to fall. How could this have happened? She felt that there must be a way to relive the day before, some way to take it back. His arms held her close, and she shut her eyes, half believing that it was still possible to erase it all and start fresh.

"Ben," she murmured, "I would never have done that if I'd known. You realize that, don't you?"

He kissed her on the forehead, the fondness of the gesture sending a wave of relief through her. He said, "I wish that was all it took." Then he pulled away from her slightly, so that he was looking into her eyes with an intensity that was at once tender and resolute. She was strangely stirred to see that his eyes, too, were filled with tears.

He said, "I've never wanted a woman as much as I wanted you last night. And before that, I'd never wanted a woman as much as I wanted you the day I first saw you."

"I feel the same way," Lila breathed. She put her hand to his cheek. "I wanted you so badly."

"But did it really have to be me?" he asked, and his eyes bored into hers.

"Ben," Lila said in confusion. "You know that what I did last night—any girl at Babylona could have done it. It doesn't mean anything about how I feel about you. Under certain circumstances, people just lose control. Hasn't that ever happened to you?"

Ben flinched. His eyes suddenly moved away from hers, and Lila couldn't help smiling at his obvious guilty reaction. He sighed and said quietly, "Of course it's happened. You know because you were there. It happened when I met you."

She swallowed. For a moment she was overwhelmed by the memory—Ben touching the tender insides of her thighs, how she had pretended that nothing surprising was happening, longing for him to fuck her. But the memory was already altered by what had happened in the intervening months. She was now remembering it as if she was already in love with him, and it carried an almost unbearable freight of sweet nostalgia. She said in a tremulous voice, "I lost control then, too. I'd never—you know you were only the second man I'd ever had sex with. I didn't know what I was doing at all. I wanted you so much."

"God, Lila. Don't cry." He touched her hair, and his eyes looked misty, too. "I know I'm wrong. But you have to see. I lost control then because . . ." He frowned and seemed to bite his tongue, ashamed.

She said lightly, "Love at first sight?"

"I know. It's funny." His voice had a tinge of bitterness.

"No, it's not. I felt the same way. I did. It was as if I'd always known you."

"Then you know. It kills me to think that you could feel that way about anyone else."

"But I don't!" She pulled away from him sharply, shocked. "Look, this is so wrong. You were at Babylona yourself! You must have come here for a reason! Ben, you can't tell me you never felt plain lust for someone? Just silly, dirty lust that you didn't *want* to control? I mean, you were the one who told me that it was a kind of innocence. And you were right."

"Lila, I know. I was right. And now I'm wrong." He shook his head. "I lost control just that way a few weeks ago. For no reason. For fun. *And* with another student." He smiled at her, the sadness in his beautiful green eyes making his expression wistful. "I don't have a leg to stand on. I'm as mad at me as you are. But I keep seeing you . . . with those other men." His face contorted and he looked away from her again.

Lila felt an utter, black despair. Somehow it was particularly painful that she couldn't see herself with those other men; having been blindfolded, she had no mental picture of the men, no idea what he was imagining. "I should go," she said listlessly.

He seemed about to say something, but changed his mind and crossed his arms, the tension in his shoulders making him the picture of misery.

She got up from the couch, stepping around a half-filled carton. But as she turned to the door, a shock of desperation hit her, and she turned to him once more, saying, "Ben? Can't you try to get over it? Will you at least try?"

He stared at her bleakly. At last he said, "I am trying. But you can't imagine how it feels."

Lila shut her eyes for a second. "Yes, I can," she said simply. Then she opened her eyes. "Who was the other girl? The second student you had sex with?"

"Oh! It was Brandi. I don't know if you know her. The big blond girl. She chased me. But that one was my fault. I really do know better now. I just lost control one night, because she was taunting me so relentlessly, and I was all messed up about you. Lila? What's wrong?"

She was staring at him with an involuntary grimace of outrage. Brandi! It had to be Brandi! She blurted, "Well, after fucking Brandi, I guess you have every right to be shocked by my behavior. I mean, I'm disgusting. I'm a slut. Not like Brandi."

"Lila? What's wrong? Do you have something against her? Honestly, I never would have done it if I'd known it would hurt you."

Lila looked at him with a sudden overwhelming bitterness in her heart. It was always the double standard. First Tad, now Ben. Only men were allowed to be human. Only men were allowed to be out of control of their desires. She couldn't believe she was being punished again, in the same way, by the same kind of fucked-up guy who—as incredible as it seemed—had betrayed her with the same girl!

"Well, it hurts me. Just like what I did hurt you." She turned to leave, but at the doorway, she paused to deliver a parting shot. "I guess it doesn't matter, but I don't forgive you, either. I don't care how unreasonable it seems. I'll never forgive you!" Then she was running down the hallway, tears flooding her eyes, fighting the desperate urge to go back and beg him to forget everything she'd said, everything she'd done, everything she was, if he would only love her.

Chapter Twenty

"Thank you," Miss Foré purred, as Judd fucked her against the school desk. "That's exactly right." The other students watched intently, following the gleaming curve of his dick as it sailed in and out of the teacher's glistening pussy. She was leaning back against the desk with her dress pulled up over her hips. It was a plain black long-sleeved dress, a schoolmarm dress; from the waist up, she was the picture of decorum. The primness of that dress had made her spread legs and naked cunt that much more arresting when she'd first pulled up her skirt and asked for a volunteer.

Finally she held up a graceful hand to ask Judd to stop. He did, though as he pulled out of her, he was gritting his teeth in frustration. Miss Foré let her skirt fall back into place. She turned to the class and said, "I think we can split up into pairs now. Would the gentlemen please practice finding the G-spot *without verbal cues*? And, girls, give them two minutes; two minutes only." She smiled. "I know the temptation may be to cheat and go on beyond two minutes. Don't. And do tell the boys the truth afterward. This isn't about ego—it's about . . ." She raised her eyebrows, letting them supply the word.

They said in ragged unison: "Satisfaction."

"Right. Go to it. And *you* . . ." She pointed at Andy. "Come here and practice with me."

Despite Judd's pleading glance at her, Lila hung back, shaking her head. There were only seven guys and ten girls in the class, so she had a perfect right to skip this exercise if she wanted to. After all, the girls weren't even learning anything. So it was fairly easy to slink to the corner of the classroom and sit this one out.

What was considerably harder was getting Brandi to do the same.

"What could be that important?" Brandi whispered to her disconsolately, watching the others pair off. "Can't this wait until after class? Damn!"

"Come on! They don't need us!"

"But we need them. I need them. I need *all* of them!"

"Brandi!" Lila gave her a look that was, if possible, even more disconsolate than Brandi's.

Brandi sighed. "Oh, well, hell. I guess I can always get laid after this. I think that whole penal regime left me with posttraumatic stress."

Lila led the way to an armchair that sat in the corner of the room and had already done service for a couple of demonstrations. They each perched on an arm, and Lila blurted immediately, "I'm coming to the Virgin Islands."

Brandi squinted at her. "Okay. Great. Was that it?" She looked back at the others, who were now all busily screwing in various poses. Then she laughed. "Look, they're all doing it in lockstep."

Lila looked, and started to laugh, too. It was true; being in the same room together, all the students had fallen into fucking in the same rhythm. The two girls watched for a second, smiling. Then Brandi said, with a certain sly carelessness, "But of course, I know that's not all you dragged me over here for. Couldn't be."

Lila said, "Well, maybe it isn't."

"Does it have anything to do with why you're suddenly free to go to the Virgin Islands?"

"No. Yes. I don't know. Should it?" Lila was watching the ongoing sex with a strange sinking in her heart. That was supposed to be her life from now on. And she still loved it. Not the sex itself, but the intimacy, the lightheartedness of it, as Ben (the hypocrite) had told her on her first day here.

"Excuse me!" Brandi said. "If that's all it is, I'm going back. *And* I'm giving you an official Brandi reprimand for interrupting my appointed duties." Brandi got up, tugging her peekaboo bra back into place.

"Okay! There's something else," Lila said, and immediately regretted it.

"Ha!" Brandi settled back down. "I knew it. Spill."

Lila looked at her soulfully and said, "I think I have a crush on someone. You know, I'm not saying I'm even sure it's a real crush. And he had a crush on me, if that's what it was. So we were good for a little while, except that it was someone I shouldn't have had a crush on. And then it all went wrong." A tear had begun to form in her eye.

"Hm," Brandi said. "As unlikely as it seems, I'm following you. So how did it go wrong?"

Lila made a face. "Well, partly . . . he fucked you."

"Well, that's just stupid," Brandi said easily. "Everybody fucks me. That's like saying he's got two legs. What else?"

"And I . . ." Lila made another, worse face. "I fucked a couple of guys in front of him. I mean, at that party for Babylona. Which made him really upset."

Brandi nodded. "And *that's* stupid. So you're both stupid. Looks to me like you're made for each other."

"Brandi, you're not taking this seriously!"

Brandi scowled, offended. "I am too taking it seriously. I'm taking it so seriously that I can tell you right now that going to Seduction, the premier vacation spot for liberated singles from eighteen to thirty, is going to fix your problem once and for all."

"Now you're *really* not taking it seriously."

"And I say I am. And I say that going to Seduction, the premier—"

"How?" Lila shook her head in frustration. "How, exactly, is that going to solve my problem?"

"Wait and see." Brandi smiled mysteriously.

"Okay, I'll wait and see. But I'm not going to see, because my problem can't be solved."

"Then why did you drag me out of class?" Brandi shrugged. "This is getting stupider and stupider."

"Because . . . well, listen, if I didn't take the job at Babylona TV, do you think my problem might be solved someday? Because it seems like that's bound to make it worse."

"Stupidest." Brandi sighed. "Listen, girl, just carry on as if you didn't have a problem, and Mistress Brandi will work her magic for you."

Lila frowned at the fucking couples in front of her—the men scowling in concentration while the girls smiled dreamily. She was beginning to be uncomfortably aware of her G-spot, and that made her aware all over again of the contract she'd just signed to star, along-side Anna, Miguel, and Drew, in Babylona TV's quasi-documentary about the school: *The Institute*. It was exactly the job she'd dreamed of just a few days ago. She would get to stay at the institute *and* be part of the TV channel. Unless she did something horribly wrong, she would have a future in the Babylona empire assured. And she was going to be a star, of course. It did mean that certain awkward conversations with her parents were going to have to take place sooner rather than later. ("Oh, forgot to mention, I'm at a sex institute, Mom. Oh, and also, I have hefty student loans for the sex institute that I'll have to pay off. But don't worry! That will all be taken care of by the new job I have as a cable porn star!") But Lila would have had to tell her parents someday.

The Ben problem was entirely different. She still had some hope that he would get over what he had seen. She was already over him sleeping with Brandi; in fact just talking to Brandi made the whole thing seem ridiculous. Everybody did fuck Brandi, and it wasn't any more of a betrayal than any other interaction he might have with

Brandi. It would mean just as much if he'd borrowed ten dollars from Brandi, or eaten some cookies she had baked. The fact that Tad had eaten the same cookies, well, that had just become one of those ironies that makes you feel sick to your stomach—for a couple of hours. So she had some hope that the party performance could fall into the same category for Ben someday.

But if he had to see her having sex with other men on video all the time, if he had to know that millions of other people were watching her do that . . . there didn't seem to be any point in even asking him to get over it. It didn't help, either, that the idea that he was spoiling her feeling of triumph about the job made her furious. She should be in seventh heaven right now. But, thanks to Ben, she was cruelly depressed.

"What if he has an incurable Madonna/whore complex?" she said suddenly.

"Oh, God!" Brandi gave her a shove. "You have got to get over this absolutely *now* because you're getting impossible and boring. Now, first things first. I know it's Ben, so you can stop with the lame routine."

"You know—" Lila's eyes flew open. "Did he tell you?"

Brandi shrugged. "Well, I kind of got it out of him."

Lila swallowed. Of course it meant nothing that Ben was telling his secrets to Brandi. At least, it meant nothing bad. It meant . . . and suddenly she found herself saying, "You got it out of him how? By sleeping with him?"

Brandi frowned at her as if she'd sprouted a second head. "Excuse me? If you want to know, I got it out of him by *threatening* to sleep with him."

"But then you slept with him," Lila insisted.

Brandi rolled her eyes. "Well, he's got two legs, hasn't he? Come on, kid. Listen, the last time I saw Mr. Ben he was so head over heels with a certain depressingly irresistible girl—yes, you, don't play dumb—it was sick to watch. So if you even want your problem solved, I'll go hunt him down and solve him. But for now I'm going to get laid, *which is what we're here for*. And in fact, just to show that I have some principles . . ." Brandi narrowed her eyes at Lila, who was staring at her with the words "head over heels" playing over and over, in her mind.

"Principles?" Lila said finally. "Wait, did he say he was head over heels? Or were you just assuming?"

"Principles," Brandi said. "That means no problem solving, no reserving vacation rentals, no nada, *until* I see you having some Babylona-style meaningless sex, to convince me you haven't gone nuts and you're not going to leave us to become some kind of a monogamous nun."

Lila looked at her haughtily. "That's so unnecessary it's gratuitous. Watch this." She got up, hiding her creeping feelings of guilt (stupid! stupid!) as she looked for a guy who was approaching the end of his two minutes. Within a minute and a half, she had several men approaching her with hopeful looks in their eyes. She smiled inwardly; obviously her star status was already taking effect.

The first man to reach her side was Judd. He was visibly losing his composure after the five couplings he had just undergone; his long blond hair had succumbed to a kind of waking bed head, the work of several passionate girls. His pants and boxers had gotten lost somewhere, as had all the buttons on his shirt. Drifting in a zone of dreamy sexuality that Lila knew all too well herself, he immediately embraced her and began to kiss her expertly, thoroughly, as if he had been fucking her all this time. Then, without a word, he turned her around by the shoulders and began kissing the nape of her neck in the same absorbed fashion while he lifted her skirt.

As always, being exposed—molested—made Lila react instantly. Her ass prickled all over as Judd began to stroke it with one hand, appreciating its firm shape. When he hooked her thong over one finger and stripped it down, she felt the twinge as an arrow of fire that shot up her pussy and set her whole belly alight. Then his dick entered her unceremoniously, and the naturalness of the act made the glow spread all over her skin. She leaned forward and braced herself with her hands on the arm of the chair she'd been sitting on. She vaguely noticed that Brandi was long gone; she vaguely noticed the other men, disappointed, straying off to find new partners. But she keenly, profoundly noticed every nanometer of Judd's cock as it gradually, almost cautiously, invaded her pussy. He leaned over her, pressing his lean, sculpted chest to her back, cupping her breasts in his palms to support her as he pushed his dick in.

It went deep, spreading her with that perfectly blissful discomfort that she loved; she was already melting, weakening, the sensations multiplying and robbing her of self-control. She arched her back, offering her pussy to Judd's luscious cock, which immediately pressed in another impossible inch. Then he was fucking her, slowly and attentively. While she was being possessed by his cock, his beautiful body, his lust—she was also being possessed by the delightfully filthy thought that she was the last of several women he'd done this to in the past ten minutes. She stole a glance around the room at the other couples, and the now comfortable feeling of debauchery stole into her like a sedative taking effect. She began to come, just gently this time. She recognized it as a baseline orgasm, from which she could build complex and ever-rising structures of climax; or which, cheated of further satisfaction, could become a profound, ambient arousal that would linger with her like a fragrance all day, coloring everything with pleasure. And then, as if reacting to that thought, Judd pulled out of her abruptly.

"Lila," he said huskily, his lips hotly at her nape, "that was fantastic. And—did I get your G-spot?"

"Oh, shit," she said. "I don't know."

He recoiled from her and when she turned around his face was stricken. He said, "How can you not know?"

She made a face. "I never knew where it was. I'm sorry. It's like it's all G-spot in there. I guess I shouldn't even be doing this exercise."

Then his face creased up into a grin, and he leaned forward to kiss her on the cheek. "Well," he said, looking around already for his next victim. "Never mind. I guess that's why you get the big bucks."

Chapter Twenty-one

"It won't be relentless, not at all," Babylona said, smiling reassuringly. "We'll film a couple of interviews every week, just about your experiences and feelings. If you don't know what to say, we'll write you a script. That part isn't crucial; it's really, you know, about the sex." She ran one hand through her long red hair, pulling it over her breasts with a habitual, sensuous gesture. She added, "And, of course, if you need any help, you can always ask any of us. We'll be spending more time close to home this year." She looked around the room, and her entourage all smiled back at her—except for Mangialina, a blond girl with porcelain-doll-like beauty, who had been curled up on a sofa sleeping peacefully from the beginning.

Lila, Anna, Drew, and Miguel all nodded dutifully. They were sitting up stiffly, all in a row, on a sofa. All of them, after frenzied consultation, had played it safe and worn interview clothes—Lila was actually in a suit with a white office shirt. Now they were feeling distinctly ridiculous.

The meeting was taking place in Babylona's office, which was crammed with extra furniture for the purpose—luxurious sofas and armchairs purloined at random from other rooms. The entourage was distributed across this furniture with a fantastic disregard for the posture the chair or sofa was designed for. Mariko, a Japanese girl with the most spectacularly beautiful legs Lila had ever seen, was lying on a sofa upside down with the legs in question straddled over the sofa back. From that pose, she had been offering input in the most serious and businesslike manner imaginable. Javier and

Jorge, Chilean identical twins who were dressed for the meeting in identical peacock-blue silk robes and apparently nothing else, sat cross-legged—one on Babylona's desk, and one on the floor directly beneath. Every time Lila looked at them, she briefly had the dizzying impression that she was seeing only one man and hallucinating the other. Then the slight differences in pose and hairstyle would register, and her sense of reality would reassert itself. Babylona herself was lying full length with her head on a gold-tasseled cushion, which was in turn on the lap of Friselle Belesci, a frighteningly tall, slender, and beautiful brunette with huge slanting eyes that were actually a bluish violet. Her only garment was a pair of dainty and ornate nipple rings. The nipples were a delicate lavender shade that echoed the color of her eyes, and the rings were dainty confections: silver thread in the shape of fuchsias dangling from each nipple. Despite her embellished nudity, she, like Mariko, took part in the conversation for all the world as if she were wearing a business suit and sitting at a desk. She had even interrupted Babylona to make a point about percentages on earnings from publicity appearances, which Lila was unable to follow, being too caught up in the way the silver fuchsias danced while Belesci spoke.

The only one who was behaving more or less as Lila would have anticipated was Mr. Banks, who had now officially been taken into the entourage—though he apparently was *not* going to appear in the notorious sex show. (When Miguel had innocently asked, the entire entourage burst into laughter, and Babylona said hastily, "No, John lacks the exhibitionist streak, sadly . . .") In fact, it seemed he was being taken on purely in the role of consort to Babylona, and Lila kept studying his face, wondering if he was happy or sad about the change in his circumstances. He was sitting in an armchair, with one of Babylona's Russian wolfhounds sprawled at his feet, and the only sign that he might be under any stress was that he chain-smoked through the entire meeting. She couldn't help thinking that whatever he was feeling might be what Ben would feel. But of course Ben wasn't going to feel anything, because he wasn't even going out with her, and that was that.

Still, when the meeting was winding down, and Babylona asked them if they had any questions that hadn't been covered, Lila found herself asking, "Do you think it's possible to have a long-term relationship in this kind of job?"

Then she blushed bright red. Drew and Miguel didn't seem to find anything strange in her question; Drew was even smiling at her as if he was grateful that she'd had the nerve to ask. But Anna was frowning at her in consternation, and she knew she was going to have to endure some hard questioning after the meeting was over. Still, it was about time she told Anna the whole story. Now that it wasn't going to get Ben fired.

Babylona smiled at her a bit wearily. "Oh dear," she said. "Everyone does like to ask that question." And she gave Mr. Banks a sly glance, which he met with his usual inscrutable look. Then he lit another cigarette, the flash of the lighter making the wolfhound look up and whimper in disapproval.

"The short answer," Babylona said, stretching languorously over Belesci's lap, "is yes. The long answer . . . is long." She gathered her arms back over herself, stroking down the green satin dress she was wearing. "But I suppose since we *do* have all afternoon."

"I would say the short answer is no," Belesci put in, with a mischievous glint in her violet eyes. Her Italian accent gave the words an exotic twist in combination with her extravagantly presented nudity.

"Oh, you couldn't have a long-term relationship if you were a housewife for a living. You aren't allowed to weigh in on this," Babylona said.

"Perhaps when someone explains to me what the purpose is of long terms," Belesci said. "It is like prison, I think."

"Don't listen to her," Javier told Lila, and Jorge chimed in, saying, "She's a freak of nature; she has no idea what earthlings feel."

Babylona said, "Yes, Jorge is the one to talk to. He was married, you know."

"*Was* married?" Anna said.

"Well, anyone can get divorced," Jorge said, annoyed. "It wasn't a work-related accident."

"You can't really call it a marriage if you can't get divorced," Javier put in.

Lila felt the conversation getting away from what she needed to know. She said quickly, "But most guys are going to get jealous. How do you handle that?" She forced herself not to look at Mr. Banks, but she felt his eyes on her, and again her cheeks burned.

Babylona smiled indulgently now. "Well, sweetie, so he gets jealous. That's not necessarily a problem."

"But it is a problem, because then he won't be happy. And . . . you know, he'll leave," Lila said.

"And when they get left, you know, some people feel *sad,*" Javier said, and Jorge started laughing. Jorge said, "You may have heard of an earth disease called 'heartbreak.'"

"Well, don't let them leave," Babylona said to Javier, in a short-tempered tone. "You don't have to let them leave, you know."

"You don't?" said Lila. "But won't they just leave anyway?"

"Not at all. Never happened to me." Babylona looked around the room as if daring anyone to challenge this statement.

Belesci looked up at Lila with a smile and said, "Now, this is very true. No one leaves the Big Baby."

"Because I don't let them," Babylona said, a little mollified. "After all, nobody wants to leave anyone. At least, they wouldn't want to leave any of us. They'd be crazy, in fact, unless they were leaving one of us for another one of us."

"And none of us would ever steal someone from another of us," Mariko said complacently, and crossed her legs on the top of the sofa back. "*Borrow* them, perhaps. But steal—never."

"Exactly," Babylona said happily. "So you just have to make your lover see his own interests. Or hers," she said to Drew, who had been following all this intently.

"But what if she says no?" Drew said.

"What if she does?" Babylona looked at him quizzically. "Let her say whatever she wants to say. It's a free country. And then you go and make her accept you as you are."

There was a pause while everyone mulled this over. Finally Babylona sat up, shaking her hair out over her shoulders, and said, "Well, enough of these technical problems, my dears. I think we can call this meeting finished, and if anyone has any further questions . . . well, you know what I always say."

"Ask your mother," drawled Belesci.

"Exactly. Ask your mother. She always knows best." And Babylona rose with a graceful shaking out of her long satin skirt, and went to the door, with Belesci following after, the silver fuchsias dancing in fantastic circles at the lavender tips of her breasts.

As soon as they judged that Babylona and Belesci were well gone, Anna, Drew, Miguel, and Lila were on their feet. Giving way at last to their intense nervousness, they all began to slink toward the door, scattering awkward good-byes as they went. On the stairs, Anna immediately grabbed Lila by the arm and said, "Well?"

They stopped on the stairwell, letting Drew and Miguel go on ahead.

"Well, I hid something from you," Lila said uncomfortably. "But you know there's a reason."

"Yeah, like you're a big fat liar." Anna put her hands on her hips.

"No." Lila's voice went weak. "Because . . . it was Ben."

Anna's face contorted into a scowl of consternation. "Our Ben? Advising Ben?"

"Yes. So you see—"

Just then they heard someone coming down the stairs behind them. They looked up, startled, and both instinctively tried to act as if nothing was going on when they saw that it was Mr. Banks. Lila's heart skipped a beat. She whispered as he approached, "Can

I catch up with you, Anna? There's something that I need to talk to Mr. Banks about."

Anna squinted at her. She whispered, "Really? Something I can't hear? What a surprise." And she turned and went on down the stairs with a pointedly aggrieved air.

Mr. Banks had almost arrived at the stairwell. He nodded at Lila and was about to pass her, when she blurted out, "Mr. Banks? Could I talk to you? Could we maybe talk in your office?"

He stopped and looked at her with a smile that just barely brushed the edges of his mouth. A long moment passed before he said, "You can talk to me here."

Lila stared at him. She had been imagining an office much like Babylona's, but smaller, with a big soft chair she could sit in while she gradually broached the topic of her personal jealousies and heartbreaks. And a leisurely hour or so while she developed that topic, with Mr. Banks playing the role of kindly older person. He would say wise things about sadness and inevitability. There might even be a box of tissues shoved toward her at some point.

It was a scene, anyway, that couldn't be played in a stairwell. And Mr. Banks showed no sign of being willing to listen to her troubles in a wiser, older, disinterested way. Instead he was looking at her with a knowing and very interested surmise.

Lila cleared her throat. "Um, I wanted to ask you about . . . It was something we talked about when we . . . you know, met at Halloween?"

There was another long moment of silence. At last he said, "I really liked fucking you."

That was all it took. All her troubles, everything she was about to say, just evaporated from Lila's head. She wanted him. On the stairwell, in his office, in a tent—it didn't matter. "So . . . would you like to . . . again?"

He reached forward without a word and took the lapels of her jacket. He pulled her in for a quick kiss that immediately made her head spin. His mouth moved over hers with an intoxicatingly direct communication of his desire, and his lips were dry and sweet with the faint, seductive scent of tobacco smoke. Then he was pulling the jacket back and off her shoulders. She held still, moving only to facilitate his movements as he quickly stripped her. Her white blouse and skirt soon joined the jacket on the floor, and she waited, holding her breath, while he unfastened her bra, the contact of his fingers waking her skin into prickling hypersensitivity. He stood back from her then and took one nipple between his thumb and index finger, looking her up and down as he teased it, making her whole body sing with response. It was amazing how he could control what she felt with a single tiny contact.

But even as she thought that, he crouched down to pull her panties over her hips, and then he was moving her legs apart with his hands, the tender skin of her thighs instantly aflame from the deft manipulation by his slightly rough palms. Before she could prepare herself, his tongue had touched the very tip of her clitoris. And he drew his tongue rapidly back and forth over her swelling clit, a minute motion that nonetheless made it hard for her to stay on her feet. She wanted to beg him to lick her more deeply, but he moved back and then she could only feel his light breath on her pussy. She was panting, inwardly imploring him to lick her again. But something warned her that if she asked, he might desert her entirely; she could clearly imagine herself standing naked, abandoned, in the stairwell. And she knew, with a lightning flash of shame, that she would have to masturbate there and then. It would take only a second for her to come, but she couldn't wait for the time it would take to get to the nearest empty room. She leaned back, letting her shoulders rest against the wall, opening her thighs in a mute gesture of supplication.

Just when she thought she couldn't stand it any more—she would have to touch herself—his hand spread her pussy lips, and he began to lick her in intense, flickering bursts. Her pussy went wild with sensation, the frantic orgasm she was going to have began to press inside her. But Mr. Banks seemed to know exactly how much she could take before crossing the threshold into explosive satisfaction; every time she felt the moment coming, he pulled back, and all she got was his maddening breath on her increasingly dripping pussy. She began to imagine her orgasm as a match about to be struck in a room full of gasoline; she began to feel the pleasure as an exquisite agony; and finally she began to be afraid of it ever ending. She didn't know how much time had passed while she stood there, her thighs aching from bending her knees to allow her hips to arch farther and farther forward, desperately inviting the caress of his mouth. And again he dipped his tongue into her and let it roam swiftly, snaking all over her tormented clitoris, stabbing into her cunt. And again it was stopped in a split second, and his breath tortured her with her need and helplessness. Then she was lost in her own shut eyes. Somewhere she felt her fingernails digging into her palms. All she wanted was for it to go on forever; and to come *now, now,* before she tore her own pussy out trying to find the orgasm only he could give her.

And then suddenly he was standing up. She opened her eyes, ready to finally beg him out loud—but before she could do anything, she felt his long, absolutely stone-hard dick slide into her. Immediately she came with an explosiveness beyond anything she had anticipated. He was holding her in his arms, lifting and supporting her as her legs first gave way and then reached up blindly to wrap around his waist. And he was fucking her, pressing her against the wall and digging into her with sure, hungry thrusts. It seemed to go on for a second eternity that took all her strength, again and again, in the form of devastating blows of pleasure.

His orgasm raised her to a final pitch of heat—and then dropped her. She was clinging to him, her feet again on the ground, with his semen dripping down her thighs. She opened her eyes and looked around as if she were looking for herself. Her eyes met his, and he was looking at her with some unappeasable desire; it was as if he were on the threshold of entering her, rather than pulling out of her after a massive orgasm.

Something about the look in his eyes made her whisper, "Are you all right?"

Then he smiled, and the hunger in his eyes was replaced by his usual inscrutable coolness. He said, "What did you want to ask me about?"

She said without thinking, "Jealousy."

"And now you remember," he said evenly, "that I'm the wrong person to ask."

And then behind him, Lila heard the sweet, teasing voice of Babylona, brightened by a hint of affectionate laughter. "Come on, John, darling. The poor girl will have enough of you all year. She can spare you now."

And the most confusing thing of all was that Lila's immediate reaction was one of delight—she would get to fuck him *more!* It all seemed horribly out of tune with any ambition for a settled relationship. As she gathered her clothes, waving her distracted good-byes to Banks and Babylona, she considered that perhaps she would be better off trying to be like Belesci. Couldn't she, someday, just lose her earthling ideas about love and "long-terms"?

She decided that she should count her blessings. Other girls lost their lovers without the outrageous consolations of a Mr. Banks. But as she struggled back into her suit, a voice inside her insisted that just wasn't good enough. And, elated by the light-headed feeling of perfect sexual satisfaction, a feeling like fairy dust in her blood, Lila felt irrationally sure it would all work out. She would make it work out—she knew it. She could have her career and her real love; she could sleep with both Mr. Banks and Ben; she could have her cake and eat it, too. It would all be fine—if only she knew how!

Chapter Twenty-two

Brandi tugged her coat around and then back again, trying to get it to settle comfortably over her baggy sweatshirt. No matter what she did, these clothes felt wrong, like they were suffocating her skin. Real clothes were basically a pain; she had no idea why people put up with them. Even according to the crazy, dumb, uptight law, you only had to wear underwear or a bathing suit, a certain bare minimum. And when it was cold, you wore a coat—out-of-doors. The whole clothes thing was basically a source of unhappiness and stress, which could eventually lead to serious health conditions. That was Brandi's opinion. Yet here she was, wearing long pants and a goddamn sweatshirt. And why? Because she was going to see a gorgeous guy who might want to fuck her. It went against everything she believed. Or everything except the top golden rule of all golden rules: anything for a friend.

As she went through the parking lot, she went over her plan. The first thing was to get Ben to let her into his apartment. That was easy; she'd faint if that was what it took. Any old manipulative lie would do; she knew an assortment.

The next thing was to tell Ben what to do. That was easy: He should forget all his crazy, dumb, uptight ideas and go have sex with Lila. And then he should carry on doing it as long as it took. Fall in love. Maybe go out to dinner with the girl once in a while. That was stage two of the plan.

Stage three was making him do it. This part was still a little fuzzy. Usually Brandi counted on sex to get her anything she wanted. But screwing Ben to get him to screw Lila . . . for one thing, it was per-

242 of 270 Carole Hart

haps the one way of manipulating him Lila wouldn't care for. And for another, it wasn't going to work.

The good news was, it shouldn't take much to convince him. It was only what he wanted to do. She'd seen that dumb, love-struck look in his eyes when he was talking about his feelings for Lila. So it was mainly a matter of making it seem like it was his idea. Or making it seem like there was some other reason to do it—like to save the school. To provide a role model to children. Anything that would even halfway confuse him into thinking he wasn't just acting like a lovesick fool.

She was so lost in thought that as she wandered among the cars, she ran smack into a man coming in the other direction. She tee-tered, flailed in space for a second, and was about to take a spectacu-lar pratfall when the man caught her out of midair and lifted her up into a big bear hug. It took the best part of a minute before he put her down and let her see his face.

"Choo-Choo!" she screamed, her heart leaping with delight.

"You got it, Bran Muffin! Goddammit, you look good!"

"You lying old smut merchant! I look good why? Because I'm all covered up? That's the worst insult I heard in my life!" She threw her arms around him again and this time he swung her around and around, squeezing her against him in a way that felt good down to the tips of her toes. When he set her down again, she gave him a once-over. He had the same slim, boyish frame as ever, the same bushy black hair, the same almost ridiculous movie star looks, with the cleft in his chin and the blazing blue eyes. At last she said, "Well, you can insult me all you like, but you look fantastic to me. That's fantastic with a capital F for Fuck me, beautiful."

"Oh, I wasn't insulting you, anyway. But you know that, angel. I guess you have to give me a hard time, though, or you wouldn't be you."

"So what are you doing here, all unannounced?" Brandi put her arms around him again. He embraced her, too, and they settled into their usual talking pose: her body pressed up against his, with her weight leaning back into his encircling arms.

He smiled down at her. "I'm here to take you back to New York for Christmas."

She squinted at him. "Back to New York? And you drove all the way out here without asking me?"

"No, dummy. I drove all the way out here because my folks live five miles away. I stopped off here without asking you because I'm not taking no for an answer."

Brandi sighed. "But I can't go."

Choo-Choo slowly moved one hand down her back, letting it rest finally on her ass. Then he pressed his groin against her, letting her feel his stiffening cock. And she *could* feel it, even through her pants, her coat, his coat, his pants—the damn thing was that unprecedentedly big.

"Even if I say pretty please?"

"Oh, God. You drive me crazy with that thing. Is it still like it was?"

"What do you think?"

"Ouch." She sighed. Even at Babylona, she'd never seen anyone with a dick anything like Choo-Choo's. It was magnificent. It made other guy's dicks look like poodles put next to a Great Dane. In fact, the only reason his porn career had never taken off was, he still insisted on making the films himself, with their old friend Rooney. Rooney and Choo-Choo were pretty smart guys in Brandi's book, but they were absolutely not businessmen. The root of the problem was that they had no work ethic whatsoever (a problem she identified with one hundred percent). Once the fun was over, their participation was over. So they had a vast and extensive oeuvre of pornos that they'd made. But when it came to getting distribution, they had a few lame ideas and that was it.

"Listen," she said. "You know I would love to spend Christmas with you guys, but I already got my ticket to go to the Virgin Islands."

She briefly sketched out for him the glory and wonder that was Seduction, the most debauched holiday destination in the Western hemisphere and the Eastern, Southern, and Northern hemispheres combined. Then, seeing that he wasn't at all impressed, she made a case that she needed to go to comfort her heartbroken friend, Lila. "The poor girl needs a holiday badly. She's got a lot of new responsibility, and in the meantime, the boy trouble thing. And I know she wouldn't go without me."

"Somebody else could go," Choo-Choo said placidly. He was rubbing his now well-developed hard-on against her, pressing it into her pussy so that the memory of what it was like inside her made her gulp.

"Oh, damn. Why do you do this to me?"

"I didn't even do it to you yet. But I want to do it to you." He pressed his hard-on into her again, and she groaned. It was getting hard to even talk to him. If it went on any longer, she was going to have to screw him right up against whoever's car it was she was next to.

Then she noticed a certain look in his eye, a look she knew of old. "Wait," she said suspiciously. "You don't want me to be in another one of your porn flicks, do you?" She tried to pull away from him, but he held her fast.

"Of course I do. And you know why?"

Brandi nodded. "I know, I know. Because you'd rather fuck me than anyone else. And so would Rooney. And blah blah. And then it never gets distributed, though. So why can't we just fuck and leave it at that?"

"But this is my best idea ever. It's a porn slasher film. *Booty Bloodbath*. 'Cause, you know most slasher films are just sex movies, anyway.

Except they never go far enough. This would be like a real sex film *plus* a slasher film." His eyes were shining with the vision of the masterpiece he had in mind. "It's a surefire hit."

Brandi shook her head disapprovingly. "For one thing, Chewy, that's sick. You want to make a film of me getting chopped to pieces and fucked at the same time? Damn, what's the matter with you? I mean, it's a totally bad influence."

He made a dismissive face. "Oh, yeah, that's going to be the thing that turns someone into a serial killer. You know, they used to say that about comic books."

"They did not."

"Pretty much they did."

"Make it a musical porn film. Make it a Western. Make it a porn film about a boy's love for his goddamn pet dolphin, only don't chop me to pieces while you're fucking me."

He gave her a guilty smile. "So you'll come?"

Brandi's jaw fell open. "How could I not see that coming?"

"Come on, I'm changing my movie for you."

"No, no, and no way."

But then he was kissing her. And pressing that beautiful dick against her so that her pussy ached and ached. She could feel that familiar sloppy feeling in her panties that she always had whenever Choo-Choo was around. In fact, whenever Choo-Choo was around, she was happy. In fact, now that he was here, she realized how much she'd been missing him. And if she went to New York, she'd spend the holiday fucking him again and again.

At last she pulled back from his kiss, all her resolve in tatters.

"Well, maybe," she said.

"Well, yes, you mean." He grinned. "You're the best. Let's go fuck in your car."

"Hang on. I already bought the whole vacation to the Virgin Islands. Hotel, flight, dancing shoes."

"Oh, don't tell me you can't sell the reservation to someone else? Somebody's got to want to go to the Caribbean. Best sex holiday and all that. Come on."

Then Brandi stared at him while all the pieces fell into place. "Choo, darling," she said. "I think I got me a plan."

Chapter Twenty-three

The flight had seemed endless, and Lila stepped out of the cab and onto the premises of Seduction with a weak-kneed feeling she recognized from stepping off of particularly hairy roller coaster rides. It had been strange, after a semester at Babylona, to be among so many civilians again. The very fact that all ages were represented struck her; it was like being in a foreign country where they had the peculiar customs of aging and having babies. There was a certain sense of: "Wow, this was going on all the time!" It made her a little too aware of what these people would think if they knew what she'd been up to.

Brandi was coming on a later flight; because Lila had only agreed to come late, she'd said, she couldn't get seats on the same plane. And Lila had missed her. She felt certain that Brandi would have made friends with everyone on the flight, told them unselfconsciously (proudly, in fact) all about Babylona Institute, and turned them into fierce proponents of free love by the time the flight had landed. As well as having sex with two or three of them.

Now, as Lila walked into the lobby of Seduction, she was relieved to see a naked couple sitting on a sofa reading the paper. There was another couple in a clinch by the flower arrangement, with all four of their hands delving inventively under each other's clothes. And the fashion choices made by the other visitors who were passing through reminded Lila powerfully of Babylona when she first arrived, when the weather was warm enough to make nudity and near nudity an option everywhere. There was even a girl wearing what Lila finally realized was a "string bikini"—one length of string looped around her hips and pussy, and another tied around her breasts just tightly enough to make them bulge in an interesting fashion.

The man at the reception desk also looked like a refugee from Babylona. Though he was fully dressed, his biceps bulged noticeably even in the act of tapping her name into the computer. His square jaw and white teeth were matinee-idol perfect, and when he handed Lila her room key, his blue eyes lingered on her face. Then he looked down, admiring her curves in her light summer dress, and his smile was a naked invitation.

But Lila just thanked him politely and followed the bellboy to the elevators. She wasn't ready for any assignations just yet. There would be all too much of that after Brandi appeared and began to work her wicked magic. For the next four or five hours she would savor the peace. Just lie on the beach and let her mind wander.

The room was like any hotel room anywhere; the impersonal beige tones, the quilted bedspread made of some artificial fabric that seemed like it had originally been invented for use in space. Lila looked around with a grimace, and had to smile at herself. She'd become so spoiled in such a short period of time. Nothing but posh designer furniture and fresh-cut flowers for her. But, she reminded herself, the beauty here would be outside, not inside. The priority was to hit the beach.

When she'd changed into her bathing suit, she wandered out first to the patio bar for a drink. She got an improbably tall piña colada and sipped it while idly, comfortably watching the other drinkers fondle one another. One man sitting at the bar was getting a blow job from a girl crouched in front of him. He continued to sip his drink, occasionally freezing and staring into space as an especially telling stroke hit home. At a table, a topless girl was saying something very earnest and heartfelt to a young man who stared, hypnotized, at her chest. She had pretty, pointy breasts whose dark red nipples looked like candy; as Lila watched, the man gave up his struggle against temptation and leaned forward to take one nipple in his mouth. At another table, a threesome grappled, their bathing suits zanily askew until it seemed they were worn on arbitrarily chosen parts of their bodies. And at still other tables, people in ordinary street clothes conversed as if there was nothing unusual going on. Lila smiled, back in her element again.

The air was balmy and fresh, with a hint of the ocean in it. From where she sat, under the broad roof of the bar, it was comfortably cool, but there was a taste of sunlight in everything. Since the bar was open to the beach, she could see the golden world of sun outside, the rays blinding where they mingled with the pure white sand, or where they threw the shaggy crowns of palms into sharp relief. The heat alone was relaxing her in a subtle but profound way. No problem could seem that serious while she was sitting here, looking out at the glare on the ocean.

A few hopeful men approached Lila, but she managed to get rid of them politely enough. With so many willing partners around, there was no point in pursuing a reluctant one. One guy did insist on writing down his room number, but there was no harm in that. Anyway, he was sandy haired and handsome, with a deep caramel tan and a raffish smile—potentially just the guy with whom to break her sexual fast later that night.

Finally, fortified by sweet booze and the sleepy sunlight, Lila wandered out onto the beach itself. The fine sand was pleasantly hot on her bare soles, and the combination of cool breeze and warm sun was lulling her further into a state of unquestioning happiness. The sea was a brilliant turquoise blue, decorated with snowy ribbons of breaker that drifted to shore in lazy slow motion, borne by the gentle surf. There were only a few people on the beach, and Lila took the trouble to walk some distance before spreading her towel, putting a decent space between herself and the nearest other sunbather. The key was to be out of earshot. She wanted absolute peace.

Then she lay down and let all the worries of the past few months seep out of her, gazing at the few fine clouds that seemed to be stretched out fast asleep in the sky. The sound of the waves rushing forward and then hushing themselves back into the sea made her feel almost as if she were being rocked to sleep. It was like floating in sunlight. For a little patch of forever, she simply lay on the beach and let the serenity take her over.

But soon she realized she'd better get some sunscreen on or else she would be spending the rest of the vacation in a darkened room with cold cream all over her body. She sat up reluctantly, blinking as she opened her eyes into the bright sun. When she dug in her bag, she found that it had somehow already got sand in it. The suntan lotion had opened, furthermore, spilling just enough cream that sand had stuck all over the top, making it an absolute certainty that she would be spreading grains of it all over her skin. She sighed as this first trivial annoyance marred her little paradise. And then she looked up and saw the man coming toward her.

He was still just a silhouette in the distance, but something about his bearing made her certain he was heading out to see her personally. It might even be one of the guys who had approached her in the bar, coming to have a second try. The worst thing was that once the man had taken the trouble to trudge out here, he was unlikely to walk all the way back again. He would probably set up his towel near her. Even if he left her alone, there he would be, and his presence would ruin her sense of flawless tranquillity. Of course, she could get up and move—but that would seem like a reaction to him personally, as if she were leaving in a huff. It might even hurt his feelings.

Oh well, she thought as she watched the figure approach. *It couldn't stay that perfect.* She began to slather sun lotion on herself, noticing all the grains of sand that were sticking to her skin, each one an emblem of the destruction of her heavenly moment.

As he came closer, though, she began to notice the man's striking silhouette: the broad shoulders, the rangy height of him, the muscular thighs. Lila felt her resolve weakening; perhaps she would start her career of Seduction waywardness a little early. If she couldn't enjoy her planned solitude, perhaps she should make the most of what was available.

It became increasingly clear that he really was walking to her; he was gazing at her as he came. She stared back without meaning to. Something about the way he moved appealed to her, and she could already feel a certain tense excitement building, the beginnings of the kind of instant crush she'd had when she was twelve or thirteen, when she was first discovering boys, a few years before they discovered her. The man was responding to her intent gaze, smiling with an expression that might have been friendly or wry. She couldn't tell with the sun in her eyes, though he was only a dozen yards away now. But she could tell that he was good-looking, more good-looking than any man she'd seen since . . .

Ben. It was Ben. She froze and she must have been gaping, because he paused and began to laugh. It was his laugh—it really was him. And Lila began to smile in a sloppy, entirely happy way. This was better than any of the beach bliss she'd planned. In a second she was on her feet, joyously noticing that he looked down automatically at her bikini, and that his face changed in response, becoming almost grave.

"Hi, Ben," she said. "I guess I should say I'm really surprised."

"But you're not?" he said gruffly.

She caught her breath, realizing just how surprised she was. "A better word would be amazed. This isn't a coincidence, is it?"

He shook his head. "No, Brandi put me up to it. She sold me her ticket, actually." Then he became uncertain, seeking in her eyes confirmation that he was welcome. "It was probably a bad idea. I mean, you came here to get away from your troubles, right?"

"You're not one of my troubles," she said evenly.

They looked at each other then in silence. The open expanse of the beach and ocean, the rushing of the waves, all seemed unreal and insignificant beside the fact of Ben's presence in front of her. Inwardly Lila was exulting: He had flown all the way here to see her, to be with her. He had bought Brandi's ticket; he would be staying in her room.

He said, "Well, you're one of my troubles." And then he reached forward and took her by the shoulders, drawing her in gently for a kiss. Her hands went to his chest, gratefully feeling the hard planes of muscle there, the smooth bare skin. Just kissing him gave her a vertiginous joy. But then he stepped back, ending the kiss firmly. Her hands fell away from him, and he crossed his arms to shut her out.

"What's wrong?" she said, trying to smile.

He looked away at the ocean, frowning. "I don't know if I should have come here," he said. Then he was scowling fiercely, obviously struggling with himself. "In the cab driving from the airport, I almost decided to go to a different resort. I don't even know what I'm doing anymore."

"You're coming on vacation with me."

"I know. But I shouldn't have."

Lila looked at him in a kind of sweet despair. Just having him there, within reach, was so wonderful it made her realize how much she'd missed him. She guessed this was what was meant by chemistry. It was as if an electric current came off him that lit up all her pleasure circuits.

She said, "Just to be really clear, I would give it all up for you. I actually would. The job, the school, everything."

"But I wouldn't let you."

"But I would."

"Listen, Lila. Not only wouldn't I let you, but I'm not going to let my problems ruin it for you. If we try to be an item, you'll end up running around trying to make it all right for me. And I don't know if it'll ever be all right." He was looking at her intently, and she could so easily imagine his hands reaching out to her that she knew intuitively he was thinking of it, too. At last he said, his voice hoarse and tired, "I shouldn't have come. Dammit, I knew I shouldn't come."

It was all so senseless, such a waste of the potential between them that something in her rebelled. She said, "Listen, you can't tell me you came all this way and you didn't intend to try this. You must have wanted to . . ."

He shrugged, but his face was agonized. He said, softly now, "I needed to see you. I was dying to see you."

"That can't have been all."

"I don't know."

She forced her voice to be light. "On the flight down here, you didn't look out the window at the clouds and think about how silly you were being, and how life is too short to let something like this go by?"

He smiled. "I think someone has all the answers."

"I think," she said, "that was a question."

"Okay." He put his hands on her shoulders again. "The truth. I did look out the window and think about how stupid I was being, and I did decide that I would never let you go. But then I got off the plane, and I actually had to see you. And I began thinking about you on television, having sex a thousand ways with a thousand men . . ."

She realized her eyes were filling with tears. She said, "That again. So that's it?"

"No, that can't be it. I didn't fly a thousand miles just to say there's no hope. But . . ." He shook his head, and his brow was creased with frustration.

She'd had enough. "Well, if you don't know, I do." And then she moved her hands up to the back of her neck and untied her bikini top.

Ben obviously couldn't help staring as her breasts fell out. He began to say something, but she put her hand over his mouth and felt his lips smiling under it. "No resisting."

Then she lifted her hand away from his mouth as she pulled his face down to kiss her. He didn't kiss her back, but she ignored that, letting her lips drift over his soft lips, then crush them hungrily. Her tongue stroked the sensitive skin there, tasting the sweat on his upper lip.

Then she took his hands and moved them behind his back. He didn't oppose her as she tied them together there with her bikini top. But while her hands were both engaged with knotting the top around his wrists, he moved away from her kiss and said, "Sex isn't going to change anything."

She smiled at him in exasperation. She said, "Well, tell me when something changes. I'll take care of changing it, and you just pay attention and let me know when it happens."

"You're very sure of yourself."

Lila took a deep breath. She said, "I am sure of myself. But what's more important, I'm sure of us."

Then she drew him to her. His skin was cool and lightly sweaty, and her breasts chilled and sparkled with the sudden contact. She crushed them against him, kissing his throat, tasting his sweat with the tip of her amorous tongue. Her hands traveled down his back, feeling the strong muscles there and the ridge between them that ran down his spine. She could feel his desire in the tension with which he held himself, but he was stubbornly still, refusing to openly respond to her caresses.

Now she moved her mouth down, feeling his beautiful chest with her lips until they found his nipple. There she stopped, nipping at it once, twice, and then sucking hard, smiling inside when she heard his sharpened breathing. Her hand traveled down his belly, and her fingers hooked lightly under the elastic of his bathing suit. He was breathing harder now, obviously trying but failing to control it. And when she licked her way down his stomach and let her cheek rest against the front of his swimsuit, she was gratified to feel the stiffening length of his dick there.

She turned to kiss the front of his trunks, letting her mouth form over his growing hard-on. As the fabric pressed against the tip of his dick, she felt a lubricating drop of precome under the cloth. Crouching, she let herself sit on her heels, and smiled as she felt how wet her pussy was already becoming. And then she reached up with both hands and swiftly lifted his trunks down over his hard-on and pulled them to his ankles.

At that, he briefly tried to reach forward, forgetting about his bound hands. And she heard him faintly laugh at himself. Then he said, "Lila, don't," but his voice was vague, uncertain.

That was enough. She took the tip of his dick in her mouth and began to suck on it. At first she concentrated on the tip, nibbling on it gently, licking the sensitive underside, letting her tongue play over its silky smoothness. And in between teasing and licking, she fastened her lips on the glans and sucked until he gasped with the intensity of it. She was bringing him to the brink of pain, making him almost afraid while at the same time he couldn't move away from the incredible pleasure she was giving him.

Finally, she was rewarded. His hips tipped forward, straining to press his cock deeper into her mouth. Then as quick as lightning, she moved her head away and looked up at him with deliberate provocation in her half-lidded eyes.

"Has anything changed yet?" she said.

He looked at her with miserable need, and she was amazed once more at the beauty of his body, his face. When he didn't say anything, she said, "Perhaps you need more."

And she took his cock in her mouth again and moved her head forward, suddenly swallowing it all. He made a low sound and tilted his hips forward to press his cock into the back of her throat. Lila let the muscles there relax and took it for a long unbearable second. Then he was pulling out—but he thrust forward again, and she shut her eyes with pleasure as he began to fuck her mouth. Her hands moved up to cup his balls, and she let her thumb play at the base of his cock, gliding in the lubrication there from her mouth. She sucked him harder and harder, again bringing him to the edge of discomfort, until at last he pulled out of her mouth, glaring down at her.

"Lila, what are you doing?" he said.

She smiled up at him. "I'm changing something." And she reached up to his waist and pulled him down. He obediently kneeled, and when she kissed him on the mouth, he kissed her back, his strong tongue moving in her mouth where his cock had just been. At last she pulled back from it, afraid of losing her courage. She said, "It's time for you to fuck me."

She pulled him over her, cradling him against her so that his chest was pressed against her full breasts. In a moment he was between her legs, lying on top of her, just as she had imagined every night since she'd last seen him. Then she couldn't stand it anymore. She said, "Ben?"

He looked down at her with a mingled passion and desperation that almost made her lose her nerve completely. "You can seduce me," he said. "It doesn't have to change anything."

"But it does," she said. "Since I last saw you . . . when you said this couldn't work. Well, I've never felt so alone."

"You're hardly alone. That's the problem." His eyes narrowed.

She swallowed, and the whole scene seemed to go pale with the power of her feelings. At last she made herself say, "I'm in love with you, Ben. Without you, I'll always be alone."

He stared at her, obviously dumbstruck. The green of his eyes seemed to intensify as he took in what she'd just said.

She kept her legs around his hips for another moment, stroking his chest. Then, very simply, she reached behind him and untied his hands. She opened her legs and said, "There. You're free. I don't want to seduce you. I know it's not that simple."

At first he just put his hands down in the sand and stared at her. Then he growled deep in his throat and kissed her, his mouth fierce on hers. His hands moved into her hair and took handfuls of it, pulling her mouth to him violently. And then she felt his dick pressing against her pussy, opening her to a rush of competing pleasure and joy.

He muttered, "Okay, something's changed."

She pulled her face away. "What? What's changed?"

Then he pressed his dick deep into her, making her cry out and pull him to her convulsively. He said, "What's changed is that I'm in love with you, too."

And he was fucking her into oblivion, everything blasted away by the feelings he sent into her cunt. She was whispering, "I love you, I love you," as her body melted into absolute acceptance. He twisted down and began to suck her breasts as he fucked her, thrusting into her so hard she could hardly feel her own orgasm begin. And she was weeping again, with a different and freshly overwhelming abandon. When the orgasm came at last, it blinded her with its force. And Ben cried out as he came in his turn, making her buttocks sting with the force with which he pressed her into the sand.

Minutes passed then while the two of them held each other, hearing the surf roar, hearing their feelings roar. At last, Lila dared to say, "I do love you—so much."

Ben shifted, and she opened her eyes to find him smiling at her. He said, "So you said."

She shook her head stubbornly. "I mean it. I mean, I don't want to let you go."

"And you didn't let me go."

She looked at him with her frail hope growing stronger. She said, "You'll try?"

He smiled, his eyes shining into hers with amused fondness. "That's what I came here for, isn't it?"

"I thought you came here to drive me crazy by changing your mind back and forth."

"Well. Let's just say I'll keep on doing that for a long, long time."

She caught her breath, aware of the tears on her cheeks, and the new tears that were flooding from her eyes. Her voice was weak and husky as she said to him, "That sounds like a plan."

Then he was kissing her again, and the rushing sound of the breakers seemed like the sound of all her fears rushing away, washing off the edge of the world.